CW00549157

Also by Ray Hobbs and Published by Wingspan Press

Published Elsewhere

LAST WICKET PAIR

RAY HOBBS

Wingspan Press

Published in the United States and the United Kingdom
by WingSpan Press, Livermore, CA

The WingSpan name, logo and colophon are the trademarks
of WingSpan Publishing.

ISBN 978-1-63683-038-4 (pbk.)
ISBN 978-1-63683-969-1 (ebook)

First edition 2022

Printed in the United States of America

www.wingspanpress.com

This book is dedicated to the memory of those
who suffered because of the intolerance of others,
and to those whose suffering continues.

Sources and Acknowledgements

Overy, R., Interrogations (London, Penguin Books Ltd, 2001).
Williams, A. T., A Passing Fury (London, Jonathan Cape, 2016).
Sands, P., The Ratline (London, Weidenfeld & Nicolson, 2020).

As ever, I am indebted to my brother Chris, who was a ready source of ideas, and who acted as a soundboard throughout the writing of the manuscript.
RH

LAST WICKET PAIR

September 1945

A West Riding Town

1

Relative Importance

The maid placed a rack of fresh toast on the table, saying, 'I'm afraid the butter's a mixture of butter and margarine, Miss Dorothy. It's all we have.'

'Thank you, Gladys. I'm sure we'll survive it. I spent most of the war making do with margarine.'

Her mother adjusted her hold on *The Times*, allowing the top half to fall like a stern drawbridge, and said, 'You had only yourself to blame for that, Dorothy.'

'I'm not complaining, Mother.'

Gladys withdrew diplomatically into the kitchen.

'If you'd only shrugged off your fanciful, bohemian ways and accepted a commission in the WAAF, as any sensible girl would, your life would have been infinitely more comfortable.'

'And when all's said and done, our prime motivation in going to war was the pursuit of comfort.'

'There's no need for sarcasm. I blame spending the war in the company of all those common girls.'

'Many of whom were excellent people.' Dorothy had already arranged to keep in touch with Connie from Jarrow.

Mrs Needham took a piece of toast from the rack, grimaced at the concoction in the butter dish, and transferred some of it to her plate. 'I just don't know what you're going to do next. You were so determined to take that job at Rimmington's, and they held it for you for five years, only for you to resign. What on earth possessed you to do that, Dorothy?'

'You weren't there, Mother, not that it would have made much difference, I imagine, if you had been, but I'll try to explain. When I arrived at Rimmington's, they introduced me to the person who'd been doing my job very much to their satisfaction throughout the war—'

'They were obliged by law to hold your job open.'

'Let me finish, Mother.' Tiresome though the task was of explaining human frailty to a non-believer, Dorothy made the effort for the sake of politeness. 'She's a war widow with a child to provide for, and it wasn't difficult for me to see that she'd been dreading my return, because it meant she'd be out of work. To put it simply, her need was greater than mine. She didn't have Needham's Pickles to fall back on.'

'How ridiculous. You treat wealth as something to be ashamed of.'

'Not wealth itself, but the misuse of it, yes, I see that as shameful.'

'You're impossible, Dorothy. That and breaking off your engagement to Bill was just typical of your chaotic approach to life.'

Dorothy pushed her plate aside and dropped her napkin on to the table. 'If every breakfast time is going to be an opportunity for a dressing-down, it's clearly time I went to live elsewhere.'

'You've only been home two minutes,' said her mother, whose growing anger was quite discernible.

'That only makes it worse.' She resented having to explain the circumstances of the parting, but she decided she must. 'Bill and I came to the conclusion together that it was better for us to part. We were simply not the harmonious pair we'd believed ourselves to be.'

'Problems can be worked out. Married life wasn't always straightforward for your father and me.'

'That I can believe.'

'I don't know what you mean by that, and I think I'd rather not know. I was about to say that we had to make allowances for each other's foibles.'

Dorothy could only imagine that her father made most of those allowances, her mother being the determined soul she was.

Now in top gear, her mother moved on to say, 'You're almost a carbon copy of your Aunt Sarah.' Her tone conveyed her long-held view that her youngest sister was beyond redemption.

'Am I?' Her mother had levelled the general criticism on many occasions, but at least, her aunt was providing a new yardstick. In the past, Dorothy's father had always been the convenient black sheep, even after he'd perished so inconveniently on Messines Ridge in 1917.

'She was always unreliable, always up to some scatter-brained scheme or other. I blame your grandmother for spoiling her.'

The comparison pleased Dorothy. Aunt Sarah had been one of the bright lights of her childhood, always accommodating, affectionate and fun. It was true that she'd never been a ready correspondent; Dorothy had written to her several times after joining the WAAF, but received no reply, which only demonstrated quite unnecessarily that no one was perfect. Almost to herself, she said, 'I wonder what she's doing now.'

'That's anybody's guess.' It was a verbal shrug. 'She disappeared shortly before the war.'

'Did she?' Dorothy had no idea.

'She was on holiday, visiting a friend in France when war broke out,' she said dismissively. 'After that, who knows what became of her?'

In disbelief, Dorothy managed to say, 'She's your sister, and you don't seem to care about her safety or… about her at all.'

'We were never close.' Her mother delivered the memorable understatement with absolutely no emotion.

* * *

A telephone call to her other aunt revealed that she, too, had never enjoyed a happy relationship with Aunt Sarah, but Dorothy did learn a little more about her disappearance.

'Sarah went to stay with a friend in Orléans. She had friends everywhere, but I remember her joking about the "Maid of Orléans". That's how I remembered it after all this time.'

'Do you know the friend's name, Aunt Alice?'

'Oh, yes. Her name was Jeanne, hence the connection with Joan of Arc, and she worked as a keeper, or some such person, at the house where Joan of Arc stayed in the Hundred Years' War. It all sounded very obsessive.'

'Thank you, Aunt Alice. That's very helpful.'

'There's no more I can tell you, I'm afraid. Your Aunt Sarah lived a capricious life, and we were content to let her get on with it.'

'Have you never been tempted to find out what happened to her?'

'After all this time, Dorothy, it would be impossible, but be assured that Sarah would always land on her feet, come what may.'

'Thanks, Aunt Alice.' Dorothy was still concerned, however, and she had no intention of following her family's indifferent example. If she represented Aunt Sarah's last chance, in effect, her last wicket, she was determined not to give up easily.

* * *

'Mother,' said Dorothy, 'apart from "capricious", "unreliable" and "scatter-brained", how would you describe Aunt Sarah?'

Her mother breathed the sigh of the long-suffering. 'You really have got the bit between your teeth, haven't you, Dorothy? Let me see. For some unfathomable reason, she was obsessed with our mother's Jewish ancestry. Frankly, I've spent most of my adult life keeping quiet about it, but she carried it like a banner.'

'But the Nazis never came, so you were as safe as houses.'

'That's not the point.' Her mother picked up the teapot and asked, 'Are you ready for more tea?'

'Yes, please.' Dorothy put her cup and saucer on the low table and placed the strainer over the cup. 'What was the point?'

'What do you mean?'

'I said that the Nazis never came to put you in a death camp, and you said that wasn't the point.'

'The point,' said her mother impatiently, 'was that Jews are not universally popular. It wasn't just about the Nazis, and I wish you wouldn't use that melodramatic language, just because the Army found that dreadful place and made a public spectacle of it.'

It was Dorothy's turn to be impatient, but she tried to control it, mindful as ever that her mother had suffered two minor strokes in the past year. 'The Allies have been finding them all over Germany and Poland. Bergen-Belsen isn't an isolated example.'

'Well, it's all in the past.'

'The recent past.'

'If you say so, dear, but I'm not going to get worked up about every little thing the Nazis got up to. It's time to move on, always supposing this excuse for a government will allow anything so sensible.'

Dorothy tried her tea, which was still too hot to drink. 'I had a similar conversation with Jake,' she said.

'Who on earth is Jake?'

'He was the Polish airman you wouldn't let me bring home for Christmas in case he ravished me with the curtains open, and set the neighbours talking. As a matter of fact, it was in a hotel room that Christmas that we had the conversation. It brought our time together to a dramatic end, I can tell you.'

'Really, Dorothy, must you be so… basic?'

'Why not, when it was the best part of the relationship? To give Jake his due, he was extremely good in bed.'

'Dorothy!'

'Oh, Mother, did you seriously expect me to spend five years in the company of healthy males and emerge as innocent as when I joined?'

'I'd rather not hear about your immoral behaviour. It's as well your father's not here to learn of it.'

'I expect he'd have made allowances for me, Mother, just as he did for you.'

* * *

'She was priceless,' said Dorothy, having recounted the story and accepted a glass of wine from Jack. He and his wife Kate were among Dorothy's oldest friends, going back to their days in the Cullington Cycling Club before the war.

'I envied you when we were young,' said Kate, 'for your unflinching ability to stand up to your mother in a way I never could with mine.'

'You never had that problem, did you, Jack? How are your folks, by the way?'

'They're fine, Dot.' Jack was no longer in uniform, and expecting daily to hear of his discharge.

'And your sister and the baby?'

'Both thriving, thank you. Little Edward's six, now.'

'We have news, too,' announced Kate, who'd clearly been containing her excitement, although the evidence was starkly obvious.

'I can see that. How long have you been…?'

'Eight months, and that's not all. We'll be moving quite soon. Farrar's have celebrated Jack's return by appointing him Deputy Manager of the new branch in Bridlington.'

'Congratulations on both achievements,' said Dorothy.

'Thank you. He'll be able to look around, now, for a boat to rebuild,' said Kate. 'I'm providing him with a baby, but he wants a boat as well.'

'Ouch,' said Dorothy playfully. She was pleased about the way life was turning out for them. Jack was obviously highly regarded at Farrar's Tours, and they'd both been keen to start a family.

Mention of his promotion had reminded her of her current preoccupation, and she said, 'I'll call into the branch to see you, Jack, probably tomorrow. If you're busy, I'll try again later.'

'What do you need, Dot?'

'Lots of things, including advice.'

'It's yours for the asking. What's on your mind?'

'I want to go to France.'

He nodded approvingly. 'Early spring's a good time.'

Kate asked, 'Aren't you going back to Rimmington's yet?'

'No, I've resigned.' She told them about her sudden decision and her mother's reaction, which still rankled with her.

'Good for you, Dot,' said Kate.

'Seconded,' said Jack, still wondering about her sudden wish to travel to France. He asked, 'Why do you want to travel so soon after your demob?'

'Basically, I'm impatient. If I can, I want to trace the whereabouts of my favourite aunt. I'll make a start in Orléans and see where it leads me.'

* * *

'Must you wear those awful trousers?'

'Yes, Mother, for as long as stockings remain as scarce as sleighbells in August, I must. Also, they're ideal for travelling in.' Dorothy was packing a suitcase, taking care only to pack essentials, a precaution that seemed lost on her mother.

'Is that all you're taking?'

'Yes, it is. I shan't need to dress for dinner, and I'm not expecting an invitation to a ball or a wild boar hunt, which is quite a relief.'

'I've told you before, Dorothy, there's no need for sarcasm.'

Dorothy stopped for a moment and said, 'As I shan't be seeing you for some time, I'll agree with you. I'm sorry, Mother. You see, when censure is heavy upon the air, that's how I find myself reacting. For every criticism, there's an equal and opposite witticism. You could call it a reflex action.'

'I'm only trying to be helpful.'

'I suppose you are.' It was time to declare a truce.

'Are you going immediately?'

'No, I haven't even got the train and ferry tickets yet.'

Her mother left the room, returning after several minutes with two cellophane packets, which she offered to her daughter.

Dorothy gasped. 'Silk stockings. No one's seen any of these since before the war. You can't give them away, just like that.'

'I bought them before the war, but I've made do with lisle, and now I don't need them. You do, so take them.'

'Oh, Mother. Thank you.' She took the stockings and kissed her mother on the cheek.

'Now you won't have to wear trousers all the time, not that you'll ever look like a man. If you haven't already noticed it, you're the image of your Aunt Sarah.'

It was true. Dorothy had the same dark hair, deep-brown eyes and fine cheekbones that she remembered when she thought of Aunt Sarah, which was increasingly often.

* * *

Jack was serving a customer when Dorothy arrived at Farrar's, but she only had to wait a short time before he became free.

7

'Come and take a seat, Dot.' He indicated the chair on the other side of his desk. 'Have you made arrangements with your bank? Travellers' cheques and that sort of thing?'

'All done,' she confirmed.

'Well done. I wish all my clients were as well-prepared as you. I've found you a street map of Orléans, by the way.' He placed the map in front of her. 'Here are your train and ferry tickets. Your train leaves Cullington at thirteen-forty, and you'll have to transfer from King's Cross to Charing Cross for Dover. You're probably right about hotel reservations. Things are still too chaotic over there to be sure of an ETA, but I'm sure you'll find a hotel easily enough.'

'I imagine so.' She smiled gratefully. 'Thank you, Jack.'

'You're welcome. Tell me about your aunt. It's obvious you're very fond of her.'

'She's lovely, always full of fun and new ideas, very clever and artistic, too. She does the most beautiful fine needlework. She's much younger than my mother and my other aunt; I'd say she's about forty-five.' She took a photograph from her bag to show him. 'This was taken shortly before the war.'

Jack looked from the photograph to Dorothy and back again. 'It's easy to see the family resemblance,' he said. 'She's a beautiful woman.'

'Thanks, Jack.' Dorothy acknowledged the compliment with a smile. 'It's difficult to believe she came from the same stable as her sisters, although my mother surprised me last evening.' She told him about the stockings.

'That's good. I think Kate would forgive her mother for quite a lot if she made that kind of gesture.' He smiled again, almost laughing.

'What's funny, Jack?'

'Last year, I won several pairs of nylon stockings in a poker game with some Americans. I managed to fix up my mother, Mary, and Kate. That was when it all began between Kate and me.' He said quickly, 'Not because of the stockings, you understand, although I have to say they were well-received.'

'I'm sure they were.' Baffled for the moment, she said, 'I didn't know you played cards, Jack.'

'I don't if I can avoid it. I was just lucky, although Kate said it might also have had something to do with my habitual scowl.'

'You don't scowl.' She pretended to examine him. 'I'm sure she didn't say that. 'You just don't give much away, that's all.'

He nodded mysteriously. ' "Poker-Face Farthing", that's me.'

'Decent, dependable, honest Jack,' she said, standing up. 'Thank you for everything.'

'Let us know what transpires. If you're not back by the time we depart for Bridlington, we'll leave our new address and number with your mother.' He kissed her cheek. '*Bon voyage*, Dot, and *bonne chance*.'

2

Begin With the Gendarmerie

Dorothy's trousers attracted several disapproving looks from women as she waited on the platform at Cullington. She wondered if French women, with their reputation for *chic*, might be more broad-minded, or simply have more important matters to concern them. Either way, she didn't really care.

When the train arrived, she found an empty first-class compartment, a luxury she intended to enjoy for as long as it lasted. Her five years in the WAAF had been illuminating, satisfying, at times challenging, and largely enjoyable, but now she was beginning to appreciate again the finer things that had survived the war and that, happily, were not rationed.

She read for a while, until the events of the past few days invaded her consciousness. The unpleasantness with her mother now made her feel unaccountably guilty, especially when she recalled the gift of stockings. Instead, she made herself think about Jack and Kate, who were now supremely happy, with everything coming together for them. They deserved the best.

It was impossible to forget that she and Jack had once been romantically involved, albeit for a short time and before Kate became the foremost person in his life. It had been most enjoyable, but inevitably, she'd called time before he was ready. Clearly, he'd forgiven her and found happiness with Kate, but that didn't make her feel any better about it. Her record of broken relationships had become an embarrassment of guilt, although she was grown-up enough to recognise that the failures hadn't always been her fault. She and Bill had parted because their relationship was no longer working, so she could put that one down in the scorebook as a draw, and she accepted no blame at all for the break-up of her fling with Jake, or Jakub Wasiliewski, to give him his real name. He'd turned out to be an unmitigated bigot, so that particular failure was down to him. Daniel, the flight engineer from New Zealand, was one of the casualties, but it wasn't really her fault that he'd been keener on her than she was on him.

She tried to read again, but found that she'd lost the thread of the story. Moreover, her conscience was still prompting her with painful reminders. Poor Maurice had tried to conceal his infatuation with her, but it was all too obvious. After much disappointment, he'd finally given up on her, eventually transferring his affection to Kate. They'd been making plans for marriage, and then he was killed over Bremen. The thought of it still filled her with anguish.

Who had she left out? Alan, of course. He'd been obsessed with her for a long time. She'd only been awful to him when he was either too full of his assumed importance or when he was teasing Maurice in that superior way he had, so there was no conscience to be wasted there. In fairness, she recalled that Alan had undergone a kind of transformation in the Army, and had even pushed a wounded soldier fifteen miles to Dunkirk in an old invalid chair but, mercifully, he'd got Dorothy out of his romantic system before any of that took place, and whilst she was pleased by the change, and the fact that he'd formed a sound relationship with an officer in the ATS, that was the extent of her interest in him.

There were others, though, who'd suffered, and for no better reason than that nature had provided her with the physical charms to which men attached so much value. She was awkwardly aware that, as a silly young girl, she'd been guilty of vanity, but now, if such a thing had been possible, she would readily have handed over her looks, like her job at Rimmington's, to some woman whose need was greater than hers.

* * *

She made the Channel crossing and the train journey from Calais to the Paris Gare du Nord, and having changed stations to the Gare d' Austerlitz, fell asleep and roused herself just in time to get off the train in Orléans at almost five o' clock in the morning. More than fifteen hours had elapsed since leaving Cullington, and she felt more tired than she ever had, even after an all-night duty. Happily, the Hôtel de la Loire was next door to the station, so she picked up her case and walked into reception.

'*Bon jour,*' she said. '*Est-ce que vous avez des chambres?*'

'*Mais oui, madame.*' The porter smiled in a way that seemed remarkably friendly for five in the morning. '*Pour une personne?*'

'*Oui.*'

'*Pour combien de nuits, madame?*'

'*Je ne sais pas. Sept nuits, peut-être.*'

The porter said something she only half understood, but the gist of it was that she might revise the period of her stay later. She thanked him, and he turned the register so that she could add her name, address and signature.

'*Merci bien, madame, et votre passeport, sil vous plaît?*'

'My passport? Oh, of course.' She fished in her bag and retrieved it, remembering that hotels always kept a resident's passport for police checks. '*Voilà.*'

He opened it, saying apologetically, '*Je suis désolé, excusez-moi... mademoiselle.*'

'*Ça ne fait rien,*' she assured him. She was wearing gloves, so it was hardly surprising that the porter had assumed she was married.

Eventually, he produced a key and advised her that breakfast might be served in her room if she so desired. She declined the latter, but took the key, thankful in her weariness that she'd been able to muster sufficient school French to make the booking without embarrassment.

The porter called a colleague, who carried her case to Room 142. She tipped him gratefully.

Alone in her room, she undressed, taking only her pyjamas from her case.

Finally, she hung the '*Pas Déranger*' sign on her door handle for the chambermaid's benefit and slept until noon.

* * *

Lunch was only a vague reminder of pre-war French catering, but Dorothy had to admit that most things she'd taken for granted in pre-war Britain, were in short supply, if they were available at all, so she made the best of it before enquiring at reception for directions to La Maison de Jeanne d' Arc.

It turned out to be particularly easy to find, but quite busy, Joan of Arc being almost as popular in Orléans as she had been five hundred years earlier, so Dorothy settled, for the time being, for a conducted tour, of which she understood about three-quarters. Fortunately, the artefacts helped to some extent with the translation, so she emerged considerably better-informed about the eighteen-year-old girl who had led an army to a series of victories in the Hundred Years' War. In spite of her turning out for the enemy, it was impossible not to admire her.

At the end of the tour, several people stopped to speak to the guide, and eventually it was Dorothy's turn.

'Excuse me,' she said in her halting French. 'I'm trying to find a lady called Jeanne, who worked here before the war. I'm afraid I don't know her surname.'

The girl smiled sadly and said in English, 'Unfortunately, mademoiselle, I have only worked here since last year, and I was a young child before the war.'

'Oh dear.'

'However, the other guide has been here longer. She is a dedicated… student of the life of Jeanne d' Arc, and she will be here tomorrow.'

'*Merci beaucoup, mademoiselle. Comment elle s' appelle, cette dame*?'

The girl smiled, as the French often did when an English person made the effort to speak their language. '*Elle s' appelle* Madame Clothilde Leblanc.'

'*Merci beaucoup, mademoiselle.*'

'*C' est rien, mademoiselle.*'

It was a step forward, and Dorothy felt quite heartened, so she spent the rest of the day sightseeing in the old town and the beautiful Cathédrale de Saint Croix. The city seemed to have escaped most of the bombing, a fact that gave her much satisfaction.

* * *

The next day, she revisited the Maison de Jeanne d' Arc, where there was no sign of anyone who might be Clothilde Leblanc. Only an elderly and almost toothless woman occupied the open-sided kiosk.

'*Bon jour, madame*,' said Dorothy. '*Je voudrai parler avec* Madame Leblanc, *sil vous plait*.'

The old woman told her sternly that the next conducted tour would be in twenty minutes' time.

'I took the tour yesterday. I only want to speak with Madame Leblanc.'

'The next tour is at ten hours, *madame*.'

'I have already taken the tour. I wish to speak with Madame Leblanc, *madame*.'

The old woman was adamant. 'The next tour is at ten hours, *madame*.'

It could go on forever, like a song about a hole in a bucket, that they used to sing in the Girl Guides, at least, during the embarrassingly short time Dorothy was with them. 'All right, I'll come back at ten o' clock.'

It was now only fifteen minutes to ten, so Dorothy walked around the locale, thinking about what she would ask Madame Leblanc, supposing she were ever allowed to speak to her.

Eventually, the time came, and Dorothy went to the kiosk. The old woman took her money and said, 'Madame Leblanc will lead the tour, *madame*.'

'Thank you, *madame*.' It seemed that the old woman lived according to her own, inflexible rules.

The tour commenced with only half-a-dozen in the party, including Dorothy, and once again, she steeped herself in the story of the maiden from Domrémy, who had made herself a pain in the neck to the English, though a different kind of pain, she imagined, from that which the old woman in the kiosk had been earlier that morning.

Madame Leblanc appeared to be forty or thereabouts, with a stern manner and what appeared to be an encyclopaedic knowledge of the Hundred Years' War, doubtless from the French perspective, but no less thorough.

The tour ended, and two of the other five members of the party engaged Mme Leblanc in conversation, which seemed to be the accepted thing. When they had gone, Dorothy introduced herself.

'*Bon jour*, Madame Leblanc. My name is Dorothy Needham, and

I am trying to trace my aunt, who was, I believe, a friend of someone called Jeanne, who worked here before the war.'

Mme Leblanc closed her eyes for several seconds before saying, 'You refer, I believe, to Jeanne Garnier. There was an Englishwoman who spent much time here.'

Dorothy felt a tingle of excitement. 'That would be Sarah Moore, my aunt.'

'I do not recall her name, but I have no reason to contradict you, *madame*.'

Dorothy was almost afraid to ask her next question. 'Do you know what happened to them?'

Again, Mme Leblanc closed her eyes, as if summoning her inner strength. 'Ultimately, no, I do not. They were both Jewish, I believe.'

Clinging resolutely to the present tense, Dorothy said, 'My aunt is half-Jewish.'

'They were all the same to the Boche,' she said resignedly. 'Full-blooded, half-Jewish, quarter-Jewish…. All the same. They were taken away. I believe it was in the summer of nineteen forty-one.'

'By the Germans?' As she spoke, she realised it was probably a silly question.

'On the orders of the Boche. They were arrested by the *gendarmes*, who had no choice in the matter.'

Dorothy had been preparing herself, but the news was no less devastating. 'Do you know…. Have you any idea where the *gendarmes* might have taken them?'

'They might have taken them anywhere, madame, but they handed them over to the Boche. You might almost say that they washed their hands of them.' In case of misunderstanding, she added, 'Like Pontius Pilate with Christ on the Feast of the Passover.'

'That's too awful for words.'

'It was a familiar occurrence, *mademoiselle*.'

'I mean that I've travelled all the way from the north of England, only to find myself in a *cul de sac*.'

'What do you mean about the *cul de sac*, madame? I do not understand you. You say you are in the bottom of a bag?'

'I'm sorry, *madame*. In England the term is used to mean a street with only one opening, or a dead-end situation.'

Mme Leblanc nodded, finally understanding the reference. 'You mean you have reached an *impasse*.'

'I'm afraid so.' Whatever name she chose to give it, her predicament was the same.

Mme Leblanc shrugged in the equivocal way that Dorothy associated with the French, and said, 'In that case, I advise you to leave the bottom of your bag and look further. You could begin with the Gendarmerie.'

3

Somewhere in Germany

Dorothy waited for almost half-an-hour in a bare and draughty corridor, before a gendarme, who introduced himself as Constable Duprés, invited her to follow him.

He led her up one flight of stairs to an office with ornate, mahogany panelling and a frosted glass window that seemed incapable of letting in any appreciable light.

'Please seat yourself,' he said in a heavy accent, 'and tell me about your difficulty.'

Dorothy took the seat in front of his desk, conscious of the strong smell of furniture polish. Looking at all the panelling and furniture in the office, she imagined that the cleaners would have an enormous task on their hands, and she hoped for their sakes that the polishing took place only periodically.

'I am trying to find the whereabouts of my aunt, who was arrested in the summer of nineteen forty-one.'

'What crime had she committed, for her to be arrested?'

'None whatsoever. She is half-Jewish.'

'Ah.' He made a note and asked, 'You have her name?'

She ignored the stupidity of the question and said, 'Her name is Sarah Moore. She is a British citizen and she was travelling with a British passport.' She could say that with confidence, because she wouldn't have been allowed to enter France without it.

'Please assist me in the spelling of her name.'

Dorothy obliged.

'So, it appears that Sarah Moore, a British citizen, although of Jewish blood, was arrested in the summer of nineteen forty-one.'

'That's what I said.' She wasn't keen on the phrase, '…although of Jewish blood.' It was almost as if the Germans had never left, but she had to remain civil. 'I need to know where she was taken after that.'

'She would be passed to the occupying force.'

'I've no doubt she was, but surely you have some record of the incident that gives more information than that.'

Constable Duprés looked at her earnestly for several seconds and then said, 'Please wait here, *madame*.' He left the room, closing the door behind him.

Dorothy got up and walked around the room, which contained nothing of interest, so she went to the window. It was partly open, so that she could hear the conversations of people below. Unfortunately, hearing and understanding were two distinct entities, so she was no wiser until a Citroen pulled up beneath the window, and a gendarme got out, followed by another man. It appeared that they were handcuffed together, and that the prisoner was less than pleased about it. Dorothy remembered seeing a deserter being brought back to Humby-on-the-Wold. He was handcuffed, and marched between two RAF Policemen and, whilst she had little sympathy for him as a deserter, the way his escorts were treating him was quite shameful.

The constable's voice interrupted her thoughts. 'The sub-brigadier is coming to speak with you, *madame*,' he said.

A sub-brigadier, eh? He sounded like top brass, so she was surprised when the officer who came into the room wore three stripes on his arm.

'This is Sub-Brigadier of Police Toussaint,' the constable announced proudly.

'How d' you do.' Dorothy offered her hand, which the sub-brigadier ignored. She waited for him to take his seat, and said, 'I, too, had three chevrons on my arm until a couple of weeks ago.'

'This is the badge of a sub-brigadier of police,' he told her coldly.

'I'd already gathered that. I was a sergeant-instructor in the Women's Auxiliary Air Force. I served for more than five years.'

He seemed as unimpressed by that information as she was with his attitude.

'You are looking for this Englishwoman who was arrested in June, nineteen forty-one, I believe.'

'I didn't know the date, but yes, she was arrested in the summer of that year.'

He turned to the constable and issued an order that Dorothy found unintelligible, but which resulted in the junior officer making a hasty exit. 'I have sent the constable to find the appropriate documents,' he said. He looked less than friendly when he went on to say, 'We are busy enough without this kind of enquiry, but we are obliged, for diplomatic reasons, to attend to such matters.'

'I'm grateful to you.' She was also grateful for the unintentional tip about the diplomatic situation. There could be a time when a little extra persuasion might be necessary.

'I understand your aunt was Jewish.'

'She's half-Jewish.'

He gave a Gallic shrug and said, 'Even so, you are looking for *une aiguille*....'

'A needle in a haystack, I know.'

'It is good that you understand that.'

The door opened and the constable came in, bearing a large tome bound between stiff boards that looked, incredibly, like wood. As he placed it on the sub-brigadier's desk, it gave a loud 'clunk', which seemed to confirm Dorothy's suspicion.

'*Maintenant,*' said the sub-brigadier, '*Juin, quarante-et-un.*' He proceeded to turn the pages quickly until he reached the month in question, when he searched more carefully.

Continuing in English, he said, 'There were several political arrests, that is to say, on behalf of the Gestapo, on the nineteenth of June. Two young women were arrested at one address. They were Jeanne Marie Garnier and Sarah Elizabeth Moore.' He sat back with an air of satisfaction.

'Thank you, *monsieur*. Can you tell me where they were taken after that?'

'Yes, they were taken to Paris.'

'By the Germans?'

'*Non, madame.* At that stage, they would still be in French hands. They would only be handed over to the Germans in Paris.'

Dorothy wasn't sure whether that was a setback or a step forward, but she had another question. 'This agency that ordered the arrests, what was its name?'

'The Gestapo, *madame*, the Geheime Staatspolizei. It means—'

'The secret police, I know.'

'They were the Nazi secret police, *madame*, and they had almost absolute power. You must understand that when they ordered arrests to be made, we had no alternative but to make those arrests.'

'I understand. I'm not blaming you or the French police for anything. I know who the real villains were.' She stood up to leave. 'I'm very grateful to you, *monsieur*. Will you answer me one last question?'

'If I can.'

'Where in Paris would they be taken?'

'They should be able to help you at the Central Police Station.'

* * *

Three nights after she booked into the Hôtel de la Loire, Dorothy paid her bill and left for Paris. She suspected she was about to reach another dead end, but she had to try.

Mercifully, the journey to Paris was fairly quick, and taxis at the Gare d'Austerlitz were plentiful. She went straight to the Central Police Station.

She had to wait more than ten minutes before a receptionist came free, but her turn came, and she explained her quest to a serious-looking woman, who shook her head dismissively.

'The officers are far too busy to be distracted by that kind of thing,' she said. At least, that was the gist as Dorothy understood it.

'I'm very surprised. The man I spoke to at the Foreign Office in London said I'd be sure to receive a sympathetic hearing.' She wouldn't normally have resorted to that ploy, but the woman was so off-hand that she invited it.

The receptionist blinked. 'You have spoken to the British Bureau d' Affaires Étrangers?'

'Of course. This is important to me.'

'Please wait one minute.' She spoke to someone on the internal telephone, and Dorothy distinctly heard the words 'Bureau d' Affaires

Étrangers.' There was a brief conversation, and the receptionist said, 'An officer will see you, but he is occupied at this time. Can you return tomorrow morning at eleven hours?'

'Yes, I'll book into an hotel for the night. Thank you.' She was about to leave, when she remembered to ask, 'What is the officer's name, the man I'm going to see?'

'He is Major Bernard of the Sûreté Nationale.'

'Thank you for your help.' She left the station ever thankful for the sub-brigadier's reference to diplomatic persuasion.

* * *

The hotel was more expensive, but more luxurious as well than the one in Orléans, and Dorothy felt as rested as she could be in the circumstances when she returned to the Central Police Station in Rue Louis Blanc.

The receptionist was not the one Dorothy had spoken to on her previous visit, but she was similarly dismissive, until Dorothy insisted that she had an appointment to see Major Bernard, whereupon she spoke to someone on the internal telephone.

'Major Bernard will see you shortly,' she said. 'Please take a seat in the waiting area.'

Dorothy sat, conscious of the silk stockings she was wearing, and of the glances she'd received from various people, male and female. The stockings belonged to the pre-war age, but most of the French women she'd seen were bare-legged. Somehow, the war refused to go away.

Major Bernard was taking his time, and Dorothy wished she'd bought a newspaper. Then she remembered the book in her bag. She was trying to find her way back into the plot, when a uniformed figure stood before her.

'Mademoiselle Needham? I am Major Bernard of the Sûreté Nationale.'

Dorothy accepted his handshake and said, '*Bon jour*, Major Bernard.'

'Please come this way, *mademoiselle*.' He led the way along a mahogany-panelled passage and opened a door, inviting her in.

Like the passageway, the office was panelled, but only up to about four feet, where a dado rail separated it from the distempered wall, which might have been cream at one time. Cigarette or cigar smoke had deepened it to an unpleasant shade of brown.

Major Bernard invited her to take a seat whilst he took his place behind a large, ornate, walnut desk.

'And now, *mademoiselle*, how may I help you?' He was dark and good-looking in a dated, matinee-idol kind of way. Even his pencil moustache belonged to the nineteen-thirties, and Dorothy had the impression that he was extremely conscious of his appearance and persona.

'I wish to trace the whereabouts of my aunt, who was arrested on the orders of the Gestapo in Orléans on the nineteenth of June, nineteen forty-one. She was brought to Paris shortly after that date, when she was taken by the Germans.'

'My dear *mademoiselle*, how distressing for you.'

'It certainly is.' She imagined that, had the desk not been in the way, he might have patted her knee, ostensibly in sympathy.

'Let me make a note of your aunt's particulars.'

'All I can tell you is her name, which is Sarah Elizabeth Moore, and that she was arrested in Orléans, as I've told you, on the nineteenth of June, nineteen forty-one.' She spelled her aunt's name for him and watched him write it.

'Thank you, *mademoiselle*. Please excuse me for a moment.' He picked up the telephone and spoke rapidly to someone. Dorothy heard the words, '*Juin, quarante-et-un*,' but she could make out little else. She imagined that, like the sub-brigadier, he was requesting the relevant document.

'In a moment,' he said, putting the phone down, 'I may be able to tell you more.'

'Thank you, *monsieur*.'

'*C'est rien*. Tell me, mademoiselle, shall you be in Paris for long?'

'That depends on what I learn from this visit, *monsieur*, although I doubt it. I have an unpleasant feeling about my enquiry, and I cannot realistically see myself taking it much further.'

'That is very sad, *mademoiselle*. You have my sympathy.'

'Thank you, *monsieur*.' Dorothy could see exactly what the Major had in mind, and it had little to do with sympathy.

'If you are going to spend the night in Paris, for your safety's sake, you should not be alone.'

'Is Paris such a dangerous city, *monsieur*?' If that were the case, it was an awful admission for a senior policeman to make, even as an overture to a proposition, which was clearly where he was heading.

'No city is completely safe, *mademoiselle*, but if you will do me the honour of dining with me, I can guarantee both your safety and your enjoyment. I know the very best restaurants—'

'Thank you for your kind invitation, *Monsieur Major*, but the likelihood is that I shall return to England today.'

He looked rather like a child who'd been denied a treat, which, in effect, he was, but a distraction occurred in the shape of a constable bearing a large file similar to that which the sub-brigadier had consulted.

'*Merci.*' He opened the file and began searching. After maybe one or two minutes, he took a sheet of paper from the file and examined it with an expression that was far from encouraging.

'I am sorry, *mademoiselle*,' he said finally. 'All I can tell you is that your aunt was taken, along with many others, on the twentieth of June, on a train from the Gare du Nord. The train had been commandeered by the Nazis.'

Dorothy heard herself ask faintly, 'Can you tell me where she was taken?'

'Unfortunately, I can be of no further assistance, mademoiselle. I only know that she was taken to a destination somewhere in Germany.'

4

May

Ten Minutes Late

Added to the disappointment Dorothy had already encountered in France was the task of relating her experiences to her mother and Aunt Alice, neither of whom really cared, but who had the right, as Aunt Sarah's sisters, to be informed.

Fortunately, for her sake, if not theirs, Kate and Jack had still not moved to Bridlington. It seemed that work on the shop premises had been delayed by some bureaucratic difficulty regarding timber and plumbing materials. Almost every commodity was controlled by a government department that appeared inactive most of the time, only occasionally breaking into a leisurely stroll.

'As if President Truman weren't enough of a problem,' complained Jack, 'our civil service is making life impossible.'

'Not that we've invited you here to listen to a tale of woe,' said Kate with a meaningful look at her husband, 'when we really want to know about France. Come on, Dot, tell all.'

'I don't mind listening to your complaints,' said Dorothy. 'It seems to me you have plenty to be upset about.'

'Take our minds off it,' urged Kate.

'All right, top me up, and I'll make you even more miserable.'

'That's impossible,' said Jack, plying the bottle.

'Unlike you, Kate,' said Dorothy, eyeing her friend's bulge, 'I don't know what I was expecting. I spoke to someone who vaguely remembered Aunt Sarah, but who knew her friend Jeanne, and she told me they'd both been arrested and taken away some time in the summer of nineteen forty-one.'

'Oh no,' said Kate, taking a sip of water and pulling a face at the blandness of it. 'That's just what we feared.'

Dorothy asked her, 'Is that all you're going to drink?'

'She won't touch alcohol,' Jack told her. 'She's afraid the baby will be born incapable of walking in a straight line, aren't you, darling?'

'No, I'm not,' Kate protested. 'It's just that… nothing's been said about drinking during pregnancy, but I just have a feeling that it can't possibly do the baby any good to keep pouring booze into him.'

'Her,' corrected Jack.

'We'll see, but do go on, Dot.'

'I went to the *Gendarmerie*, where they told me that the prisoners had been taken to Paris and handed over to the Germans there, so I caught a train to Paris, where the policeman I saw tried to proposition me, and then told me that the prisoners had been taken away by train the next day to Germany. That was all he knew. She was taken to a place somewhere in Germany. At that point,' she said dejectedly, 'as they say in the worst detective stories, the trail went cold.'

'What rotten luck,' said Kate.

Jack simply nodded in agreement.

'Silk stockings,' said Dorothy absently.

'What?' Even Kate sometimes struggled to follow her friend's thought processes.

'I was wearing a pair of the silk stockings my mother gave me. It was a mistake.'

'Why was it a mistake?' A few years earlier, Jack had made no secret of his disappointment when Dorothy joined the WAAF. He'd always visualised her in a Wren's uniform, with black stockings, but he'd admitted to her in a private moment that she looked pretty good in any kind of hosiery.

'I think it encouraged Major Bernard, the policeman who propositioned me.'

After the briefest consideration, Kate asked, 'Do Frenchmen need encouragement? I've always thought it was a national characteristic, like driving on the wrong side of the road and selling onions from a bicycle. Anyway, why are you suddenly wondering about that?'

'I was using it as a diversion, to distract me from the fact that my quest turned out to be a total failure.'

'Dot, if you wore gumboots and a sack tied up with string, men would still proposition you.'

'I'm afraid so.'

'And if it was a failure,' said Jack, 'it was no fault of yours.'

* * *

He was right. So Dorothy kept telling herself. Her mother was listening to a play on the wireless, but Dorothy was lost in a series of thoughts that distracted her completely from the book she was trying to read.

'I really don't care for this,' said her mother. 'It's one of those clever plays by J B Priestley. If you ask me, he's too clever for his own good.'

Dorothy couldn't imagine that anyone would take the trouble to ask her. 'If you don't like it, why don't you switch it off? The news isn't for another half-hour, yet.'

'I think I will.'

Dorothy tried again to engage with the story, but looked up when she heard a soft grunt. Her mother's left arm was dangling over the side of her chair. The left side of her face appeared to have collapsed, so that her mouth hung open in a lopsided gape.

She leapt up and went to the phone.

'Number, please?'

'Emergency. Ambulance, please. This is Cullington one-one-eight and my mother's had a stroke.' She went through the rest of the procedure, giving her name, her mother's name, and her address. Assured that an ambulance would be with her shortly, she put the phone down. She was completely helpless, now. She would notify Gladys when she could, but there was absolutely nothing more she could do. Meanwhile, her mother sat helpless in her armchair, unreal and grotesque in her paralysed state.

For the sake of doing something, and in case she couldn't get to Gladys's cottage before morning, she wrote a note for her:

Mother had stroke. In hospital

Hastily, she tore it up, impatient with herself for her stupidity. She would be around when Gladys arrived, and she would tell her then.

After about ten more minutes, the doorbell rang, and she answered it, relieved beyond belief that the ambulance had arrived. She watched the men lift her mother on to a stretcher, and then locked up the house so that she could go to the hospital.

* * *

After what seemed an age, a nurse came to the waiting room and called her name.

'Your mother is in safe hands, Miss Needham. The best thing you can do is go home and get some sleep. We may be able to tell you more in the morning.'

It all sounded unbelievably trite, and Dorothy could imagine them giving the same clichéd advice to all relatives. However, she kept that thought to herself and took a taxi home, where she surprised herself by falling asleep almost as soon as her head touched the pillow.

Incredibly, when the alarm clock woke her in the morning, several seconds elapsed before the events of the previous evening returned to her and the adrenalin began to flow.

She bathed and dressed hurriedly, so that she was ready to speak to Gladys when she arrived.

Eventually, she heard the kitchen door open, and she went to meet her.

'Good morning, Gladys.'

'Good morning, Miss Dorothy….' She gave her an enquiring look. 'Miss Dorothy, is something wrong?'

'My mother had a stroke last night.'

'Oh, no.'

'She's in hospital. I'm going to telephone them shortly, but the things is, she won't be here to eat, obviously, and I don't know when I'll be in. Could you leave me something for dinner, please, that even I can serve up?'

In the capable way that she had, Gladys went seamlessly from shocked to reassuring. 'I'll do you something for lunch, Miss Dorothy, and I'll make a stew as well. All you'll have to do is put it in the oven for half-an-hour to warm up. I'll leave full instructions.'

'Thank you, Gladys. I'm very grateful.'

'That's all right, Miss Dorothy, and don't you worry. Mrs Needham's in the best hands.'

Dorothy looked at the clock. It was a little after eight. According to snippets gleaned from conversations with Kate, the day shift would now be on duty, so she telephoned the hospital.

'Cullington General Hospital.'

'Good morning. I'm enquiring about my mother, who was brought in last night, having suffered a stroke.'

'What is the patient's name?'

'Florence Needham.'

'Thank you. Please hold the line while I connect you with the Stroke and Cardiac Ward.'

Dorothy waited for what seemed a long time, and then someone answered the telephone, identifying herself as Sister someone, a name that Dorothy didn't quite catch.

'Good morning. My name is Dorothy Needham. I'm enquiring about my mother, Florence Needham, who was admitted last night after a stroke.'

'Ah, Florence Needham, yes. Your mother spent a comfortable night and she's responding to treatment.'

Dorothy controlled her impatience. 'Is that all you can tell me?'

'I'm afraid so, Miss Needham. Visiting time is between two-thirty and three-thirty. You'll be able to see her then, but you'll have to be patient. It's unlikely that she'll be able to speak to you yet.'

'I'm trying very hard to be patient, Sister. Thank you. Goodbye.'

'Goodbye.'

She put the phone down and went to the kitchen to relay the information, such as it was, to Gladys.

'I expect they have to be careful in case they give the wrong impression,' said Gladys.

'They're careful, all right.'

'Just keep telling yourself, Miss Dorothy, that she couldn't be in better hands. Leave it to them.'

Under normal circumstances, Dorothy would never have discussed family affairs with either Gladys or her husband, who looked after their gardens as well as several others, but today was different. 'Only a couple of weeks ago, I had a pitched battle with my mother about my private life, Gladys.'

With surprising insight, Gladys said, 'Don't give it a moment's thought, Miss Dorothy. That stroke was always going to happen, come what may. You go and sit down while I prepare your breakfast. I'll bring you a cup of coffee while you're waiting.'

* * *

She spent some time on the telephone to Kate, who was similarly soothing.

'They have to be very careful what they say, Dot.'

'I realise that, but it's like listening to a gramophone record, the way they trot it out.'

'Have you always put heart and soul into every little job, Dot? We have to give that information to relatives all the time.'

'No, you're right, Kate.'

'Are you going to visit her this afternoon?'

'Yes.'

'Don't expect too much from her at this stage. It takes time to recover from a stroke.'

Dorothy's mind returned to the previous evening. 'It happened in no time at all,' she said.

'They do.'

'One minute she was going to switch off the wireless set, and the next minute she was helpless.'

'Try not to dwell on it, Dot. You'll feel better about it when you've seen her.'

Dorothy looked up at the clock and said, 'Yes, I must get ready. I've a taxi coming in ten minutes.'

'All right, Dot. Chin up, and keep me informed. ''Bye.'

''Bye, Kate.' She put the phone down and went for her hat and coat.

* * *

29

The taxi arrived promptly. For once, the driver wasn't one of the talkative kind, a quality very much in his favour, and Dorothy had a peaceful journey to the hospital. As she got out, he asked, 'Back in an hour's time, then, love?'

'That's right. Do you want me to pay you now?'

'Nay, it'll wait while I get you home.'

'Thank you.'

There was a plan on the wall in Reception that showed the way to the ward, and she reckoned that by the time she reached it, visiting time would have begun, so she followed the signs.

Two flights of stairs and a long corridor later, she saw the sign in front of her for the Stroke and Cardiac Care Ward, and she was about to enquire at the office by the entrance, when a severe-looking woman of possibly middle years opened the door.

'Oh,' said Dorothy, 'I'm looking for my mother, Florence Needham.'

The severe look softened. 'I'm Sister Danby. I'm sorry, Miss Needham. 'Your mother died very suddenly about ten minutes ago. We tried telephoning you, but you were obviously on your way.'

5

June

A Grown-Up World

In the days that followed, Dorothy had to attend to matters of which she had no previous experience, but which nevertheless demanded her attention, and the list of tasks would have been more daunting still, had she not had Kate's support and advice, often delivered over the telephone.

'I couldn't help learning about these things when I was caring for Mrs Alcock after Maurice was killed,' said Kate modestly. 'She was distraught, and I was over the hills and far away with phenobarbitone, but some of it registered. You'll find that others will prompt you as well.'

'Which others?'

'The undertaker, the hospital, your solicitor…. It's quite normal for someone in your position to feel overwhelmed, and it's up to those people to help and guide you through the maze. You mustn't be afraid to ask for help.' She smiled suddenly.

'What's so funny, Kate?'

'Just the thought of you being in awe of any of those people.'

'Maybe I'm not as tough as you think.'

* * *

Mr Paynter, the solicitor, was one of the helpful professionals Kate had mentioned.

'Basically, Miss Needham, your mother left a bequest of five hundred pounds to the Cullington Conservative Association, and the balance of her estate, which is substantial, to you.' He shook his head confidently as he said, 'I presume she left no debts.'

'Only the monthly tradesmen's accounts, and I've informed them that I'm now responsible for them.'

'Do let me have the accounts up to your mother's demise, Miss Needham, and I will deal with them.'

'If that's how you want to do it.' She took a number of documents from her bag and said, 'Here are the bank statements and share certificates you wanted.' Having handed them over, she looked around the office, gaining the impression that little had changed since the formation of the partnership in Victorian times. In most respects, it resembled the offices she'd visited in France; in fact, only the portrait of the King and Queen, which hung above Mr Paynter's head made it different.

'Thank you. I'll deal with those as well. I'm sure your mother's bankers will release monies to cover the cost of the funeral.'

'There's no need for that, Mr Paynter. I can pay for the funeral.'

'I assure you, Miss Needham, that there is a pressing need for it. This government has increased estate duty to an extent that makes it vitally important that all allowable expenses are charged to the estate. We do not know, as yet, the full value of your mother's shareholdings, but I can tell you that you are likely to lose either fifty or seventy-five percent of it in estate duty.'

His tone was so grave that Dorothy had to bite her lip so as not to laugh. 'How perfectly appropriate. She hated Clement Attlee and his government passionately, and now she's helping to fund their policies.'

Mr Paynter eyed her sympathetically. 'I believe you're still reeling from the shock of your mother's demise, Miss Needham. It is perhaps a little early in the proceedings to expect you to grasp the enormity of the threat.'

'I'll bear it in mind, Mr Paynter. In the meantime, is there anything else in the will that I need to know about?'

'Only a wish on your mother's part for the funeral to be held at the church of St Philip and St James, by the Reverend Nicholas Sykes. Unfortunately, the Reverend Sykes departed this life three years ago, but I'm sure his successor, the Reverend Thomas White will be happy to oblige.'

'In that case, I'll speak to him and set things in motion.' She stood up and offered her hand. 'Thank you for your help, Mr Paynter.' She hoped, though not too earnestly, that she hadn't offended him.

* * *

Having completed the undertaker's checklist, she made an appointment to see the Reverend White. She'd gone to the vicarage with a rough, preconceived, and therefore pre-judged, idea of what to expect, and then the vicar promptly bowled her a googly.

'What are you feeling, Miss Needham?' He was a young man with none of the stereotypical attributes of Dorothy's limited experience. 'It probably sounds like a daft question, but I do think it's important to talk about these things.'

'Yes, you've just caught me on the back foot, that's all.'

'Take your time,' he advised matter of-factly. 'Tell you what. Would you like a drink? I know I should.'

It was a welcome suggestion. 'Yes, please. What have you got?' It was a fair question at a time of continuing shortages.

'Anything you like, as long as it's wine, whisky or gin.'

'Gin would be oh, so welcome.'

'With tonic water or cordial?'

'You continue to surprise me. With tonic, please.'

'Excuse me for a moment.' He left her alone with her surroundings. The room was small, but presumably adequate for its purpose, and the ancient desk, with what appeared to be a tooled leather surface, was otherwise host to several piles of documents. If he had a system for keeping track of them, she imagined it was either a chaotic one or an extremely clever one.

He returned with the drinks. 'Excuse the mess, won't you? My housekeeper's not allowed to touch anything in here. It's absolutely out of bounds and therefore disgracefully untidy.' He handed her a glass containing gin, and placed a bottle of Indian tonic water on the desk. 'Say when,' he said, opening the bottle.

'Dorothy watched him pour tonic on to the gin. 'When,' she said, still in a state of disbelief.

'I'm hardly the stage vicar, you'll have deduced,' he said, as if

33

reading her thoughts. 'I was an RAF chaplain until a short time ago, stationed at Humby-on-the-Wold.'

'When?'

'Since May, nineteen forty-four.'

'I just missed you. I left Humby in February, forty-four, when I was posted to Cranwell. I was a sergeant-instructor there.'

'Good for you, Miss Needham.' Reverting to his initial question, he asked, 'Have you thought about what I asked you earlier? I mean, how you feel at this stage?'

'If you'd asked that question a few days ago, I'd have struggled to give you an answer, I was so confused, but I'm thinking more clearly, now.'

He said nothing, but waited for her to continue.

'More than anything else, I feel guilty on a number of counts.' She began counting on her fingers. 'Firstly, I'm not overcome with grief, when convention dictates that I should be. Secondly, there's the fact that my mother and I always had a stormy relationship because I couldn't live the kind of life she wanted me to lead. Because of my rebellious ways, I was expelled from school, and even drummed out of the Girl Guides. I insisted on taking a job for my own satisfaction, even though I was financially independent. I refused to apply for a commission in the WAAF, preferring to associate with those whom my mother called "common girls", and I resigned from my job at Rimmington's just as my mother had begun to accept it.' She left out the shock revelation that she was no longer a virgin, reasoning that there must be a limit to the confessions a cleric could be expected to hear with equanimity.

'What was your job at Rimmington's. Miss Needham?'

'I was Assistant Buyer in Women's Fashions.'

He nodded, clearly impressed. 'And why did you resign from that job?'

'Without wishing to sound impossibly pious, I took the line that the person who'd been doing my job since nineteen-forty had more need of it than I. She's a war widow and a mother. Needless to say, my mother saw it as a ridiculous reason for resigning.'

'And of course, you resented your mother's reaction. A clear picture is emerging, Miss Needham. Tell me, though, why you refused a commission.'

She shrugged, having explained her reasons so many times. 'I couldn't see the point. I was doing a useful job as a wireless operator, and then as an instructor. Also, for the first time in my life I was able to share the experiences of girls from every conceivable background, the girls my mother called 'common', but who were, in many cases, true friends. I wrote to one of them only a few days ago.' She took a sip from her glass and said, 'The war was the most terrible thing imaginable; I lost two particularly close friends, one to enemy action and the other to a training accident, but I have to admit that I benefited from my service in the WAAF.'

The Reverend White smiled and nodded. 'I'm not used to hearing individual confessions,' he said. 'I usually leave that to my Roman Catholic counterparts, but as confessions go, and as I understand them, yours leaves you almost blameless. You can't make yourself feel any kind of emotion. That's an impossibility.' As Dorothy had earlier, he was counting with his fingers. 'I don't have to tell you that it takes two to argue, and my faith tells me there's not the slightest doubt that your mother has forgiven you for your part in any disagreement.' Taking his middle finger, he said, 'Maybe the fault that resulted in your being expelled from school and the Girl Guides was simply that you were an untamed individual, and goodness knows, history is full of great men and women who enjoyed that characteristic. Our previous prime minister springs readily to mind.' Finally, he touched his fourth finger. 'Taking the job at Rimmington's showed character, but relinquishing it in favour of someone less well-off than yourself was an act of true kindness. Bless you, Miss Needham.' He reached for a notepad and took a pen from his pocket. 'Now, if you're feeling better about things, perhaps we should organise the funeral.'

'Yes, let's.' Dorothy was feeling a great deal better for their conversation. He'd only told her what she already knew. She just needed to hear someone else say those things.

* * *

The funeral went extremely smoothly, after which Gladys performed one of her culinary miracles, turning the humble rations into a feast at the reception.

When everyone was gone, Dorothy spoke to her. 'Gladys, thank you ever so much for what you've done. I can't think of anyone who could have done it half as well.'

'Oh, it's not difficult when you know how, Miss Dorothy, and If everybody was happy with it as well, that's all that matters.' Her words were as genuine as ever, but she seemed somehow preoccupied.

'Is something troubling you, Gladys?' It had occurred to her that Gladys and her husband might be apprehensive about their future, although Kirby did have work elsewhere.

'Miss Dorothy, I've been meaning to speak to you, but it's never been the right time, with Mrs Needham being carried away, and things being as they are.'

'Don't worry about that, Gladys. Just tell me what's on your mind.'

Gladys hesitated, nerving herself. 'The thing is, Miss Dorothy, Kirby and me, for some time now, we've been wanting to retire, only we've held off until you were home from the WAAFs. We wanted you to be settled, and then Mrs Needham being taken as she was....' Clearly, the rest was difficult to put into words.

'If you both want to retire, of course you must. I have to sell this house, anyway, and buy something smaller.'

'Have you, Miss Dorothy?' Evidently, the possibility had never occurred to her.

'Yes, you see, there'll be a massive estate duty to pay to the government when the will's proved, and I don't want to sell any shares to pay it.'

'Why ever not, Miss Dorothy? This house belonged to your grandparents, as I recall.'

'That's right.' Her mother would have been appalled at the idea of her discussing such a thing with a servant, but Dorothy was mistress of the house, and Gladys had asked her a perfectly normal question. 'To sell a large block of Needham's shares, I'd need the consent of the other shareholders, and I couldn't guarantee that happening.'

'Oh, I see.'

'I would be equally reluctant to sell them. You see, it would enable someone to acquire a large holding in the company, and not everyone has the family's best interests at heart. So, you see, it makes sense to sell the house. Then you and Kirby can retire, and I can deal with the Chancellor's demands.'

'I'll tell you what I'll do, Miss Dorothy. I know cooking isn't what you're best at.'

Dorothy laughed good-naturedly. 'As a model of understatement, that should be mounted, framed and hung on the wall, Gladys.'

'Right, Miss Dorothy. I was going to say, you know me and my instructions, don't you?'

'I'm thankful to say I do.' Gladys's step-by-step instructions were a triumph of plain English and acceptance that some people needed the minutest of directions, all achieved without ever patronising her clueless mistress.

'Well, just until you find another cook-general, I'm going to leave you instructions about basic cookery. I won't leave you in the lurch, don't you worry.'

'Gladys,' said Dorothy, 'you're not just a cook-general. You've always been a fairy godmother to me, and I'll be heartbroken to see you go, but I want you and Kirby to have a happy retirement.'

There was still a great deal for Dorothy to do; it was a grown-up world for a new orphan, but the greatest drama occurred partway through the following month.

6

Room for Growth

The trials of tidying up her mother's affairs seemed never-ending, so Dorothy was always grateful for a distraction, and especially when it involved friends. Her latest came on the twentieth of the month with a telephone call from Jack.

'Dot, will you do me a gigantic favour?'

'Oh, I don't know, Jack. It depends on what you have in mind.'

'Say you will, Dot. Please.'

It was unusual for Jack to beg; in fact, it was unknown in Dorothy's experience, so she stopped teasing. 'If I can help you, of course I will. What's the problem?'

'I have to take a party to London Airport tomorrow, and I won't be back until late. I can't leave Kate on her own at this late stage, but there's no one else to do the job.'

'Don't tell me. You want me to take your party to London Airport. Consider it done.'

'No.' He sounded quite desperate.

'Only joking, Jack. Do you want me to stay with Kate?'

'Please, will you?'

'Of course I will. Don't worry.'

'You should be all right. The baby's not due until next week, but you never know.'

'If it starts,' she assured him, 'I'll push a cork in until you get back.'

'Now I know you're joking, but thanks, Dot.'

Joke was all she could do. She would never leave Kate on her own, but she found the very idea of childbirth terrifying. She could only rely on the baby's sense of timing and hope that nothing would happen until the scheduled date, when Jack would be on hand. Failing that, she could only hope that the ambulance would arrive promptly.

* * *

She reached the house shortly before Jack was due to leave, so he showed her where the panic bag and various other things were kept.

'Off you go, Jack,' she said, 'and stop worrying. There's every likelihood the bump will still be there when you come home.'

'Thanks again, Dot.' He kissed her cheek before taking his leave of Kate.

'He's worrying himself silly,' said Kate. 'I wish he wouldn't. I keep telling him it's the most natural thing in the world.'

'If he takes some convincing, I'm not exactly surprised.' Dorothy certainly wasn't won over.

'Anyway, I'm a rotten host, because I have to wash some clothes.'

'I'll help you, Kate.'

'Do you know how?'

'Basically, but I'm sure you'll take me through the finer points.'

'How do you do yours?'

'Gladys does it.'

Kate gave her a meaningful look and said, 'Maybe I should give you a few pointers. Gladys won't be there much longer.'

'That has a scary sound, Kate. Just supervise, and I'll do the donkey work.'

The next hour was an education for Dorothy in proper laundering, during which she learned to soak the clothes and then heat the water in a copper. Finally, when the washing was done, she learned how to position the mangle over the draining board and wring out the clothes.

'When we move to Bridlington,' said Kate with heavy emphasis on the word 'when', 'we're going to get an electric washing machine.'

'Why don't you get one now?'

'We're waiting until Jack gets his increase in salary as Deputy Manager. Until then, it's just hard work.'

'You're telling me.' Even so, Dorothy had learned a great deal, and she was keen to learn more. After lunch, which she'd provided, she said, 'I imagine we hang the clothes on the rope-thing outside.'

'The *clothes line*, yes. How did you wash your clothes in the WAAF?'

'By hand and with difficulty, but after a couple of goes I took to using the laundry. I mean, you can take the pioneering life just so far before the appeal begins to wear off.'

Kate looked out of the window and said, 'It's a lovely, sunny day and it's quite windy as well. These things will be dry in no time at all.'

'Let me help you. You mustn't reach up there.'

'Move the prop, and the line comes down far enough,' explained Kate patiently.

'Okay,' said Dorothy, picking up the laundry basket, 'let's go pegging.'

Kate demonstrated with the first item, one of Jack's shirts, and then it was Dorothy's turn.

'It's quite easy when you get the hang of it.'

'You were born to hang out washing, Dot. I mean, credit where it's—' Suddenly, she stopped, and Dorothy was conscious of a pattering noise, like water hitting a hard surface.

'Kate,' she said in disbelief, 'you're pee-ing on the grass!'

'No, I'm not. My waters have just broken.'

'What does that mean?'

'It's the fluid that protects the baby in the womb. I'll have to clean myself up and change my clothes.'

'Is the baby on its way?' It seemed that Dorothy's fears were about to become reality.

'Yes, but it could be hours yet.' She gestured towards the laundry basket and said, 'If you'll see to the rest of it, I'll go and do what I have to do.'

'Shouldn't we phone for an ambulance?'

'Not yet. Just carry on with the pegging out. It'll take your mind off things.'

With some misgivings, Dorothy pegged out the last of the clothes and carried the basket and peg bag indoors.

Kate's voice came from upstairs. 'Dot?' Thankfully, she sounded quite calm.

'Yes?'

'Will you get me a bath towel from the airing cupboard, please? I should have put clean towels out when I took the others for washing.'

'All right. Are you okay?'

'Yes. I told you, it could be hours yet.'

Dorothy took out a bath towel and handed it to Kate. 'Do you need anything else?'

'No, thanks. I'm all right, honestly. Don't fuss.' After drying herself, Kate went into the bedroom and took a clean pair of knickers from a chest of drawers.

'Are you sure you're all right?'

'Relax, Dot,' she said, stepping into them. 'Will you pass me the grey skirt that's hanging in the wardrobe?'

Dorothy found the skirt, took it from its hanger and handed it to her.

'Thanks,' said Kate, pulling the skirt up and fastening the waistband over the bulge. 'After that excitement, let's go downstairs and have a cup of tea.'

With her nerves stretched to what threatened to be their limit, Dorothy welcomed the suggestion.

She made tea, and they sat with it at the kitchen table.

Kate asked, 'Do you know how to iron clothes?'

'Yes,' said Dorothy confidently. 'I had to press my uniform and iron my shirts and collars. When they've taken you to hospital, I'll do your ironing, if you like.'

'Thanks, but don't worry too much about it. Jack's quite handy at that kind of thing.'

'Is he?' The picture of Jack washing and ironing seemed an unlikely one.

'He wasn't always an officer, you know, and sailors lead an enclosed sort of existence. They had to do their own washing, ironing and everything else.' Kate seemed to tire of the subject, because she asked, 'Have you had any more thoughts about your Aunt Sarah?'

'Lots and lots of thoughts, but not even a hint of a solution. Let's not worry about it until this is out of the way,' she said, waving a hand in the general direction of Kate's bump. 'It's too much of a distraction.' To avoid possible misunderstanding, she said, 'I mean my problem would be a distraction, not the baby.'

'Oh, it'll be a distraction all right. They're usually at their most demanding in the middle of the night,' she said, appearing remarkably unfazed by the prospect.

After a few seconds, she twitched.

'What is it, Kate?'

'Nothing to worry about. What can you hear?'

Dorothy was listening for something.

'What is it, Dot?'

'I thought I could hear bells. I was right.'

'They seem to be coming closer.'

'Yes, it sounds as if there's a major problem somewhere.'

'Dot?'

'Yes?'

'I was wrong. I think the baby's coming.'

'I'll phone for an ambulance.' Dorothy picked up the phone, conscious that she was reporting an emergency for the second time in a month.

'Number, please?'

'Emergency. Ambulance, please.' She gave Kate's and Jack's number.

'Ambulance station.'

'My friend is about to have a baby. Any minute now, I think.'

'Will you give me the name and address of the patient, please?'

Dorothy obliged, wondering how the ambulance people could remain so calm, until she remembered the girls on 'Darky' Watch, talking matter-of-factly to bomber pilots in cases of dire emergency. It was the same kind of thing.

'We'll get an ambulance to you as soon as we can.'

'Thank you.' Dorothy put down the phone.

The bells were very much louder, now, but Dorothy had to ignore them because Kate was calling her. 'What is it, Kate?'

'Will you get all the towels out of the airing cupboard and put them on the kitchen floor?'

'All right, but there's an ambulance on its way.'

'I can't guarantee that the baby will wait that long. My firstborn appears to be a pushy little blighter. He probably takes after his dad.' She added, 'Or *she* does.'

'Right.' Dorothy raced upstairs, thankful that she knew the whereabouts of the airing cupboard, and grabbed armfuls of towels.

'Oh!'

'I'm coming, Kate.' As she spoke, she knew it was a silly thing to say. What comfort or help could she give? She could only take instructions from her.

She dumped the towels on the kitchen floor and helped Kate lower herself on to them. 'What now?' She could hear bells in the distance, but there was no guarantee that one of them was on their ambulance.

Kate was hauling her skirt up. 'I've got to get my knickers off,' she said. 'I don't want the baby to be born inside them.'

'It could scar a child's mind for life,' said Dorothy, pulling them over her feet and tossing them aside. She realised to her embarrassment that the awful situation was causing her to make silly jokes. She had to concentrate. 'What next?'

'Is the baby's head visible?'

Dorothy nerved herself and lifted the hem of Kate's skirt. 'Something's visible,' she reported, looking at the smooth dome that was now clearly in sight.

'Aargh!' Kate's face was beaded with perspiration. 'Get a peg from the peg bag and scissors from the kitchen.'

'Okay.' Dorothy had only the vaguest idea of their purpose, but she found a peg and, after some rummaging, a pair of scissors.

'Aah!'

'Does it hurt?'

'Of course it bloody hurts! It's like trying to push a football down a drainpipe! Aargh! And the drainpipe is me!'

'What do I do now?'

'Bloody hell! This one's in a hurry! Support the baby's head when it comes through. Aaargh!'

'Okay. Take it easy.' Something told Dorothy that she should encourage calm.'

'There's nothing easy about it. Aaaaargh!'

Dorothy placed a hand where the head was trying to make its exit, or entrance – she wasn't at all sure – and said, 'You're doing fine, Kate. Keep at it.'

'It's coming. Support it, but don't pull!'

'I'm ready to support it.'

Suddenly, the head was born.

'I'm steadying the head now, Kate.'

'Goo-od! Aargh!' She gave a convulsive jerk, and the baby was born. 'Rub the baby's back, Dot. Make it cry!'

After all the hearts she'd allegedly broken, Dorothy now had to make the baby cry for its own good. It was just possible that she was born for this moment. 'Come on,' she urged, 'cry.'

Suddenly, there was a wailing such as she'd never heard in her life, and it sounded like music.

'Clean its nose and mouth.'

'I'm doing that now. Who's flying this thing? You or me?'

'You're doing fine, Dot.' Kate was sobbing for sheer joy. Usually so self-contained, Dorothy joined her a moment later, and the baby made up the crying trio.

'Is it a boy or a girl, Dot?'

'It's a.... Good lord! It's a boy,' sobbed Dorothy.

'What's the surprise?'

'Only that a tiny baby like this can have such massive balls!'

'Wrap him with towels, Dot. We have to wait for the placenta to come away.'

Dorothy busied herself with towels, making the wailing infant warm and secure. 'Where is it?'

'Where's what?'

'The placenta-thing you mentioned.'

'It's still inside me. Oh, dear, I want to hold my baby, but I have to clear the placenta first.'

'What can I do?'

'Use the clothes peg to peg the cord about two inches from the baby's navel.'

'Right.' Dorothy felt for the umbilical cord. It was quite squidgy and not at all pleasant to handle, but she pushed the peg firmly on to it.

'Is it a tight fit?'

'Very.'

'Good. Use the scissors to cut the cord on my side of the peg.'

'Are you sure?'

'Positive. Cut the cord.' Kate had pulled up her skirt and was massaging the area below her navel.

'What on earth are you doing?'

'I'm trying to move the placenta.'

After a few minutes, she gave an involuntary heave and deposited the remaining contents of her womb on to the towel below. 'Just wrap it in a towel, Dot. Tie the four corners to contain it. They'll want to inspect it at the hospital.'

'Rather them than me,' she said handing the crying bundle to Kate. 'I've just discovered something else.'

'What?' Kate wasn't really listening. All her attention was centred on the baby, and Dorothy didn't find that at all surprising.

'Delivering babies is bad for my grammar. I keep saying "me" instead of "I".'

'Shame on you.' Kate had uncovered the baby's lower body to inspect it. 'What were you saying about his balls?'

'I said they were out of proportion to the rest of him.'

'Oh, that's quite normal. Baby's balls are always well-developed. I'm thankful they're both in place, though.' A moment later, she remembered her manners and said, 'Thank you, Dot. You were absolutely wonderful.'

'Well, I couldn't leave my best friend to cope alone.'

'And you rose magnificently to the occasion.' Kate looked down again adoringly at the baby, who was still exercising his lungs. 'I suppose I'll have to feed him soon.'

'Yes, and that's something I can't do for you.' She was about to say more, when the doorbell rang. 'I'll go,' she said, only realising then that she'd just said something downright silly, because she was the only one who could answer the doorbell. She went to the door and opened it to two ambulance men.

'I'm sorry it's taken so long,' said one of them. 'There's been an almighty traffic incident in the town centre, and we've had to come the long way round, along with everybody else. The traffic's ridiculous.'

'It's all right,' said Dorothy. 'The baby's born, the cord's cut, the placenta's wrapped in a towel, and everything's fine.'

'Who delivered it?'

'I did,' she said, realising that she sounded surprised, as if she'd only just realised the fact. 'I delivered it, and it's the best thing I've ever done.'

* * *

Later, when Jack came home from the hospital, Dorothy had washed the towels and they were ready to be pegged out the next day.

'Coming back from London Airport,' said Jack, 'I thought that if the baby was born while I was away, we'd call it Dorothy.'

'You'd have attracted some strange looks. In case you haven't noticed, he's a boy.'

'Yes, I noticed.'

'There was no mistaking it,' said Dorothy. 'I still can't get over the size of his balls. Kate says that all boys are born with big ones. I suppose they grow into them, like puppies and their feet.'

That set Jack off reminiscing. 'My mum always bought my school clothes two sizes too big. You know how quickly children grow.'

'I've never really thought about it, but yes, I suppose they do.'

'She said it left room for growth.'

7

A Farewell And A Reunion

The letter was postmarked 'Morpeth, Northumberland', and Dorothy knew only one person up there. She opened the envelope and took out the letter.

15th October, 1945
Dear Dot,
I was really sorry to hear about your mam. Even though you didn't always get on with her, it must have been a shock. Let me know if I can do anything, and that's not bull – I mean it.

As you might have twigged from the postmark, I've still got a job of sorts, working for the same family, but only for another week, thank goodness! I've got a new job as a switchboard operator at the Shire Hall in Durham City. It's trained ape work after what we did in the WAAF, but I don't care. As far as I'm concerned, it's steady employment. The only thing is, it doesn't start until the fifth of November, so I've got a week to spare, and I'd love to see you again. Is there any chance of you putting me up for a few days?

Sorry this letter has to be short, but I'm still at the beck and call of a demanding family. I'd forgotten what it was like, but I soon got a reminder.

Let me know as soon as you can.
Lots of love,
Connie.

Dorothy replied immediately.

Last Wicket Pair

17th October, 1945.

Dear Connie,

Of course I'll put you up. Come as soon as you like and stay for as long as you like.

That's excellent news about the job. You'll find it less demanding, and according to my friend Jack, who works at a travel agency, there's always scope for promotion in a large concern.

I can't wait to tell you my news. You'll never guess what happened yesterday. I was staying with my old friend Kate, Jack's wife, because Jack had to be away, and Kate was near her time. Anyway, the baby started to arrive early, and the ambulance was delayed by a traffic accident, so I delivered the baby! Fair enough, Kate told me what to do – she's a midwife – but I did everything else, and I'm cock-a-hoop about it. By the way, did you know that boys are born with big balls that they have to grow into? No wonder men are so full of themselves!

Let me know when you're coming. My phone number is Cullington 118. I'm looking forward to seeing you again and catching up on everything.

Lots of love,

Dot.

Connie had been demobbed two months earlier than Dorothy, so there would be a great deal of catching up.

Before that, though, was Gladys's last day at the house. Kirby, her husband, would be returning to mow the lawns until either the house was sold or until Dorothy could find someone else to look after the gardens, but Gladys would be leaving at four o' clock in the afternoon after preparing something for Dorothy to heat up for dinner. It was in a sober frame of mind that Dorothy received her in the drawing room.

'Are you all set for retirement, now, Gladys?'

'Yes, Miss Dorothy.' Tears were already threatening.

'You were always fond of my mother's fob watch, weren't you?'

'Yes, Miss Dorothy.' She looked uncertain.

'I found a note among her personal things. Here it is.' She handed the note to Gladys, who unfolded it. Dorothy knew exactly what was written on it. It was a deed of gift that had slipped her mother's memory, possibly in the confusion caused by her first stroke.

'I can't take this, Miss Dorothy. They won't have settled the will yet.'

'It's a deed of gift, Gladys. It has nothing to do with the will. Look at the date.'

Gladys looked again at the note and read, 'The tenth of February, nineteen-forty.'

'She'd forgotten about it, Gladys. Strokes can affect people that way.'

'Well, I never.'

'Take the watch, Gladys. She wanted you to have it, and it's perfectly legal. I checked that with the solicitor.' She handed her the watch and chain in their original box.

'Miss Dorothy, I don't know what to say.'

'Just enjoy it. You've earned it.' It was true. The deed of gift was a rare example of Mrs Needham's generosity to her staff, and she demanded a great deal. 'Now, I gave both of you your wages this morning, I know, but there's something else. Rather than buy you a retirement present, I thought you might prefer some money so that you can buy something you really want.' She took a sealed envelope and pressed it into Gladys's hand. 'That's for twenty-five years' faithful and excellent service. It *is* twenty-five years, isn't it?'

'That's right, Miss Dorothy. Nineteen twenty-one we came here.'

'I was three years old.'

'I remember you as a little girl.'

'A little minx.'

'No, Miss Dorothy. I could always see the good in you, and I'm so proud of you for what you did yesterday.'

Dorothy could see the tears forming in Gladys's eyelids and she held out her arms and hugged her. Her mother would have been horrified at such intimacy with a servant, and that made it all the more appropriate. 'Have a long and happy retirement, Gladys.'

'Thank you, Miss Dorothy. Thank you for everything.'

'No, Gladys. Thank *you* for everything.'

* * *

Just as Dorothy expected, the phone rang on Monday morning.

'Dot, you bugger. Thanks for your note. I can come down today, if that's all right.'

'Of course it is. Do you know the train times?'

'There's a one at ten-fifteen that gets into Cullington at twelve-thirty. Is that convenient?'

'Absolutely. You'll find out about inconvenience when you arrive. I had to say goodbye to my cook-general yesterday. She and her husband have retired.'

'Oh Dorothy my dear, how perfectly ghastly for you to have to cope without servants, and how boring of them to place their retirement before your convenience.'

Dorothy laughed. 'You can still do the accent, can't you?'

'How do you think I got the job at the Shire Hall, bonny lass?'

'It's going to be marvellous. Get on that train and I'll meet you at the station, Connie.' Dorothy had business in the town, but she would have ample time to meet the train as well.

* * *

Farah's Tours were quiet when Dorothy called in. She picked up a brochure from the rack and took it to Jack's desk.

'Hello, Dot. What are you doing?'

'I'm pretending to discuss with you the possibility of an expensive holiday, but in reality, I'm asking you when your next day-off is likely to take place.'

Puzzled, Jack said, 'On Wednesday. It's when I'm bringing Kate and the baby home.'

'Perfect. I have a surprise for you both, and it will be delivered on Wednesday. I'll find out exactly when and let you know.'

'This is very mysterious, Dot.'

'That's the essence of a surprise. Let me just say that it will make coping with a new baby much easier.' She returned her attention to the brochure and looked thoughtful. 'I'll think hard about this,' she said as she stood up to leave, 'and I'll let you know.'

Her next stop was the railway station. Connie's train was due to arrive at twelve-thirty, which gave her almost ten minutes, so she called at the electrical shop, where she was told that the delivery would be made to Jack's and Kate's address at between nine and ten a.m. on Wednesday.

The train arrived on time, and Dorothy saw Connie's red hair clearly through the smoke and steam.

'Connie.'

'Dot, you bugger.'

They embraced and then walked out to the taxi rank.

Connie asked, 'Is it a long way, like?'

'No, not far.'

'In that case, why are we takin' a taxi?'

'Because you're an honoured guest and because that's a heavy case you're carrying.'

'I've carried many a heavy load, but I've never been an honoured guest until now.'

On the way to Dorothy's house, Connie chatted excitedly. 'Tell us about these friends of yours,' she said, 'the people who've got the new baby.'

'They're old friends from before the war. Kate's a nurse when she's not having a baby. Actually, she's a midwife, which was just as well last Friday, because she could tell me what to do.'

'I can't get over that, Dot. You deliverin' a baby! Whatever next?'

'We're never too old to learn something new, Connie.' She smiled at her friend's disbelief.

'You said the baby had big balls, so he's obviously a lad. What are they going to call him?'

They both laughed silently at the taxi driver's reaction to Connie's remark. Dorothy controlled herself and said, 'Maurice.'

'That's nice. It's unusual, though, for a little lad.'

'I think I once told you about Maurice. He was engaged to Kate, but then he was shot down and killed over Germany.'

'That's tragic, but is her husband standing for that? His baby takin' the ex-fiancé's name?'

'Maurice was Jack's friend as well, and there's no insecurity about Jack.'

The driver turned into the drive and pulled up outside the door.

'Thank you.' Dorothy paid him and took Connie's case from the cab. Connie was standing, open-mouthed.

51

'What is it, Connie?'

As the taxi left them, Connie said, 'Is this your house, Dot?'

'Yes.'

'All of it?'

'Yes, but not for much longer. It'll go up for sale as soon as the change of ownership is registered. Come inside, Connie, you're making me feel guilty.'

Connie followed her into the house, still mesmerised. 'Guilty about what?'

'Being one of the idle rich.'

'Ah never realised you were as rich as this.'

'Make the most of it, because I won't be for long.'

'Why's that, like?'

'Put your case down and we'll have a cup of tea. The reason I'm going to sell the house is so that I can pay a staggering death duty bill to the taxman.' She led the way to the kitchen and filled the kettle.

'That must make you hopping mad.'

'No, It doesn't, Connie. It's indecent that I have a house like this while people are living on top of each other in tiny rooms.' She lit the gas and spooned tea into the pot.

'That's a very generous attitude, Dot. There won't be many taking that line.'

'I wasn't always so generous. It was the war that changed my way of thinking.' Changing the subject, she said, 'Before the kettle boils, I'll take you up to your room.'

Connie picked up her case and followed her upstairs to one of the spare rooms. 'Why-yer-bugger, man, this room's gigantic!'

'They all are,' said Dorothy, pointing to an adjoining door, 'and your bathroom's through there.'

'*My* bathroom? D' you mean I have a one to meself?'

'As I said earlier, make the most of it, because if you come to stay with me in a few months' time, we'll have to share one.'

Connie shook her head in disbelief. 'Where I live, any bathroom at all is posh.'

'You're making me feel guilty again. Drop your case, and we'll have that cup of tea.'

'I've brought some rations with me to help out, Dot.'

'Thanks, Connie. Rationing is a great leveller.'

They went downstairs, and Dorothy scalded the tea. While they waited for it to brew, she said, 'The first time I went to a restaurant with Jake, it was at my invitation, but he couldn't allow me to pay the bill. Even though I'd just told him that my family owned Needham's Pickles, he insisted on paying for dinner.'

'Oh well, that's normal, though, isn't it? A working man won't let a woman pay her way. It's a matter of pride.'

'I suppose so.'

Connie's curiosity was now alight. 'Which one was Jake, anyway?'

'The Polish airman at Market Linfield. I told you about him.'

'Ah believe you did. Didn't you say you had your first time with him?'

Only a little embarrassed, Dorothy answered, 'Since you ask, yes.'

'Go on, Dot. What was it like?'

Dorothy smiled coyly, playing for time by pouring the tea.

'Go on, you bugger. Tell us what it was like.'

Dorothy couldn't refuse. 'Subsequent events have tainted the memory to some extent, but I can still describe the event itself as… simply glorious.' The admission caused her to subside into laughter, to be joined readily by Connie, for whom laughter was a way of life.

When her laughter had subsided, she said, 'My first time was a dead loss.'

'I'm sorry to hear that, Connie.'

'Oh, the poor lad was nervous, and neither of us had a clue what we were doin'. He couldn't get… ready for it… you know. It was like tryin' to push a marshmallow into a penny slot machine. We had a few more goes, though, and it was okay.' She laughed again, still eager to hear more about Dorothy's experience. 'What happened with Jake after that?'

'We had a good old time, and then I learned more about him. In particular, I discovered that he was horribly prejudiced against Jews.'

'Was he, now?' She thought about that briefly and said, 'Ah cannot say Ah've ever met a one, meself.'

'You have, although I'm only a quarter Jewish.'

'You bugger! Ah never knew that! It's impossible to tell with women, though, isn't it? I mean, they don't have anythin' cut off, like.'

'Thank goodness.' Dorothy had never considered that.

'That's a turn-up for the book, though, you bein' Jewish. Ah'd never have known.'

'Ah well, we haven't been made to wear badges like the Jews in Europe. That's why I went to France just after I was demobbed.'

Connie's face was blank. She asked, 'What did you going to France have to do with wearin' badges?'

'I'm sorry, I'll explain. My Aunt Sarah, my favourite aunt, who's half-Jewish, was arrested and handed over to the Germans in nineteen forty-one, except I didn't know that at first. I just knew she was missing. All I know now is that she was sent from Paris to Germany by train. Nothing more than that, and it's frustrating as well as worrying.'

'Of course it is, bonny lass.' She bit her lower lip in thought and said, 'There must be somebody who can help you find out more. Now that they're trying war criminals, lots of facts are comin' out into the open. Let's go to the library tomorrow, and see what they know.'

8

Straight Talk And Baby Talk

A visit to Cullington Public Library elicited the name of the office that dealt with refugees. It was called the United Nations Relief and Rehabilitation Administration, and that was a step forward, except that neither Dorothy nor Connie could find an address that was closer than Dupont Circle Building, Washington D C. As the sub-brigadier in Orléans had said somewhat unnecessarily, Dorothy was searching for a needle in a haystack. All the same, she bought a pad of lightweight air-mail notepaper and some envelopes, and returned to the library to write to the agency with her enquiry. A short time later, she posted it by air mail.

'Nothing venture, nothing win,' said Connie. 'What are we going to do now?'

'There's a café just off the market place that does excellent bacon sandwiches. I think we've earned a treat.'

'Lead the way.'

They were almost at the market place when Dorothy recognised a woman coming towards them. As they drew closer, she said, 'Hello, Mrs Lofthouse. How are you?'

'Good heavens, it's Dorothy Needham.' Her manner was business-like, rather than friendly. 'I didn't realise you were home. I presume you've been demobbed.'

'Yes, it's only a memory, now.'

After they'd exchanged the usual greetings, Dorothy said, 'This is Connie Sellers. We served in the WAAF together. Connie, I'd like you to meet Mrs Lofthouse. Her son Alan was one of the original five I told you about.'

'Oh, the cycling club, of course,' said Connie in her switchboard accent. 'How do you do, Mrs Lofthouse.'

Mrs Lofthouse's response was polite, but it lacked the warmth of Connie's greeting. 'How do you do.'

Dorothy asked, 'How is Alan, Mrs Lofthouse?'

'You heard about Gwen, surely.' Her expression was as bleak as ever.

'No, no one's told me anything.' Gwen was a junior officer in the ATS. She and Alan had married in nineteen forty-four.

'Oh, I thought everyone knew. Gwen was killed by a V-Two rocket. What made it particularly cruel was that it was the last one to fall on London.'

'Oh, Mrs Lofthouse, I'm truly sorry, and I can't begin to imagine what it did to Alan. As I said, I had no idea, and I can't imagine that Kate and Jack will know, or they'd have told me.'

'I've seen nothing of either of them, so you're probably right.'

'Where is Alan now? Is he still in the Army?'

'Yes, he's in Germany.'

'If you'll give me his address, I'll write to him, naturally.'

Mrs Lofthouse nodded. 'I haven't got it with me, but give me a ring. We're in the phone book.'

When Mrs Lofthouse had gone on her way, Connie said, 'Maybe a bacon sandwich and a cuppa will warm us up after that frosty reception.'

'I hope so, but don't take it personally, Connie. The icy touch was for me. I'm the *femme fatale* who broke Alan's heart, and she's never forgiven me for it.'

'How did you do that?'

'By spurning his advances and by giving him a verbal slap on the wrist whenever he was rotten to Maurice.' She stopped outside the café. 'Let's give ourselves a treat.'

Connie found a table while Dorothy went to the counter to order two bacon sandwiches and two cups of tea. When she returned to the table, Connie said impishly, 'A verbal slap on the wrist sounds very restrained.'

'I had to restrain myself. I could have strangled him sometimes.' She smiled briefly and said, 'Actually, what I did to him was more like verbal castration. He seemed to think so, anyway.'

'He probably needed it, but whatever he did, the poor bugger didn't deserve to lose his wife like that. It was his wife he lost, wasn't it?'

'Yes, it was. By all accounts, they'd been very happy together.'

'Aye, you just don't know what's going to happen next.' Connie was playing with the ketchup bottle when she noticed the label. 'Look what I have here. Needham's ketchup.'

'Of course. They knew I was coming.'

'I'm sure they did, bonny lass. Go on, then. Tell us all about Alan and Maurice. He was the lad who was killed, wasn't he?'

'Yes, that's right. Alan is that cliché of romantic fiction – tall, dark and handsome in a Fitzwilliam Darcy sort of way.'

'Oh, Lawrence Olivier. I remember the film.'

'Actually, he's not unlike Lawrence Olivier, although you'd be able to tell them apart in the same room.'

'Lovely.'

'He's also clever, and he was insufferable at one time.'

'Because he was clever?'

'Because he knew he was clever. Having met his mother, you can see where his superior attitude came from, and the trouble was that Maurice, who was a lovely boy, went to the elementary school and got a job at Needham's as an apprentice in the maintenance department.'

'What's wrong with that?'

'Nothing at all, but Alan treated him as a figure of fun. Maurice was popular with all of us, and we all "stuck up" for him, as he called it, but I was the one best placed to bring Alan to heel.'

The café owner came to them with their bacon sandwiches, and Connie waited until she was gone before saying, 'You know, Ah'm feelin' less sympathetic all the time towards that Alan character.'

'Ah well, the last time I saw him, he was a changed man. It was just before he left for France in nineteen-forty.' Dorothy looked around her.

'What are you lookin' for, Dot?'

'The brown sauce.' She spotted some on a nearby table and asked a woman sitting there, 'Do you mind if I have a dribble of brown sauce?'

The woman gave her a friendly smile. 'Take it, love.'

Dorothy helped herself and then returned it to the woman, saying, 'There you are, delivered to your table personally. Needham's always try to oblige.'

'Oh, aye? My name's Crosse and Blackwell, and I've got a dog called Heinz.' They both laughed.

'They never believe me,' she told Connie as she returned to their table.

Connie was far more interested in the story than she was in fun and games with other diners. 'You were tellin' us about Alan,' she prompted.

'Yes, he was so quiet and unassuming, I wondered if I was talking to his long-lost twin brother. I asked him if he'd had a visit from three spirits, or if he'd been posted to Damascus and got a bit too close to a star shell, but he didn't rise to it as he had in the past.'

'That's odd.'

'He said that the Army had made him think differently about things. In the light of my own experience, I can understand that, although I couldn't at the time.' She tried her sandwich, and her features morphed into a look of wanton ecstasy.

'Yes, I can see how that could happen.'

'Not only that, I learned later that he'd pushed a wounded soldier – I think it was fifteen miles, but I can't be sure – along those dreadful French roads in an old invalid chair, all the way to Dunkirk.'

'All right, he's startin' to win me over again.' She bit into her sandwich and said, 'If Hitler had known about these, he'd have been over in nineteen-forty, and there'd have been no stoppin' the bugger.' She examined it more closely and said, 'These miniature stotties are good an' all.'

'Miniature whats?'

'Stotties. A stottie cake is a big one of these.'

'That's a plain teacake here, a barm cake in Lancashire, and a bap or sometimes a huffkin down south.'

'I bet you speak lots of languages, don't you, Dot?'

'Only when it's about food.'

'Speakin' about food,' and it was evident that Connie was thinking about it, 'how are you going to manage without a cook? We had what your cook left for us last night, but now she's gone, what next?'

'Ah, Gladys has left me her masterwork: "Cooking for Silly Buggers". It's so simply written, I can't go wrong.'

'It sounds like a good idea, but I still think I'd better give you a few tips while I'm here.'

'I appreciate that. We can start tonight, if you like.'

'All right.'

'Then, tomorrow evening, Jack's going to cook for us. We're pooling rations, of course, but we have to celebrate the new baby, and Jack's giving Kate a rest from all the housework.'

Unusually, Connie appeared to have lost the power of speech. Eventually, she managed to say, 'You mean, a fella's goin' to cook for us?'

'That's right. He's a good cook, too.'

'Ye gods. What kind of a place have Ah come to?'

'When you and I were at Cranwell, I stayed at the cottage he was minding for someone, and he cooked a superb meal. We hadn't seen each other for ages, so he pushed the boat out.'

'Hang on, Dot.' Thoughts of food were suddenly set aside. 'You stayed at a cottage with him?'

'Yes, and he cooked an excellent meal.'

'Then what?'

Dorothy feigned innocence. 'What do you mean?'

'After you'd eaten, what did you do? And don't tell me you did the washing-up, or Ah'll be cross. You slept with him, didn't you?'

'Well, it seemed only right after such a superb meal.'

'You bugger, Dot. I didn't know you'd had him an' all.'

'It didn't last long.' She corrected herself hurriedly, 'I mean the relationship didn't. He was quite good at making it last, now I think of it.'

'And then he married Kate?'

'Eventually. I just felt bad about ditching him. I still do.'

Clearly, Connie was trying hard to understand. 'But he's happily married, isn't he?'

'Oh, yes, but I feel guilty when I think of how I hurt him.'

'Oh, Dot,' said Connie, like a despairing parent, 'you may have left a trail of broken hearts behind you, but yours must be the only one that's still hurtin'. They'll all have got over it by now.'

* * *

Jack met them at the door. He kissed Dorothy and shook Connie's hand. 'Dot,' he said, 'thanks ever so much. You really shouldn't have done it.'

'Well, I think a new baby's worth celebrating, and I learned last week about washing clothes the hard way. Anyway, Jack, this is Connie. Where's Kate, by the way?'

'How d' you do, Connie. I'm glad to meet you.'

'And you, Jack. Ah've heard a lot about you.'

'Kate will be here shortly. She has to take gentle exercise, so she's just gone up to the shop on the corner. Maurice, on the other hand, is fast asleep.'

With the greetings out of the way, Dorothy became serious. 'We bumped into Mrs Lofthouse yesterday. You haven't heard about Alan's wife, have you, Jack?'

Jack looked bemused. 'No,' he said, 'what's happened?'

'She was killed by a V-Two in London. Mrs Lofthouse said it was the last one to come over.'

Jack closed his eyes. 'Bugger.' Remembering he had another guest, he said, 'I'm sorry, Connie.'

'Don't be sorry, bonny lad. Ah think it's a bugger an' all.'

A third response came from Maurice, waking up in his cot and wailing loudly.

'Oh, good,' said Connie, 'Ah've been wantin' to see this young fella.'

Jack lifted the bawling baby out of his cot and tried to soothe him. 'I'm not very good at this,' he admitted.

Connie held out her arms. 'Give us him, Jack.' She took Maurice into her arms and rocked him. In a matter of seconds, he was quiet. 'He probably needs his nappy changed,' she said, sniffing. 'In fact, Ah'm sure he does. You do, don't you, pet lamb?' She addressed the last few words to Maurice, who remained silent.

'You have hidden depths, Connie,' said Dorothy.

'Haddaway. Ah've got brothers an' sisters, an' that's trainin' enough for lookin' after babies.'

Kate walked in, and the introductions continued with Connie still holding Maurice.

'He's filled his nappy,' she told his mother helpfully.

'Thanks, Connie. I'll take him and change him.'

'Rather you than me,' said Jack, as she disappeared into the kitchen. 'Now that I've changed a few nappies, I'll never be able to face English mustard again. Sorry, Dot.'

'I don't think you'll dent the profits all that much, Jack, but I wish you hadn't painted that picture quite so vividly.' Remembering her duty, she said, 'I'll tell Kate about Gwen.'

She went to the kitchen and was immediately reminded of Jack's unfortunate analogy. 'Kate,' she said, 'there's bad news about Gwen, Alan's wife. She was in London when the last of the V-Twos came over.'

'Was she killed?'

'I'm afraid so.'

'How awful. Poor old Alan.'

'I phoned Mrs Lofthouse this morning and got Alan's address in Germany.'

'Oh, good. We'll write to him. I wondered why he was so strangely silent. I think his last letter came more than a year ago.'

'It would,' said Dorothy, passing the nappy bucket. 'It's been more than a year since they stopped.'

Kate set about washing Maurice, who seemed to find the process enjoyable. 'How was Mrs Lofthouse with you, Dot?'

Dorothy laughed. 'As icy as ever.'

'It was his own fault, but his mother really knows how to carry a grudge.'

Changing the subject to one of more immediate concern, Dorothy asked, 'How do you feel after the major event?'

'Oh, I'm fine. It's as if nothing's happened.'

With Maurice now bathed and in a clean nappy, they re-joined Jack and Connie in the sitting room.

Connie said, 'Don't babies smell lovely when they're clean?'

'They certainly do the two extremes,' said Jack.

'Here, Dot,' said Kate, 'I know you two have met before, but now that the circumstances are less dramatic, would you like to get to know each other?'

Dorothy took the bundle carefully, never having held a baby in her life, and found the experience surprisingly pleasing.

'When they smile, when they're as young as that,' said Connie, 'it's usually wind that causes it.'

Dorothy didn't care. It was good just to see him happy and comfortable. Almost without thinking, she began talking to him. 'You're a lovely little chap, aren't you? You didn't look so lovely when you were born, but you were very welcome.'

'Accordin' to what you told me, Dot,' said Connie, 'you were admirin' his balls, and no fella looks lovely from that angle.'

'Don't listen to her, Maurice. You're a lovely, lovely boy.' She kissed him to add emphasis to the words that had taken even her by surprise.

9

November

Sympathy And A Sewing Lesson

Dear Alan,

I met your mother yesterday quite by accident, and she told me the awful news about Gwen. I am so sorry. It's been more than a year, now, but you must still be devastated, and for that reason, this letter will be brief. There are just so many ways of expressing sympathy, and they all mean the same thing, so just be assured that your old friends in Cullington are thinking about you. I've told Jack and Kate, so I imagine they'll be in touch.

The news from over here is that my mother died of a stroke last month. She'd had a series of them, so it wasn't entirely unexpected.

On a happier note, Kate gave birth to a boy last week. They're both fine, and the baby, perhaps not surprisingly, is called Maurice.

Jack's going to be Deputy Manager at Farrar's in Bridlington, supposing the Ministry of Supply gets its finger out, but for now, he's languishing at Head Office in Cullington.

I have an old friend from the WAAF staying with me this week. I told her how you pushed a wounded soldier fifteen miles to Dunkirk in an invalid chair, and she was terribly impressed. I still am, so let that be one happy thought.

Take care.

Love and sympathy,

Dot (still Needham. The thing with Bill didn't work out. I know, I'm hopeless.)

Dorothy sealed the envelope, wondering again what the designation WCIT in his address stood for, and then put it on the hall table, ready to go to the Post Office. She met Connie in the sitting room.

'I've just written to Alan,' she said.

'Ah thought that was what you were doin'. It's never easy, writing them things, is it?'

Dorothy was inclined to agree. 'Loss affects people in different ways,' she said, 'but Alan must have been crushed when he got the news.'

'Why aye, but you're still thinkin' about your mam, aren't you?' Typically, Connie had put her finger on the problem immediately.

'Yes, I am. I've never given way easily to emotion, as you know, but to experience something like that and not feel the loss in the usual way just doesn't seem right.'

'It's not a matter of duty, Dot. You cannot make it happen. It either does or it doesn't.'

'I won't argue with that, but when I said goodbye to Gladys, I was heartbroken. We clung to each other in this very room, both of us in tears.'

'She meant a lot to you, didn't she, bonny lass?'

'Yes, she did. When I was little and when I was growing up, I had two sources of affection. I had Aunt Sarah and I had Gladys.'

'It makes you bloody think, doesn't it?'

In spite of the seriousness of the conversation, Dorothy smiled. 'What makes you bloody think?'

'You had just about everything money could buy, but you couldn't get love from the right quarter. Poor as we were, there was never any shortage of love at our house. Me mam and dad even demonstrated it by havin' kids until they were both worn out.'

It was no surprise to Dorothy. 'It shows.'

'What do you mean?'

'You behave like someone who's always known affection.'

'What about you, then? Ah'm bein' nosey, but what was the present you sent to Jack and Kate that they were so excited about?'

'I bought them an electric washing machine.'

'You bugger! What a brilliant present! Ah've never even seen a one.' She laughed shortly and said, 'Mind you, it wouldn't make any difference to our lives, 'cause we haven't got electric power. They say it'll come when they nationalise it, but we're not goin' to get excited yet.' Returning to the topic, she said, 'You've got a lot of love to give, Dot. Your auntie and the cook must have done a thorough job on you when they stood in for your mam.' She stood up and beckoned to her. 'Howay to the kitchen, bonny lass, an' Ah'll show you how to make panacalty.'

'What on earth is that?'

'When everybody has their own, it's called Pan Haggerty, and it's a good way to use your bacon and corned beef ration when you're sick of havin' 'em the way you usually have 'em.' She led Dorothy to the kitchen and said, 'You can make it with all kinds of meat, or even vegetables. It's as versatile as that.'

'I'm going to miss you when you go, Connie.'

'Aye, but you'll know how to make panacalty.Just remember to let me know your new address.'

* * *

The house felt empty after Connie left for home, and it occurred to Dorothy that, because of various events both within and beyond her control, her homecoming had been anything but normal. She'd naturally sought out the company of Kate and Jack, who were her oldest friends, and Connie's visit had been a tonic, but that had been the extent of her social life so far. It was clearly time to broaden her sphere of activity. She wondered if the cycling club were still dominated by the older end, or if maybe there'd been an influx of younger members. Now that she'd thought of it, it was time she brought her bicycle out of mothballs, to use one of Jack's curious naval expressions.

Its frame and wheels hung separately from the garage rafters and behind the sheeted Rover that stood on its axle stands, looking like an amputee about to wake up and take its first faltering steps down the ward, except that the event was unlikely to take place soon. Like most commodities, petrol was still rationed and in extremely short supply. The bicycle was of far more use, she thought. At least, it would be if she could get it down from the rafters.

She took the stepladder from the far wall, being careful to avoid touching the car, and positioned it so that she could reach the bicycle frame. Meticulous as ever, Kirby had fastened it with slip-knots, so that with any luck, she might be able to release it without breaking her nails.

Taking the weight of the frame with her left hand, she unfastened the knot with her right, which she quickly transferred to the frame, lowering it gratefully to the floor.

Next came the wheels, which were deceptively heavy, especially the rear one, with its three-speed gearbox, but she got them down and emerged breathless and with her hands liberally coated with Vaseline. Kirby had smeared it all over the metal parts as a precaution against rust. He must have known that the war would be a long one.

Fearful of damaging the car, she took the frame and the wheels out of the garage in three separate trips, and now she tried to put the wheels back on. Kirby had always been around to attend to mechanical problems, but she no longer had the benefit of his services. He would be back to attend to the lawns, but she was reluctant to ask him to do more than that. This was the pattern for the future, in which the new, independent and capable Dot must emerge.

With much painstaking, and searching the bicycle toolkit for the right spanner, she managed to fix the front wheel. She was feeling quite proud of herself, but now, she had to fix the rear wheel, and with the chain off and soaking in a can of oil, she found the prospect daunting. She looked at the problem from all angles, trying to ascertain what went where, finally looking at her watch to see if Jack was likely to have arrived home yet. The new, independent and capable Dot needed masculine help after all. Life could be a bugger at times.

* * *

Some men might have been gleeful at her failure. Some might have seen it as a huge, on-going joke that provided them with endless merriment until she wanted to hit them with the bicycle pump. Thankfully, Jack wasn't one of them. He checked the front wheel and said, 'You did a good job with this one, Dot. The only problem is that the tyres are in a parlous state. You need new ones, but I don't know where you'll find them.'

'I was thinking of taking it to Turner's bike shop for a general tidy-up. Maybe he has some tyres.'

'He's worth a try.' He thought briefly. 'I'll put your rear wheel and chain on, and then you can wheel the whole thing to Turner's. You could try pumping your tyres up, but I can't guarantee they'll stay up.'

One disappointment seemed to follow another. 'I don't understand. The tyres haven't been anywhere, so why are they damaged?'

'Rubber's a natural substance, Dot. Like all living things, it deteriorates. You and I will, eventually.'

'What a horrible thought. Would you like a cup of tea before it happens?'

'Now, that's a happy thought.'

'I'll bring it out to you.'

She went inside to make tea, and then another question occurred to her, so she put the kettle on the gas and re-joined Jack outside. 'Jack,' she asked, 'what can I use to clean Vaseline off the metal parts?'

'Have you any nail varnish remover?'

'Yes, I bought a big bottle in Orléans. It's almost impossible to find here.'

'It's just as well, because that's your answer.'

When she brought the tea out to him, she said, 'I was looking forward to being independent. Maybe I'm not cut out for it.'

'You can't expect to do everything all at once. Give yourself time, Dot.'

* * *

Mr Turner looked at the tyres and then at Dorothy. 'I remember you now,' he said. 'You used to come here for your bits and pieces.'

'I bought this bike from you. It'll be ten... no, eleven years ago.'

'So you did, and that means I've got to do my best for you. What happened to the other youngsters you used to hang around with?'

'Two of them are back in Cullington and they've just had a baby, one's still in the Army in Germany, and one was killed in the war.'

'Eh, I'm sorry to hear that, love.'

'So were we.' She'd been thinking about Maurice and the others. Getting her old bike out had revived lots of memories.

'Your tyres have had it, I'm afraid.'

'I realise that.'

'And your brake blocks. Your pedals will survive.' He thought for a minute. 'I can change your brake blocks.... Just a minute.' He disappeared into the back of the shop and returned with a smile on his face. 'Because you bought the bike from me and because you've been a regular customer, I've got two nearly-new tyre covers you can have, and I've got two new inner tubes in the back. Do you want me to fit 'em for you?'

'Yes, please. I'm ever so relieved. I've been away for six years, and I just want to go back to my old life with the cycling club and everything I knew.'

That seemed to please him. He asked, 'Have you been in the forces?'

'Yes, the WAAF.'

'Officer?' It was a common assumption.

'No, sergeant-instructor.'

He smiled broadly. 'I were a sergeant in t' first war. I bet you looked better in your stripes nor what I did in mine.'

She eyed his expanding figure and had to agree with him. 'I probably did,' she said, 'but it was about more than that, wasn't it?'

'You're right, there, love.'

'Anyway, I'd better settle up with you. What do I owe you, Mr Turner?'

'Let's call it eighteen bob, have we? That includes fittin' an' brake adjustment.'

'Eighteen shillings? That suits me.'

They completed the transaction, and Dorothy left the bicycle with him, having arranged to collect it the next day.

She went home to hunt out her old cycling shorts and flat leather shoes. She remembered giving her cycling shoes a generous treatment of dubbin, and she was reasonably sure they'd still be serviceable.

It turned out that she was right about the shoes; they were in tip-top condition, but her shorts were nowhere to be found. She knew she'd left them in the wardrobe with her blouses, skirts and dresses, but as hard as she searched, there was no sign of them. It was when she was pondering the various places where she could possibly find a new pair that she remembered a letter from her mother. It was when she was stationed at Cranwell the first time round, as early as that, that she learned her mother had given some clothes 'that couldn't possibly be of any further use' to the WVS. She'd evidently decided that her daughter had done enough cycling, and that she should find a more sedate pursuit that befitted a young lady. It was infuriating.

She phoned Kate more to have a good moan than for any other reason, but Kate was instantly helpful.

'Mine would have fitted you,' she said, 'but they disappeared in like manner. I'll tell you what, though. Have you a pair of summer slacks you can sacrifice?'

She had two pairs that fitted that description. 'Yes, but I don't fancy cycling in them.'

'I was going to suggest that you cut them down and hem them. Have you an old chamois leather about the house?'

Dorothy thought. It was something that had naturally been left to Gladys in the past. 'I'll have a look. Do you mean for lining them?'

'Yes, you can treat it with a softening agent and it'll be fine.'

'You know, Kate, everyone is suddenly more practical than I am.'

'They always were, Dot. This one's been lying in wait for you for some time.'

'It's not funny.' She could hear Kate laughing.

'I'm sorry. How are you with a sewing machine?'

'Very basic. I never really caught up at school.' When she was expelled from her independent school, she'd joined Cullington Girls' Grammar School, where she found the practical curriculum both advanced and forbidding.

'If you've got the slacks and a wash leather, bring them over, and I'll show you how to hem them up on my old machine.'

It was a welcome offer, so Dorothy mounted a search.

Having drawn a blank with the domestic implements, she tried the garage, where she vaguely remembered watching Kirby leather the Rover after washing it.

Sure enough, she found a large chamois leather in the box of cleaning materials, and decided to give it a new home. After all, the car was going nowhere for the time being.

* * *

Kate's sewing machine was an ancient, hand-wound Jones that was primitive enough not to make Dorothy freeze with apprehension.

'Slowly and carefully,' said Kate, watching every move.

'It's easier than I thought.'

'Many things are, Dot.'

Dorothy completed the first hem, having surprised herself. 'I wish I'd had someone like you to teach me this at school,' she said. 'I wouldn't have felt so inept and ham-fisted.'

'I was three years behind you. A tiny tot, you might say.'

'So you were, Kate. You and Maurice were very much of an age, just as Jack and Alan and I were.'

'I don't suppose you'll have heard anything yet from Alan.'

'No, it's a little soon.' Thinking about her letter to him reminded her of something. 'His address is in Hanover,' she said.

'I know. I've written to him, too.'

'Of course. I was just wondering about the mysterious WCIT, because that's the name of his unit.'

'We also wondered about that, so Jack asked around. Apparently, it stands for War Crimes Investigation Team.'

10
A Bicycle Ride And A Reunion

*D*ear Dot,
Thank you for your kind sympathy. It's been a year-and-a-half now, and I'm beginning to see daylight. I have to say, also, that the good wishes of my old friends mean a great deal to me.

I was sorry to hear about your mother's passing. I know she'd had a series of strokes, but it must still have been a shock for you.

Thank goodness for brighter news. I've congratulated Jack and Kate, and I understand that you're to be congratulated too, for delivering the baby in dire emergency. Well done indeed, Dot! I'm full of admiration for you, because it was a wonderful thing to do.

I'm glad they've named the baby after Maurice. To my undying shame, I only realised a short time before his death what an excellent chap he was, and I'm ever thankful for a chance meeting in a York pub, when he and I were able to bury the hatchet that should never have seen the light of day in the first place. I stopped in Bremen on my way here to pay my respects to him. I knew from Kate that he'd had been brought up in the Methodist Church, and I had it in mind to visit their church in Bremen, but they don't go in for symbols and ritual, and I felt that I needed to pay a physical tribute. In the end, I went to the Lutheran Church and lit a prayer candle for him. I remember kneeling there in uniform beside so many Germans who'd lost relatives in the war, and it seemed somehow right. We're not exactly popular over here, but no one in that church offered me an unkind word.

You said very little about yourself in your letter. By this time, I imagine you're back at Rimmington's and working under great difficulty amid rationing and shortages.

My work is no longer sensitive, and I can tell you that, for the past several months, I've been investigating war crimes and interrogating their alleged perpetrators. Since Dunkirk, it's a close as I've come to soldiering. Incidentally, I didn't push my friend Harry fifteen miles – it was only twelve. For what it's worth, though, I would have gone the extra three miles and more, simply because we were, and still are, mates.

It was splendid to hear from you again. If you can spare the time, please write again and I shall. In the meantime, take care.

Love and total, unqualified admiration for delivering baby Maurice!
Alan.

Dorothy reread the letter several times, but her initial impression remained. This wasn't the Alan she remembered; even allowing for the change that was so evident before his embarkation for France in 1940, he sounded like a different man, and she could only imagine that the transformation had continued to develop.

In particular, she was impressed by the account of his visit to the Lutheran Church in Bremen. That he'd been moved to make that visit and perform his act of remembrance told a story of its own, that he was still burdened with guilt for his earlier treatment of Maurice. It seemed she wasn't the only one unable to doff the hair shirt.

His modest correction of the Dunkirk story, as well, was completely unlike the Alan of old, and his reaction on hearing of her part in baby Maurice's birth was genuine and clearly heartfelt. She would write to him when she'd had time to think about what she wanted to say.

Meanwhile, she was in training. She'd ridden her station bicycle regularly in the WAAF, but air stations were built on flat terrain that offered no challenge to the keen cyclist.

Her saddle was in excellent condition thanks to a quantity of saddle soap. It was just unfortunate that the part of her anatomy that occupied it needed gradual reintroduction and generous applications of Zam-Buk ointment.

Eventually, however, she felt confident to take part in the club's final ride of the year, to Ilkley. Her initial enquiry had confirmed that a number of new members had joined the club since the war, and she looked forward to making new friends.

* * *

She sat outside the Cow and Calf pub, quietly pleased with herself. It was her first proper ride since 1939, because the departure of Maurice, Jack and Alan, and Kate's new shifts at the first-aid post had caused her temporarily, at least, to lose interest in cycling. She thought of that meeting in the function room of the Bay Horse in Cullington, the last time all five of them would meet. It was probably unwise to keep revisiting it, knowing of the sadness round the corner, and she tried to dispel the mental picture. As she did, a young man took the seat next to her, thereby unwittingly providing a convenient distraction.

'Nice day,' he remarked.

'Lovely. It's a bit cold, but it's November, after all '

'Brian Gibson,' he announced, offering his hand.

'Dorothy Needham. "Dot" to my friends.' She took his hand.

'You're new, aren't you?'

'Not really. I was a member until the war took me away, and now I've re-joined.'

'What did you serve in?'

'The WAAF.' She wasn't keen on his direct, almost abrupt, manner, but she was prepared to be sociable.

'Women's Air Force, eh?'

'The same. What about you?'

'Royal Artillery, the Sixtieth Anti-Tank Division.' Having asked about her armed forces credentials, he delivered the information almost grudgingly, as if he were already bored with the subject. Then he asked, 'When were you demobbed?'

'At the end of August.'

'I came out two months ago. Not before time.'

Reluctant to press him on what was apparently an unhappy topic, she waited for him to speak again.

'What's your civvy job?'

'I'm in between jobs. I used to be an assistant buyer at Rimmington's, the department store.'

'Oh, yeah? Very posh, I must say. I'm a painter and decorator, myself.'

'Is that a good business to be in?' It was the only rejoinder she could think of, and she was about to make an excuse and go elsewhere, when, instead of replying, he asked, 'Is that what you've been doing since you were demobbed?'

'No, I've done all kinds of things. I spent some time in France after I came out.'

'What for?' He made it sound as if it were the last destination he'd ever consider.

'I was trying to find out what had happened to my aunt. She was taken away by the Germans in 'forty-one, and put on a train for Germany. That's all I know, and it's very worrying.'

He nodded. 'What did they take her for?'

'She's half-Jewish.' She decided that if he found that less than to his liking, it was his affair, and she would move away.

'Bastards,' he whispered.

'Who are?'

'The Nazis.' He seemed disinclined to enlarge on that assessment, but then surprised her by saying. 'We got to Bergen-Belsen first. Saw it with us own eyes.' He continued to whisper, looking downward all the time at his feet. 'Horrible. Hanging's too good for them evil bastards.'

Again, Dorothy kept quiet, not knowing what to say.

'Bodies everywhere, lyin' helpless. T' bastards were still tryin' to finish 'em off.' He fell silent again, clearly remembering.

'Don't talk about it if you find it difficult.'

'What's difficult after that?' He closed his eyes and said, 'They'd emptied all t' other camps into Bergen-Belsen, tryin' to put 'em where no bugger would see 'em.'

'Were they all in the one camp?'

He nodded. 'That's right. They couldn't kill 'em all, so they moved 'em to Bergen-Belsen.'

It sounded impossible, but she knew nothing at all about it, and he was an eye-witness. It was clearly a matter of great distress for him, so she waited for him to speak again.

'Bastards,' he whispered, 'savages, all of 'em.'

Two male members of the club approached them. One said, 'Come with us, Brian, and we'll get you another drink.' The other said to

Dorothy, 'Don't think ill of him, love. The poor bloke's seen things nobody should ever see.'

'I know.'

'We'll look after him.'

The man who'd spoken to Brian earlier came to her as they were all getting ready to leave. 'I hope that wasn't too awful, love,' he said. 'Brian was at the liberation of one of the Nazi concentration camps.'

'Bergen-Belsen. I know, poor man.'

'He doesn't usually talk about it at all. I think the beer might have loosened his tongue today.'

'I'm afraid I may be the culprit,' she said. 'I told him I'd been in France, trying to trace my aunt who was taken by the Germans.'

'In that case, don't blame yourself, love. Brian will be all right, anyway.' He turned to leave, and then hesitated. 'Did you find out anything about your aunt?'

'Only that they took her in a train to Germany.'

'I'm sorry, love.'

Dorothy's head was filled with unanswered questions. Suddenly, she wanted to get back on the road instead of sitting there, turning the thing over in her mind. She needed to pedal, to do something hard and physical that would let her vent her frustration.

Eventually, she got her wish, and the party formed up and left Ilkley for home.

* * *

After a night's sleep made possible in spite of her disturbing thoughts, by sheer physical tiredness, Dorothy replied to Alan's letter.

Dear Alan,

Thank you for your letter. I'm encouraged by the news that you're feeling a little better. Long may it continue.

I found your tribute to Maurice very touching, and I'm delighted that you lit a candle for him. At the same time, I'm sure he forgave you for everything, so isn't it time you forgave yourself?

I'm no longer at Rimmington's. I visited the place and then resigned. It was nothing personal, except that I'd learned that the person who'd been doing my job needed the work quite desperately, whereas I didn't, so what the heck....

I know you have plenty to occupy your time, but I have a problem I'd like to tell you about. It would be wonderful if you could help me, but if you can't or haven't the time, please don't worry about it.

My Aunt, Sarah Elizabeth Moore, was living in Orléans when war broke out. She and a friend were arrested in June, 1941 by the French police and handed over to the Germans in Paris, who sent them by train to... all I know is that it was somewhere in Germany. That's as far as my enquiries took me. Then, yesterday, I went on my first ride with the cycling club since 1939, and I met a man who was at the liberation of Bergen-Belsen. He was terribly distressed about it, but he told me that all the concentration camps had been emptied into Bergen-Belsen because the Nazis wanted to hide their victims from the Allies. Would it be possible, without a lot of trouble, for you to check the names of the surviving victims for that of my aunt? I'd be ever so grateful, but if it's not possible, as I said, I'll understand.

One final note regarding your friend Harry. I don't care if it was twelve miles or twenty. What you did was an act of compassion and great friendship.

Take care.

Love,

Dot.

* * *

Alan's reply came within the week.

Dear Dot,

I'm sorry to have to tell you that your aunt's name is not among those of the Bergen-Belsen survivors. However, that in itself, means very little. Apparently, some of the more able-bodied survivors took off immediately, without leaving a name or location, but if your aunt had been among them, I'm sure she would have been in touch with her family by now. At the same time, she's not bound to have been in B-B. Your informant in the cycling club was misinformed. The Nazis did move a great many prisoners, mainly Russians, away from the advancing armies, but the sheer numbers involved would have made it impossible to put them all into one camp, gigantic though B-B was. It's possible that he was so affected by the scenes there, that he became confused. There are many allied soldiers who will live with those horrors for the rest of their lives, and goodness only knows what the experience will have done to some of them.

This leaves us with a problem, in that the people with most of the information regarding who, when and where, are the Jewish community, who are chafing at the bit.... Is it 'chafing' or 'champing'? I can never remember. At all events, they're impatient to form the new state of Israel, and the British Government isn't moving fast enough for them, which means that they're not in a hurry to co-operate with us either. Currently, the only people who are talking to us with any degree of civility are the French and the Americans, and they know as little as you or I, whatever they tell us.

It's a pity we're so far apart, because, without wishing to build up your hopes, I'd love to help you if I possibly could. As things stand, I'm sorry to be of so little help.

Take care,
Love, and admiration for the Rimmington's thing,
Alan.

She wondered what he meant about it being a pity they were so far apart. It was obviously important, or he wouldn't have mentioned it. After a while, she decided that there was only one way to find out.

Dear Alan,
What did you mean when you said, 'It's a pity we're so far apart'? Please enlighten me.
Love.
Dot.

* * *

His reply was prompt, though not immediately promising.

Dear Dot,

Last Wicket Pair

I only meant that communication by post is slow, and there are things that, for political and legal reasons, are best not communicated in writing. I'm not suggesting for one moment that you come here; in fact, I would go as far as to advise you against it. Germany isn't the safest place just now, by any stretch of the imagination, and you could be taking your life in your hands.
Love,
Alan.

* * *

Dear Alan,
I don't care about the danger. I'm coming over. May I call on you?'
Love,
Dot.

* * *

Dear Dot,
You haven't changed at all, and I know when I'm beaten. Don't be tempted to do any of the journey by train, or you'll be on a hiding to nothing. I suggest you get a flight to Nijmegen, and then an onward flight to Hanover, because no one else does international flights to Hanover. You'll see the reason why when you arrive. When you do, phone the number at the head of this letter and ask for me, and I'll pick you up from the airfield. When I call it an airfield, rather than an airport, I'm only being literal. One last warning: it's very important that you go nowhere in Germany without an armed escort. It's as dangerous as that, but if your mind's made up, bon voyage.
Love,
Alan.

11

Devastation And Sublimation

The airfield at Hanover was, as Alan had warned her, no more than a large field that served as an airstrip. There were very few amenities, and she had to wait her turn for everything, including the telephone. Eventually it came free and she dialled the number Alan had given her. A woman's voice answered, surprisingly, in English.

'War Crimes Investigation Team, Hanover.'

'Good morning. May I speak to Captain Lofthouse, please?'

'I'll try his office. Who is calling?'

'Miss Dorothy Needham.'

'Did you say, "Readman"?'

'No, Needham.' Clearly, the telephonist had cloth ears. 'Let me spell it for you. Nan, Easy, Easy, Dog, How, Able, Mike. Needham, as in ketchup.'

'Oh, *Needham*. Please wait, Miss Needham.'

Dorothy waited for maybe a minute, before Alan came on the phone.

'Dot, you made it. Where are you?'

'Hanover Airfield. It feels like the end of the earth.'

'It's very close to the end of the earth. You can probably see it from there. Stay where you are, and I'll come for you. It's good to hear your voice again.'

'I'm more than relieved to hear yours.'

He laughed. 'I'll be over as quickly as I can. 'Bye.'

''Bye.' She put the phone down and looked for a place where she could buy a cup of coffee or any hot liquid, but there was nowhere, so she stood and waited. The arrivals hut was cold, but it was even colder outside, where snow was beginning to fall.

Most of her fellow-travellers were men, including some British officers, who stood in a group, possibly waiting for official transport into the city. None of them looked particularly happy, and there was no reason why they should. It was likely they were returning from leave, and that was seldom an occasion for rejoicing.

She'd waited a further fifteen, or possibly twenty, minutes, when she heard a once-familiar voice say, 'Hello, Dot.'

She half-turned and, even after six years, recognised him immediately. 'Hello, Alan.' She joined him in a heartfelt hug, their past differences momentarily forgotten.

'I hope your journey wasn't too grim. Are these yours?' He indicated the two suitcases that stood nearby.

'Yes, thank you. The flights weren't too bad at all, but nothing happens in a hurry nowadays. Everything seems to have been slowing down ever since I was demobbed.'

He led her out to a Mercedes saloon and deposited her cases in the boot. As he did so, a youthful second-lieutenant standing nearby saluted him and said tentatively, 'Excuse me, sir. How do I get a taxi from here?'

'By sheer serendipity, Lieutenant. That's how rare they are. I'm going into town, if you'd like a lift to barracks.'

'Thank you, sir. That's awfully good of you. It's my first time here.'

He sounded like a new boy joining his school, and his language made Dorothy smile. With the war now over, the Army was once more finding officers with the approved social background.

'There's room in the boot for your case. Put it in there and then get in the back.'

'Very good, sir. Thank you again.'

Dorothy got into the front seat, and Alan drove off.

'Have you booked a hotel, Dot?'

She forced her attention away from the seemingly endless panorama of bombed-out shells of buildings and piles of rubble. 'No,' she said, 'I've no idea which hotels are still in business.'

'If you like, I'll ask the colonel if you can have one of the spare rooms in our married quarters. You'll be safer there than in a hotel, and the food will be better.'

'That would be marvellous. I'll pay my way, naturally.' She was conscious that all the time he spoke he was looking from left to right, as if he expected trouble at any moment.

'You could always do the washing-up, of course.'

A glance at him told her he was being less than serious. 'I'll have you know, I've learned a few domestic skills since I left the WAAF.'

'Including midwifery. I told you how impressed I was.' He was still keeping a close eye on pedestrians and other traffic.

'No, you're not. You just can't believe I did something as practical as delivering a baby.'

'All right,' he admitted, 'there is that, but there's also a huge helping of admiration. How are Kate and Jack, by the way?'

'They're fine, and still waiting for the shopfitters to finish the new branch.'

He pulled up outside a building that must have belonged at one time to the German military. An armed sentry guarded the entrance. 'Off you go, Lieutenant, and good luck. Don't forget your case.' He waited for the young man to remove his case from the boot, before moving off again.

'This is a very nice car,' commented Dorothy.

'Each team has a car similar to this one. We need the room in the back when we have to transport a prisoner handcuffed between two guards. Most of the time, though, I run around in an American Jeep.' He drove for only a few more minutes, and then turned into a gated compound that served an ominous-looking building. Again, an armed sentry stood at the entrance.

Dorothy asked, 'Is this some kind of prison?'

'It was a military detention centre, similar to the glasshouse, except that I imagine the treatment of prisoners was even harsher. Don't worry about showing your identity,' he told her. 'It wouldn't mean a thing here, anyway, and I'll sign you in.'

'They're very security conscious,' she observed.

'They're continually on the lookout for troublemakers.'

'You're joking.'

'It's no laughing matter,' he assured her. 'We'll leave your cases in the boot for the time being, just until we know for sure where you're going to stay.'

The sentry came to attention when Alan approached him.

Alan waited maybe ten seconds, and asked, 'Haven't you forgotten something, Somers?'

'Sorry, sir. Can I see your identity, please, sir?'

'By all means.' Alan took out his identity card and allowed him to compare the photographs. 'I may look like the Captain Lofthouse you know and revere, but I could be a disaffected German who just looks like him. I'm not joking, Somers. Men have been killed because someone was as careless as you just were.'

'I'm sorry, sir. It won't happen again, sir.'

'Good. Miss Needham is my guest, and I can vouch for her.'

'Very good, sir.'

Alan led Dorothy into the building, where he signed them both in and put his head round a door to speak to someone. Then, re-emerging, he announced, 'We'll have coffee in a few minutes.'

'Oh, lovely.'

'Don't get too excited. It's American coffee and it's better than nothing, but it still leaves something to be desired.' He opened the door to the next room and said, 'Welcome to my place of work. Come in and take a seat while I speak to the colonel.' He pushed a button on the intercom. Dorothy heard a man's voice, and then Alan said, 'Lofthouse, sir. Regarding the visitor I spoke to you about, I wonder if, in the interests of her safety, we might offer Miss Needham one of the spare rooms in married quarters. She has offered to pay for the accommodation.'

The voice at the other end said, 'That's a good idea, Lofthouse. As she's insisted on coming here, we must give her what protection we can. Tell her that her offer to pay is appreciated, but that four can live as cheaply as three. At least, that's what my wife told me when she announced the advent of our second son.'

'Thank you, sir. I'm most grateful. May I also invite her to join us in the mess for lunch?'

'Why not, Lofthouse. She'll probably brighten the event up no end.'

'Thank you again, sir.'

'Not at all, Lofthouse. By the way, have you seen that fellow Rödermann yet?'

'No. I'm going to interrogate him this afternoon. I thought I'd make him wait.'

'Good thinking, Lofthouse. Carry on.'

'Very good, sir.'

The intercom clicked, and Alan said, 'You heard all that, Dot. You can forget about hotels now.'

'I'm terribly grateful, but how do you come to be in married quarters?'

'When I was posted here, I was married, so I asked for married quarters. Since then, no one's raised the subject of my widowed state, and I haven't reminded them either.'

'I'm sorry.' She cringed awkwardly. 'That was clumsy of me.'

'Not in the least, but I hope that's answered your question.'

'It has, but I'm puzzled as well.'

'About what?'

'This talk about German troublemakers. Were you being serious?'

'I don't joke about that kind of thing.' He broke off when there was a knock on the office door. 'Come in.'

A woman in civilian dress entered, carrying a tray of coffee things.

'Thank you, Erika. Just leave it on the desk, please. Dot, this is Erika, one of our stenographers. Erika, this is Miss Needham, an old friend of mine.'

'How do you do, Miss Needham.'

'I'm glad to meet you, Erika.'

Smiling, Erika left the office and closed the door.

Dorothy picked up the coffee pot and asked, 'Shall I pour?'

'Please do, and I'll tell you about the malcontents around here.'

'Yes, I'm fascinated.'

'There are still ardent Nazis, who refuse to accept that they've lost the war, and they're to be taken very seriously, daft though their aims are.'

'Are they active hereabouts?'

'Yes, and that's why I wasn't happy about your coming here. I'm obviously delighted to see you again, but I can't overstress the risk you're running.'

The war had been over for six months. It made no sense at all. 'What do they hope to achieve, these people?'

'They know they can't turn back the clock and defeat the allies, but they believe that by waging a war of terror, they can delay any peace settlement and gain a treaty more favourable to Germany.' He added even more soberly, 'They also enjoy killing British soldiers and anyone connected with them, including those they regard as collaborators.' His eyes lit on the tray of coffee things. 'Erika, who brought in the coffee, runs an enormous risk in working for us, but she continues to do so because she wants to help us stamp out Nazism for good.'

'Good for her. It's easy to forget that there are innocent Germans.'

'If only it were as simple as that.' He opened a drawer and asked, 'Do you smoke, Dot? I honestly can't remember.'

'No, I never have.'

'I stopped in nineteen-forty, and I still find myself reaching for them. I keep them for interrogations.'

'How very civilised.'

'They help loosen tongues.' He closed the drawer. 'You saw the bomb damage on the way from the airfield, didn't you?'

'Yes, it's horrendous.'

'That's why the German people hate us as much as they do. They believe that the true war criminals are the allied air forces; in fact, it's fair to say that if they knew of Air Chief Marshall Harris's identity, they'd regard him much as we've come think of Göring.'

'But they did the same to London, Newcastle, Hull, Glasgow....'

'It would make no difference to them even if they'd been allowed to know that. In any case, the bombing of Britain was a fraction of what the allies dropped on Germany. There's no black-and-white delineation between guilt and innocence. All we can do is punish the guiltiest, and I don't enjoy it. I do most of it in blinkers, constantly reminding myself that all I do is prepare cases against our prisoners. I leave the trial and punishment to others, thank goodness.'

In an attempt to lighten the conversation, Dorothy said, 'I'm looking forward to meeting your brother officers for lunch.'

The idea made him smile. 'They're an odd lot.'

'How?'

'They're all lawyers, from the colonel down to the most junior of them.'

'Lawyers? In the Army?'

'The investigation and interrogation of alleged war criminals is now the responsibility of the Judge Advocate General and his officers, although it's an ever-changing scene. Because of my experience in the job and, although I hesitate to mention it, my record of success, I've been allowed to stay on.' He laughed modestly. 'It also relieves them of the expense of another interpreter, as I've always done the job myself.'

Reluctant though she was to revisit the question of guilt, she had to ask, 'Hasn't losing Gwen to enemy action made it difficult for you to maintain your balanced view?'

'Of course it has.' He looked down, and he appeared to be staring at nothing in particular, as if his eyes were temporarily out of focus.

'Look, if it hurts too much to talk about her, please forget I asked the question.'

'No,' he said, looking up again, 'it's important.' He was silent again, no doubt remembering, and then he said, 'When you lose someone like that, the most natural thing is to lash out at the first person or people you associate with your loss. It would have been very easy for me to make a case against all the prisoners that were brought to me, and send them all to the scaffold simply because they were Nazis, but I didn't. Coping with my tragedy was difficult enough, but to commit all those people to trial, knowing they would most probably face the death penalty, would have meant living with that guilt for the rest of my life.'

'I can see that now.'

He got up from his desk and walked over to the window. 'Kate wrote to me after Maurice was killed,' he said. 'It was in response to my letter of sympathy, and she told me that there was nothing she could do to the people who'd killed him, but there was plenty she could do for the people they were hurting, and that was when she got her transfer to Hull Royal Infirmary.'

'I remember. She said much the same kind of thing when she answered my letter.'

'I imagine she would. I believe psychologists call it "sublimation", the redirection of an anti-social impulse into acceptable activity, in Kate's case, a mission of mercy. In my case, I simply tried to help those who I thought deserved it. There were more cases of wrongful and malicious accusation than you might imagine. The simple fact that they were German meant that they attracted denunciation by vengeful citizens. I came across many instances of it in France, but in helping them, I helped myself as well.'

'I'm glad you told me that, Alan.' She got up and stood with him at the window.

'Strangely enough, so am I. I don't know why, but I'm not going to worry about it.' He looked at the clock on the wall and said, let's go the officers' mess for a pre-prandial drink. I don't know about you, but I need one.'

'After all that, I'm hardly surprised.'

'No, not because of that.' He smiled for the first time since their conversation began. 'I have to interrogate an ex-Gestapo officer this afternoon, who I know to be as guilty as they come, and that kind of thing's always easier after a drink.'

12

Denial And Hospitality

Rimless spectacles seemed to be a Gestapo cliché. It couldn't be that there was a shortage of frames in the Reich. Alan knew that, because he'd seen a photograph of the piles of spectacles stolen from the inmates of Bergen-Belsen. No, it was more likely to be vogue and vanity, or compulsive conformity that endeared them to party members.

Rödermann approached the chair in front of Alan's desk and moved it backwards.

Alan spoke to him quietly in German. 'I wasn't aware that I'd invited you to sit, Hauptsturmführer Rödermann. Remain standing until I tell you to do otherwise.'

The prisoner made no reply, merely staring at Alan through those rimless glasses that seemed as cold as the eyes behind them.

'Why were you running away?'

'I was not running away.'

'You were caught when we discovered your ratline, Rödermann, and a ratline has only one purpose: as an escape route for Nazis fleeing from justice. Why were you running away?' For the first time, Alan detected a flicker of emotion behind the otherwise impassive features.

'I am not familiar with the word "ratline".'

'Then I shall prompt you again. A ratline is an escape route for Nazi war criminals who wish to evade justice. Why were you running away, Rödermann?'

'I can only repeat that I was not running away. The concept is unknown in the Third Reich except as a despicable activity performed by British and American forces.' The man's arrogance was astounding.

'Seltzing, Müller, Bernhardt and Klingemann were all caught running away from capture and justice, Rödermann. You were with them, therefore you were running away. Why were you running away?'

'Justice?' Suddenly, his face was alive with anger. 'Do you call this justice?'

'No, you'll meet justice when you go to trial.' Alan turned to the stenographer and said, 'The interview was terminated at fourteen-fifteen hours, when Hauptsturmführer Rödermann became too enraged to co-operate.' He said to Rödermann, 'I'm going to give you an opportunity to calm down before I speak to you again.'

'That is the very least you can do, Hauptman.'

'Guard, take this prisoner back to his cell.'

'Yes, sir.'

Alan thanked the stenographer and returned to his office, where Dorothy was waiting for him.

'That didn't take long.'

'No, the suspect was becoming overwrought, so I sent him back to his cell to calm down.'

She looked at him oddly. 'That was very humane of you.'

'Not at all. I let him almost lose his temper, and then sent him away. I'll do the same again and create the expectation of similar treatment. After that, I'll let him boil over, and that's when I expect him to be indiscreet.'

'How Machiavellian.'

'Not exactly cricket,' he agreed, 'but neither was he playing to the rules when he sent innocent people to the concentration camps.'

The intercom crackled, and Lieutenant-Colonel Rigby came on the line.

'Lofthouse here, sir.'

'Ah, Lofthouse, I'm glad you're back. Will you come to my office?'

'Very good, sir.' Alan made his apology to Dorothy and set off down the corridor, where he found the colonel's door open.

'Come in, Lofthouse. Take a seat.'

Seeing that Rigby was bareheaded, Alan took off his cap and sat down.

'How's it going with Rödermann?'

'So far, so good, sir. He was in danger of blowing a fuse, so I sent him to cool down. I'll speak to him again, shortly.'

'Splendid.' Despite his enquiry, the colonel's thoughts were clearly elsewhere. He even seemed apologetic, and his next utterance confirmed that impression. 'I'm sorry we can't keep you here, Lofthouse. You have an excellent record of success, and I value your contribution.'

'Thank you, sir.'

'I've received confirmation that you're to be posted in December to a unit run by the Corps of Military... I beg their pardon, the Royal Military Police, as they're now called.'

'Thank you for telling me that, sir. I'll try to be properly dressed at all times – I know they're keen on that kind of thing – and I'll try not to cause them too much disappointment.'

'But you're disappointed, Lofthouse, quite clearly.'

'I've enjoyed working with JAG, sir.' Perhaps 'enjoyed' wasn't the most appropriate word for his experience, but he would have preferred to remain in his current post than to be at the disposal of the RMP.

Changing the subject to a lighter one, Rigby said, 'I hope Miss Needham didn't find our lunchtime conversation too arcane.'

'If she did, sir, I'm not aware of it.'

'Excellent. Well, I'll allow you to return to your duties. I just thought you'd like to know your fate.' With his last sentence, Rigby smiled broadly.

'Thank you, sir.' Alan got to his feet.

'Not at all, Lofthouse. Carry on.'

'Very good, sir.'

He called briefly on Dorothy to apologise again and to say, 'I'll be speaking to a French person tomorrow, in connection with one of our investigations, but he may be able to shed some light on your question. Meanwhile, I have to leave you again for another cosy session with Hauptsturmführer Rödermann.'

'Don't let me get in the way of your work, Alan.' She held up a battered volume and said, 'I'm brushing up my German, as you can see.'

'*Viel Glück.*' He left her and proceeded to the interview room, where he told one of the guards to bring Rödermann.

The stenographer who'd accompanied him on the last session entered the room and sat at her machine.

'Thank you for coming, Annaliese.'

'It is a pleasure, Captain.'

The pleasure faded when the guard marched Rödermann into the room.

'Good afternoon, Rödermann. I trust I find you in an improved temper.'

Rödermann remained silent but clearly resentful.

'You may be seated.'

'*Danke.*'

Alan began with a different line of questioning. 'Were you aware of the mass-murder taking place in the concentration camps?'

'I have already answered that question. I had no knowledge that anything of that nature was taking place, and I still refuse to believe it.'

'Why were you running away, Rödermann?'

'I will tell you again. I was not running away.'

'You and the others I have mentioned were captured when we exposed the ratline. Why were you trying to evade justice?'

Rödermann's temper was rising again. 'Did you expect me to submit myself to this nonsense that you call justice?'

'So, you *were* running away, after all. Why, Rödermann? What crime had you committed, that you had to flee from justice? Why did you have to scurry down a ratline?'

The anger was there already, waiting to burst out. 'I had not committed any crime.'

'If that were the case, Rödermann, you would have nothing to fear, and yet you scurried with the others down your precious ratline.'

'I object strongly to your use of the word "ratline".'

'What would you like me to call it, Rödermann?'

Flecks of saliva had formed at the corners of his mouth. 'I see no reason why a means of escape should be given an insulting name.'

'A means of escape? Why were you running away, Rödermann, and what crime had you committed?'

'Crime? According to your decadent values it is a crime to rid the country of Jews, homosexuals, gypsies, freemasons….'

'Hunchbacks, intellectuals, Jehovah's Witnesses. Interestingly, your Führer wanted to exterminate homosexuals despite that fact that he was one of their number.'

'How dare you?' It was a full-scale rant that startled even the stenographer, and she was used to prisoners' outbursts. 'How dare you insult the Führer's memory in this way?'

'He knew what he was. He was disciplined for it during the previous war. Why would he have been insulted?' He called the guard and said, 'This prisoner is unable to control his temper. Take him back to his cell, and I'll send for him later.'

'Yes, sir.'

When the guard and prisoner were out of the room, Alan spoke to the stenographer. 'Don't go away, Annaliese. I'll send for him in ten minutes or so. Would you like a cigarette?' He offered a box to her.

'Yes, please, Herr Hauptman.' British cigarettes were always popular in Germany.

He lit it for her, and they chatted about various things until Alan looked at his watch and decided that his prisoner was probably in a more amenable mood. 'Guard.'

'Yes, sir?'

'Bring Hauptsturmführer Rödermann to me, please.'

'Yes, sir.'

The prisoner was brought in, and Alan noticed immediately that his nostrils were alerted to Annaliese's cigarette smoke.

'Ah, Hauptsturmführer, would you also care for a cigarette?'

'I should. Yes, please.' He took one from the box, and Alan lit it for him.

'Yes, I'm sure you'll agree, with your long experience of interrogation, that there's no reason why an interview should take place in an atmosphere of animosity.'

Rödermann stared at him coldly.

'What grudge had you against Jehovah's Witnesses, or were you simply tired of them ringing your doorbell every Sunday morning?'

'I have nothing against them. I never sent them into the camps. I could never understand the order to imprison them.'

'Not Jehovah's Witnesses, then. What about freemasons?'

'I never sent freemasons into captivity.'

'All right. Not Jehovah's witnesses and not freemasons. What about gypsies?'

The expected explosion came. Who cares about gypsies? Only you sentimental Engländer. Why are you so outraged by the culling of a few stinking, thieving gypsies?'

'A few?'

'I sent possibly fifty into the camps. No more than that.'

'A mere fifty murdered with your collusion. It doesn't sound all that many when you say it quickly.'

'They were of no consequence.'

Alan consulted the sheaf of documents on his desk and said, 'I have seven independent depositions stating that you committed Jews, freemasons and suspected dissidents to the concentration camps. That's in addition to your fifty or so gypsies.'

'Lies!'

'Each of the witnesses has positively identified you as the Gestapo officer who had them transported to the concentration camps. The alleged dissidents have also accused you of ordering their torture as a means of gaining confessions.'

'If you believe them, why are you asking me these questions?' There was a flicker of fear as well as anger in his eyes.

'Because I want you to make a full confession. You've already admitted to sending gypsies to the death camps. Come on, Rödermann, take the credit for the Jews, the dissidents, the freemasons, the unemployed labourers….'

'Why not?' Rödermann was shrieking, now. 'Why should they be allowed to go on living as parasites on the state?'

'You had them put to death, didn't you?'

'Not immediately.'

'But you were responsible for their deaths sooner or later.'

'I was only following orders. The German race had to be purified.'

Alan picked up one of the documents and pretended to read it. Without looking at Rödermann, he asked, 'Whose orders were they?'

'Officers of the Geheimer Staatspolizei were directly responsible to Reichsführer Himmler.'

'Not that laughable megalomaniac Hitler or that fat toad Göring?

Are you saying you took your orders from the most evil snake of them all, from Himmler?"

'How dare you?' Rödermann was out of control. 'How dare you speak in this way of the Reichsführers? Those prisoners died because they were of no use to society and because the German race had to be purified!'

'They died because you committed them.'

'I had no choice!'

'Are you really telling me that you carried out your orders, zealously torturing suspects and herding your victims on to the trains that took them to Dachau, Bergen-Belsen, Ravensbrück, Buchenwald, Auschwitz and the rest, and all because you were afraid to disobey orders?'

'Yes! Why don't you listen the first time?'

'Thank you, Rödermann. That will be all.' He walked over to the door and spoke to the guard. 'Take this prisoner back to his cell. I'll send for him when his confession is ready for his signature.' Turning to the stenographer, he said, 'Thank you, Annaliese. I hope you didn't find that too unpleasant.'

* * *

He found Dorothy in his office, where he'd left her. 'Hello, Dot,' he said. 'I hope you haven't been too bored.'

'Not in the least, and my German is somewhat improved. It was also an opportunity to digest lunch. I imagine the German civilians don't eat as well as we did.'

'I'm afraid not. Will you excuse me again while I speak to the colonel?'

'Do you want me to leave the office?'

'No, perish the thought.' He pushed the button on the intercom and waited.

'Lieutenant-Colonel Rigby.'

'Lofthouse, sir. I got Rödermann to make a general confession. Together with the depositions made by his victims, it should ensure a conviction. He wasn't very happy when I left him five minutes ago.'

Rigby chuckled. 'I don't suppose he was. Well done, Lofthouse.'

93

'Thank you, sir.'

'Good. As I told you earlier, I'm sorry we can't keep you with us, but orders are orders. Carry on, Lofthouse.'

'Very good, sir.'

Dorothy waited until the line was dead, and asked, 'Why can't the colonel keep you, or shouldn't I ask?'

'It's yet another reorganisation.' He couldn't help but sound bored, because, after six months of constantly shifting responsibility, he was very bored. 'The Judge Advocate General's staff are going to concentrate on what high-level war criminals remain alive and not in American captivity, leaving the rest of us to deal with the lesser characters.'

'How important is the man you interrogated this afternoon?'

'He was quite powerful. He was a *Hauptsturmführer*, the equivalent of a captain, in the Gestapo. Needless to say, he has a great deal of blood on his hands, if not on his… conscience.'

'Has he a conscience?'

Alan shook his head. 'None that I could detect.'

* * *

That evening, he drove Dorothy in an American Jeep to a house in the suburbs, that appeared to have been untouched by bomb damage, prompting the question, 'Whose house is this?'

'No one seems to know. In the six months or so that we've been using it as married quarters, no one's complained or tried to claim it as their own. It's quite pleasant. There are four bedrooms, two bathrooms – the couple who share it with me have the benefit of the en suite bathroom – and there are two reception rooms. We share a truly excellent cook-general, called Else.' He swung into the circular drive and stopped the engine. 'Welcome to our humble abode.'

The front door swung open, and a fair-haired maid of forty or so welcomed them into the house.

'Thank you, Else,' said Alan in German. 'Miss Needham will be staying here for a short while. Will you please prepare one of the guest bedrooms for her? She will be joining us for dinner.'

The maid smiled in response. '*Zu Befehl, Herr Hauptman.*' She took their coats and hats to hang them up.

'If I studied for the rest of my life,' said Dorothy, 'I don't think I'd ever speak German as well as you.'

'I'm sure you would. It's only a question of practice. Now, you met Nicholas Donaldson at lunchtime. Come and meet his lovely wife.'

Marigold Donaldson was an attractive redhead, who turned out to be friendly and to have a sense of fun. Her husband Nicholas was more reserved, but with a dry wit. He was the perfect foil for her.

At dinner that evening, Dorothy rediscovered the pleasure of meeting new people and enjoying their company. It was an agreeable prelude to the promise of new information about Aunt Sarah.

13

Filling In The Gaps

After breakfast, when they were alone, Alan said, 'The man I'm going to meet is currently in Bremen. If we're lucky, we'll be there in a couple of hours or so. Now, I suggest you come with me to his place, but I'll have to speak to him alone, as he and I are dealing with sensitive information. Is that all right?'

'Perfectly.'

'It shouldn't take long, and then, if you like, we could visit the Lutheran church I told you about.'

'Oh, yes. That would be perfect.'

'You'll need to wrap up warmly, because we're going in the Jeep.'

'Of course.'

They walked out together to the jeep, Alan in his greatcoat and Dorothy in a woollen coat, scarf, hat and kid gloves.

As they drove northwest towards Bremen, Dorothy said, 'When we met in Cullington shortly before you left for France, you'd undergone a major change, it seemed to me, and you told Kate and me that the Army had made you think differently about things. How did that come about?'

He was silent, and Dorothy interpreted that as reluctance to discuss the subject, so she said hurriedly, 'Tell me to mind my own business, by all means. It was clumsy of me to ask.'

'But it is your business, because it affected you and everyone else I knew.'

'Even so, if it's difficult for you to talk about it, I'm happy to forget it. I was never a likely candidate for the diplomatic service, as you know.'

'No, it's all right. The only unpleasant part about it is remembering what a conceited, insensitive, self-obsessed bore I was. I keep thinking of that last time we all met at the Bay Horse. Do you remember, after the meeting of the cycling club?'

'If I remember correctly, and I think I do, I wasn't very nice to you on that occasion.'

'I asked for it, Dot.' He drove on in silence for maybe two or more minutes, and Dorothy was about to repeat her earlier suggestion, when he said, 'I had a hell of a time in basic training at Deepcut, and that was my fault, too. My platoon officer gave me some excellent advice, which, in my single-minded way, I ignored, until I was almost at the end of signals training at Catterick.'

'What happened there, Alan?' She patted his arm with her gloved hand. 'I'm on your side now, remember.'

'All right. The Senior Medical Officer gave us a lecture about the perils of indiscriminate sexual activity.'

'Oh.' Dorothy had attended that kind of lecture, too.

'He was an ebullient, larger-than-life character from Dundee, and he treated the lecture as a performance, rather than a warning. He was like a comedian at an undergraduate entertainment.'

'In what way?' Dorothy had never been an undergraduate.

'He used language that soldiers from ordinary backgrounds couldn't possibly understand, and he snarled his warnings in a light-hearted way, as if the diseases in his photographs were the fault of his careless, and therefore laughable audience.'

'Those jobs always fell to the wrong people, didn't they?' She remembered hearing embarrassed medical officers, some of them virginal spinsters, mumble their way through Freedom From Infection lectures.

'That one did, although he was the right one from my point of view. I remember realising to my horror that he was inadvertently holding up a mirror for me. He was showing me where I'd been going wrong.'

She patted his arm again. 'Does it still hurt to think of it?'

'It doesn't hurt, so much as embarrass. I could hear him using needlessly extravagant language in describing the pitfalls of promiscuous behaviour, simply because he thought it made him sound clever.'

'That was downright irresponsible.'

'It was also a timely warning for me, because I finally admitted to myself that I'd been doing the same thing. Only the accent was different.' He slowed down to give a wide berth to some children at the roadside, and was rewarded by a chorus of '*Gottverdammter Engländer*' from the women who ushered their children to safety.

'They really do hate us, don't they?'

'Some of them do, certainly,' he agreed. 'Most of them, I suppose, if I'm honest.'

'Did your platoon go to France still ignorant and vulnerable to VD?'

'No, thank goodness. When we arrived back at the hut, they were all complaining that they hadn't understood a word of the lecture, and someone said, "I bet 'Prof' understood it." That was what they called me, and it wasn't meant as a compliment. That was when I offered to explain the subject of the lecture in plain English, and they all welcomed it.'

Suddenly, her face was alight with curiosity. 'Go on, Alan, what did you say?'

'I don't think it's fit for your ears.'

'I'm sure I'll have heard worse. Go on.'

'I told them that if they had sexual contact with someone they'd just met or, especially, with a prostitute, they stood a good chance of being infected with gonorrhoea, or even syphilis, and they'd seen pictures of those two horrors, so the warning went home.'

'The pictures probably told the story better than the MO.'

'There was no doubt about it. Then I told them that if they really had to take the risk, their best friend was the condom sheath, or "spoggie", as they called it. However, the only safe way, I told them, was to avoid intimacy with strangers and prostitutes.'

'Well done, Alan. You probably saved a few lives with that small service.'

He felt somehow easier, now he'd told Dorothy the story. 'We had quite a chat after that,' he said. 'It was the start of my friendship with Harry Bramhall, as well as the moment I began to behave as a normal human being.' He stopped talking, having realised something rather odd. 'You know,' he said, 'I never told Gwen the full story about that.'

'Maybe you had better things to do.'

'Not all the time. I think I was still too embarrassed to talk about it.'

'I hope it hasn't been too difficult.'

'Not at all.'

They drove past an endless vista of bomb-damaged property, so that, partly as a distraction, Dorothy asked, 'Will you tell me about your journey to Dunkirk?'

'If you really want me to.'

'Of course I do. Your war was much more interesting than mine.' She hesitated and said, 'That's if it's not too difficult.'

'This is another story I've never told in any detail, to Gwen or anyone else.'

'I'm honoured.'

'Not really. We were a mobile signals unit, the officer, a horrible corporal – although I shouldn't say that, really, because he was killed – and there was Harry and me, and we'd just crossed a road full of refugees, mainly French peasants, when we were attacked by an enemy aircraft. We all jumped out of the lorry and took shelter in a ditch while the aircraft strafed us and the refugees.'

'Oh, no.' It was horror mixed with disbelief.

'Oh, yes. They hit the fuel tank of the lorry, and it exploded. When the aircraft was gone, I found the officer and the corporal lying dead, and Harry with a thigh wound that was bleeding heavily, so I put a field dressing on it. He joked that if it had got him a few inches higher, he'd have been singing soprano.'

'He was joking?' It seemed impossible.

'Harry was like that.' He thought for a brief spell and said, 'You wouldn't believe the carnage. A young woman and an elderly relative, I suppose, were both killed. She'd been wheeling him in a wicker bath chair, and suddenly she was stretched across the road with her clothes half ripped off. I found a shawl and draped it over her to give her some dignity.'

She stared at him with new admiration. 'Oh, Alan, you're a.... I don't know, but you're something special, anyway.'

'I don't know about that. Anyway, I lifted Harry into the bath chair and pushed him to Dunkirk.'

* * *

They reached the address in Bremen, and Alan introduced Dorothy to the Frenchman Henri Laurent, who, it seemed, was using a bomb-damaged house as an office. Alan renewed his warning against going out alone, and Dorothy made herself as comfortable as she could while he spoke with M. Laurent.

After almost an hour, Alan joined her again.

'Was your meeting a success?'

'So far. I've asked him if he can tell me anything about that train from Paris. It was good that you could provide the date. We'll see, anyway.'

They drove to the Lutheran church, where they were relieved to find that there was no service in progress, and they put their money in the box for prayer candles, which they took to the table.

Kneeling on the carpeted step, they lit their candles and placed them in the holders provided.

Dorothy closed her eyes, remembering Maurice, youthful, innocent and eager to be accepted by the RAFVR. Before long, she was conscious that tears were pouring down her cheeks, and then she felt Alan's arm on her shoulders, and he was offering her a handkerchief.

'Stay there,' he said. 'I'll be back in a minute.'

She tried to stem her tears, and had almost succeeded when he returned with another two candles.

'You light one for Kate, and I'll do one for Jack,' he told her.

They lit their candles, and Dorothy thought of Maurice, in love with Kate, and she with him. It had been a magical, innocent and touching affair, but all too brief. She tried to tell Maurice silently that Kate was happy again, married to Jack, and that his name lived on, along with his memory, in Baby Maurice. She thought of the recent birth, and the tears returned. Alan's arm was round her shoulders again. She turned to him and buried her face in his greatcoat.

How long they knelt there she had no idea. All she knew was that Alan was there for as long as she needed him.

Eventually, she lifted her head to say, 'I'm sorry. I don't usually react like this.'

'It's an unusual situation,' he told her, gently kissing her forehead. 'Nature makes the rules, and all you can do is follow them.'

She blew her nose on the sodden handkerchief, and he produced another from a hip pocket.

'I can't fault you today,' she said, standing up.

'Are you ready to go?'

'Yes.' She took his arm and they left the church. After a while, she said, 'What a story this will be to tell Kate.'

On the way home, she asked, 'How do you feel, Alan?'

'Okay.'

'You're very quiet. Are you thinking about Maurice?'

'Yes.'

It was just as she'd suspected. 'I do understand, but you made things right with him,' she reminded him. 'He forgave you, so you've got to make the effort to forgive yourself.'

'I do. It's not easy.'

'Nothing's been easy today. I don't usually cry the way I did, and I just couldn't stop myself.'

He was quiet again, and then he said, 'I sometimes wish I had a valve I could open, like that, and let all my feelings drain away.'

'Can't you?'

'No.' He seemed to ponder that. 'It's not a male bravado thing,' he explained. 'It's just the way I'm made.'

'Can you think of something funny? I think our flagging spirits need a lift, jointly.'

'Something funny happened—'

'On the way to the theatre?'

'No, on the way to Dunkirk. Harry had been asleep, and you know what it's like when you first wake up. He needed to relieve himself, so I stopped the bath chair and helped him up. He couldn't stand up without support, you see. Well, I held him up at the side of the road, and he tried, but he couldn't do it. He said it was always like that when there was someone close by. He was quite inhibited in his own way.'

'Poor man.'

'We agreed that he needed to relax.'

'Easier said than done.'

'I reckoned that thinking of something he found amusing might start the flow, so to speak.'

'I can see how that would work,' she said, trying to put herself in Harry's situation.

'I suggested he thought of something funny that he'd seen or heard recently, and he came up with a film he'd seen, starring George Formby, so there I was, holding him upright over a trench at the side of the road and singing "When I'm Cleaning Windows". Believe it or not, that did the trick. He was shaking uncontrollably with laughter and... doing the other thing, but not at the memory of George Formby. It was my singing that was making him laugh.'

'I don't suppose you minded. What happened to Harry when you arrived in England?'

'They amputated his leg.'

'Oh,' she protested, 'you were making such a good job of cheering me up, and then you told me that.'

'Only because you asked me.' Feminine logic defeated him, as usual. 'I'll tell you what, though,' he said. 'It would have been less funny if they hadn't taken his leg off.'

'That's probably true.' She seemed unable to banish the subject, because she asked, 'What did he do in civilian life?'

'He was a painter and decorator.'

'Oh, Alan, you made that up.'

'It's true,' he protested. 'He works in a radio factory now. He said he always wanted a sitting-down job.'

* * *

Two days later, Alan received a message from Henri Laurent, which he had to pass on to Dorothy.

'The train that left Paris on that day,' he told her, 'was bound for Berlin, so the most likely destination for its prisoners was the concentration camp at Sachsenhausen. I'm sorry, Dot.'

Determined as ever not to give up, she said, 'Surely, the names of the survivors can be checked, can't they?'

'It's doubtful. The camp was liberated jointly by a Polish unit and one from Byelarus, one of the Soviet states. I'll try our Polish contacts, although they're in a state of disintegration, but if the information is in the hands of the Soviets, the answer's firmly in the negative. We were allies, but we're now potential enemies.'

Unless the Poles could provide the information, it was another dead end, and Dorothy had no alternative but to return home, at least for the time being.

14

Selling Up And Moving On

At home again, Dorothy discovered that probate on her mother's will had been approved, ownership of the house had been transferred to her, and she was free to put it up for sale. She also learned that work on Farrar's new branch was finally complete and that Jack and Kate would be there within weeks. Dot joined them for dinner shortly after her return.

Having learned that Dot's quest had come to, hopefully, a temporary halt, Kate's next question was, 'How were things between you and Alan?'

'Oh, Kate.' Jack sounded like a despairing parent.

'I mean generally. We all know that too much water's passed under the bridge for anything else to happen.'

'He couldn't have been more helpful,' said Dorothy. 'He's busy enough, interrogating Nazi war criminals, but he did everything he could. He even took me on a day excursion to Bremen.'

At the mention of Bremen, Kate's face became solemn. She asked, 'What did you do there?'

'Do you remember my telling you about Alan going to the Lutheran church there when he first arrived in Germany? It was because the Methodists didn't go in for props, such as candles, and he wanted to light a candle for Maurice.'

They both nodded.

'Well, we made it a group tribute on behalf of the four of us who survived. We lit a candle each for ourselves and then we lit two more for you and Jack.'

'Thank you for that, Dot,' said Kate softly. Jack nodded again, taking her hand.

'It's bound to sound daft, and you know I'm not fanciful, as a rule, but I'm going to tell you this, anyway. It was very easy, in that place, to imagine that I could actually communicate with Maurice. It was as if I had a direct line to him, and I told him that you were both blissfully happy with each other. Strangely, it gave me the feeling that I was able to set his mind at rest.'

Kate blinked, and a tear ran down her cheek.

'It got me like that,' Dorothy told her. 'Yes, me, Dry-Eyed Dot. Believe it or not, I went through two of Alan's handkerchiefs.' She shook her head at the silliness of it. 'I must be slipping.'

'Thank you for doing that, Dot,' said Jack. 'We both appreciate it, and we may go there ourselves, one day. What do you think, Kate? Is that a possibility?'

Kate sniffed. 'You tell me. You're the travel agent.'

'At this point,' said Jack, 'I think we should change the subject before we get maudlin. How's the house sale going, Dot?'

'I don't know. I only put it on the market yesterday.'

'It's maybe a little early for impatience. What are you going to do about the Rover? I could picture you driving around in it, as you did before the war.'

'Not with petrol rationing as it is. No, I'm going to sell it and get something a little less staid.'

'Ah.' Jack was suddenly excited. 'I know someone who has an MG for sale. That would suit you down to the ground, Dot. It's the perfect car for the independent woman.'

'No, I'm considering something more sensible than that.'

'What's happening?' Kate asked the question of no one in particular. 'Alan's become human, and Dot's become sensible and practical. Where will it all end?'

'If you remember, I became practical when Baby Maurice got impatient. As for Alan, he just grew up when he saw the error of his ways. He told me all about it on the way to Bremen.'

A wail from Baby Maurice forestalled further disclosure, and Dorothy followed Kate to the cot, to be reunited with the baby she'd delivered.

Kate changed him and handed him to her, still amused by her new and surprising attitude towards babies. 'Do you remember turning up at Jack's house when I'd just changed his dressing after he was wounded at Dunkirk, Dot?'

'It's one of my treasured wartime memories,' said Dorothy, gently rubbing noses with Maurice to his obvious pleasure.

'And mine,' said Jack, smiling at the recollection.

'Jack's newly-born nephew was an excitement for some, but not for you and Jack.'

'It was five years ago, Kate. Attitudes can change.'

'All right, it's taken five years, but you're beginning to feel broody, aren't you?'

'It's very hypothetical,' said Dorothy, 'and, if I did want to do something about it, I'd need to get a move on. I'm single and I'll be thirty next year.'

* * *

The advertisement for the Rover 12 6-Light saloon attracted several phone calls, a development that surprised Dorothy in the light of petrol rationing. The enquiries ranged from promising to downright insulting. The first call was of the latter kind.

'I'm enquiring about the Rover Twelve, which I believe is for sale.'

'Oh, yes?'

'May I speak to its owner?'

'I'm it's owner.'

'Oh.' The caller sounded taken aback. 'Perhaps I might speak to your husband.'

'That's not possible.'

'Why not?' His tone was now demanding.

'Because I have yet to meet the man in question. I am a single woman.'

'But I need to discuss technicalities.'

The receiver was quite heavy, and Dorothy moved it to her left hand. 'What do you want to know?'

'To begin with, the year of manufacture.'

'Nineteen thirty-six.'

'Also the mileage.'

'Nine thousand, two hundred and fifty-three miles.'

'Are you sure?'

'Positive. I'm very good at reading numbers.'

Her sarcasm was lost on him. 'What is the state of its tyres?'

'That's hard to say. They've done nothing for six years.'

'Are they on the car?'

'Of course not. The car is on axle stands and the wheels and tyres are wrapped in sacking.' By this time, she was losing patience with him.

'You're asking a great deal for it.'

'It's a valuable car. It cost… just a minute while I turn up the invoice... two hundred and seventy-eight pounds in nineteen thirty-six.'

'That was in nineteen thirty-six.'

'I know. I just said so.'

'This is nineteen forty-five.'

'Well done. That's right.'

'The thing is, I don't expect you to understand market forces, but the fact is that, because of petrol rationing, a car with an engine of that size is worth considerably less than it might have been in normal times.'

'Listen, Mr….'

'Worth. Ernest Worth.'

'Listen, Mr Worth, During the war, we had a saying, that "bullshit baffles brains". It wasn't true then, any more than it is today. Moreover, your attitude is overbearing and insulting. I suggest you look elsewhere, because I'm too fond of that car to sell it to an ill-mannered, imperious, supercilious, patronising bore like you. In other words, bugger off and leave me in peace!' She never heard his response as she put down the receiver.

Happily, the fourth phone call seemed likelier to bear fruit.

'Hello, is the Rover still for sale?'

'Yes.'

'Thank goodness for that. May I come and see it?'

'Please do. When do you want to come? I'm here most of the time, and I can arrange to be here if you have a particular time in mind.'

'Would lunchtime, say, twelve-thirty today, be all right? I'd like to see it in daylight, if possible.'

'Very wise. I'll be here when you arrive. Let me give you the address.'

* * *

Mr Wilkinson turned out to be around forty and as pleasant as his phone manner had promised. Dorothy had opened the garage doors so that he could see the car properly, and he walked around it, almost purring with approval.

'I imagine there's been a lot of interest in it,' he said warily.

'Some interest. Two people are considering it, and I'm expecting them to phone me today.'

'Ah.' Clearly that wasn't what he wanted to hear. 'Miss Needham,' he said, 'do you think we could shake hands on the asking price, or are you expecting more?'

'I think we can do that. As you've been a model buyer, as well, perhaps you'd like a cup of tea or coffee while we go through the arrangements.'

'How kind. Yes, please, a cup of tea would be very welcome.'

A mechanic would arrive at a convenient time to charge the battery, refit the wheels, replace the oils and fluids, and ensure that the engine ran smoothly. The sleeping beauty was about to be woken, if not by the prince, at least, on his behalf, and Mr Wilkinson was the happiest of princes. Dorothy was also happy as she phoned the other would-be buyers to give them the bad news. She wondered about phoning Mr Worth, but decided against it. He didn't even deserve to be remembered.

* * *

Later in the week, a letter arrived from Alan. The return address was in Lüneburg in Lower Saxony.

Dear Dot,

I hope you arrived home safely.

From my return address, you'll have gathered that I'm now attached to a unit of the Royal Military Police whilst awaiting demob with unprecedented impatience.

I've checked with the Polish units I know, and I'm afraid they all tell me the same story, that the records of Sachsenhausen survivors were taken by the Soviets. I really am sorry. The only good thing I have to tell you about the liberation of Sachsenhausen is that, according to the Poles, the Russians dealt sympathetically with the survivors, giving what immediate care they could and transporting the severe cases to hospital. I've already begun making enquiries of the Berlin hospitals, so far without success, but nil desperandum.

In view of the nature of my work, I should get Christmas leave, in which case, do you think we might meet at some time?

Please give my best to Jack and Kate. I hope their move will take place soon.

Take great care, I hope to see you before too long.

Love and best wishes,

Alan.

Dorothy replied immediately.

Dear Alan,

It was good to hear from you, but I'm sorry if your posting is less than you'd hoped. However, every cloud has a… something or other, as they say, and now I know where you are, I'll send you your handkerchiefs, duly washed and ironed.

Jack's new branch is now complete, and he and Kate will move soon, probably before Christmas.

I told them about Bremen, and they were very grateful, both for your earlier visit and for ours, last week. It was actually quite an emotional conversation. Meanwhile, Baby Maurice continues to delight everyone, including me, believe it or not.

My house is now up for sale, and I've sold the Rover. I'm happy that it's gone to a good home. When I find somewhere to live, I'll look for a smaller car that's lighter on petrol.

I managed to get in a final ride with the cycling club before winter, but it's not what it was. I realise now that I was being unrealistic. There's something cosy about the past, but a great many things have happened since then that were far from cosy. I remember how, during the war, we used to distance ourselves from aircrew, because their future was

109

so uncertain that we didn't want to become too involved with them. It seems awful in retrospect, but I once sort of lost someone, and that served to reinforce the way we felt. He and I had parted by the time he was killed, and I wondered for a time if that had affected his judgement. Fortunately, Jack was on hand at the time to brace me up. When he wasn't being daft, he was always good at talking common sense.

Keep your chin up – and other well-worn wartime exhortations that may apply.

Love and understanding,

Dot.

P.S. Of course we must meet when you're on leave. Phone me when you're in Cullington.

* * *

With the house on the market, Dorothy could give some thought to where she might live. With two of her closest friends moving to the coast and the other living in County Durham, there was nothing in Cullington to keep her there. The trouble was that she had too great a choice. Possibly a sense of purpose, if she could find one, would help her make the decision. Her earlier purpose seemed to have come to a full stop, although she wasn't prepared to write off Aunt Sarah just yet.

15

Lüneburg

A Square Peg

The officer in charge of the unit was Captain, soon to be Acting-Major, Bruce Cochrane of the Royal Military Police's Special Investigation Branch, and it soon became apparent that he resented the attachment of an outsider to his domain.

'We do everything by the book in the Royal Military Police, Lofthouse. You need to take a copy of the manual and study it.'

'Do you mean that someone has actually written a book that tells your people how to carry out an interrogation?' Even as he spoke, it seemed increasingly ludicrous.

'That's exactly what Ah do mean, and Ah won't have mavericks in my unit, even if you think you know everything there is to know about interrogating prisoners, which Ah very much doubt.'

'Here's a fair question, Cochrane. How long have you been investigating alleged war criminals?'

'That's none of your damned business!'

'In other words, not very long. What a mercy it is that JAG are investigating the Nazi top brass and leaving only the troops to us lesser mortals.'

Cochrane's response was almost a snarl. 'Ah'll thank you to keep your opinions to yourself, Lofthouse.'

'It's probably as well if I do.' At least, Alan could understand them.

'Another thing, Lofthouse.'

'Another?'

'Why did you send your interpreter out of the interview room during an interrogation?'

'Because I didn't need him.' He thought that was obvious.

Cochrane tapped the palm of his hand with his swagger stick. 'Maybe you can explain to me how you intend to interrogate a suspect without an interpreter.'

'I'm sure I can, Cochrane. I've never needed an interpreter, because, unlike you and your staff, I speak German. What's more, I find that the immediacy of direct communication with the suspect gives him less time to think and therefore prevaricate. It's an important advantage.' He paused to check that Cochrane was still following him, and asked, 'Doesn't your manual touch on that?'

Cochrane ignored the taunt. 'In future, Lofthouse,' he said with a final flick of his swagger stick, 'you will have an interpreter in the room with you on every occasion. Is that clear?'

'Abundantly. He can come for the ride, if that's what you want.'

'As long as that's understood.'

There was a knock on the door.

'Yes?'

The door opened, and a sergeant said, 'Two of our men have been beaten up, sir. They are being treated for their injuries, and we've made an arrest.'

'Just one arrest? How many of the sausage-eating bastards were involved?'

'There was only one of them, sir, and he's not German. He's a Queen's Own Highlander, a big bugger, sir.'

Alan smiled involuntarily at the image.

'Leave him in the cells for now.'

Alan said, 'He should have representation, Cochrane.'

'Ah don't need you to tell me that, Lofthouse. Ah know the regulations.'

'I only mentioned it because you seemed to have forgotten.'

Cochrane delivered a look of smouldering hatred and said, 'Maybe you'd like to go down there and hold his bloody hand until somebody from his own regiment arrives to do the job.'

'I'll certainly see that he's treated fairly. Then, of course, the matter will need to be brought to the attention of his CO.'

The simmering hatred became a shout. 'Did ye not hear what the sergeant said, Lofthouse?' Slowly and with great emphasis, he said, 'He's just beaten up two of my men!'

'And you know nothing of the circumstances. It's possible, of course, that the man did it because, like a great many front-line soldiers, he has little time for the Military Police. On the other hand, and for all you know, he may have had a subtler reason.'

'Go and see what you can find out.'

'It'll be a pleasure. Lead the way, Sergeant.'

The sergeant led him downstairs to a row of cells, some of which were populated by Nazi suspects. Further along, however, raised voices told a different story. Alan heard a voice say, 'Don't even bloody think about it, or you'll get the same treatment as the other two bastards got.'

'What's the prisoner's name, Sergeant?'

'McTavish, sir. He's a hard case.'

Alan stopped at the cell door. Two redcaps were squaring up to the kilted prisoner, who was quite clearly standing his ground. He was, as the sergeant had said, an extremely large man.

'McTavish, I'm coming in for a chat with you, so calm down. You two, come outside.'

The sergeant looked uncertain. 'Are you sure, sir? He's dangerous.'

'Only if he's mistreated.' He turned to McTavish and said, 'I'm not military police, McTavish. I'm with the Intelligence Corps and I'm here to see that your rights are respected until an officer from your regiment arrives. Come on, you two, out before you cause even more trouble.' He waited until the two redcaps were out of the way, and then entered the cell. 'Sit down, McTavish, and tell me why you assaulted two redcaps.'

McTavish looked as if he were about to lose his temper again, but quickly abated. 'They called out to me from across the road, sir.'

'What did they say?'

'They called me a sheep sha…. They said I… did it… with sheep, sir. It's the kilt. It sometimes takes savages that way.'

Alan smiled. 'And now they wish they hadn't. Where are you from, McTavish?'

'Wester Ross, sir.'

'A magnificent part of Scotland. You're a proud Highlander serving in a fine regiment, and you were insulted by two brainless louts.'

'That's about the size of it, sir.'

'You have to bear in mind, McTavish, that all you'll ever hear from a pig is a grunt or a squeal.'

'Aye, sir, they did plenty squealing this morning.'

'I can believe it.' It seemed to Alan that justice itself could be very unjust. 'You're going to be disciplined for this, McTavish,' he said. 'You realise that, of course, but I'm going to put in a word in your defence.'

'Thank you, sir.'

Alan was about to say more, when a redcap appeared with an officer of the Queen's Own Highlanders, also wearing a kilt. As he entered the cell, Alan saw that he was a 2nd lieutenant.

'Good morning, Lieutenant. My name's Lofthouse, and I came down here to ensure fair play.'

The officer glanced at Alan's shoulder flashes and said, 'I'm obliged to you, sir.'

'McTavish, here, was going about his lawful business, I imagine, when two redcaps made a loud, insulting and indecent remark about him. They accused him of indulging in bestial sex on a regular basis.'

The subaltern nodded sadly. 'It goes with the territory, sir, and the kilt, I'm afraid.'

'So I understand. McTavish naturally objected to the insult, to the extent that he taught the two redcaps a salutary lesson, whereupon he was arrested by yet more of their kind, who tried but failed to repay the assault.' He stopped and said, 'I'm sorry, Lieutenant. It's not at all funny.' Nevertheless, he was struggling to contain his laughter. 'It's entirely up to your CO, of course, but I recommend leniency, as McTavish was only defending his and his regiment's honour.' He answered a questioning look from McTavish by translating. 'I'm asking that your CO goes easy on you, McTavish, but do try to control your temper in future, and remember that not everyone lives according to your civilised standards.'

'Aye, sir. Thank you, sir.'

* * *

114

After a successful interrogation later that day, Cochrane met Alan on the way to the officers' mess.

'Ah spoke to your interpreter just now, Lofthouse.'

'In English, I hope.'

'Don't get clever with me. He told me that your German is better than his.'

'That's why I said I hoped he'd spoken to you in English and not German.'

'Right.' Cochrane adjusted to the revised message. 'Well, Ah suppose you might as well carry on without an interpreter, as you seem to be able to manage.'

'There, now, Cochrane, it took a while, but you got there in the end.'

'An' what's this Ah hear about you putting in a word for that thug McTavish?'

'He acted under extreme provocation. Because he was wearing a kilt, your two monkeys accused him of a bestial act. He's a proud Highlander, Cochrane.'

Cochrane raised his voice again. 'He's a criminal, Lofthouse.'

'And you're very much a Low…lander. It makes a difference, doesn't it?'

'Just you wait until my rank is confirmed, Lofthouse. You'll not be so cocky then.'

Alan could wait, because he'd received good news that day.

* * *

He went into breakfast the next morning, and in a very short time, he heard Cochrane's rasping voice.

'Captain Lofthouse, kindly explain to me why you are wearing those things on your epaulettes.'

'I'm wearing them, Cochrane, because I'm no longer Captain Lofthouse, but Major Lofthouse, not acting, but confirmed.'

The fit of apoplexy that Alan hoped for never materialised, because Cochrane made a rapid, if angry, recovery and left the mess, whereupon Alan enjoyed a peaceful breakfast.

With no pressing business, he took out his writing things to acquaint Dorothy of his good fortune.

Dear Dot,

Captain Lofthouse is dead. Long live Major Lofthouse! In the normal course of events, I wouldn't be quite so triumphant, but in this particularly exquisite case, I have trumped the egregious officer in charge of this post. Honestly, it's a running battle, but he won't be able to pull rank on me, even when his acting promotion comes through. He almost had a fit this morning when he saw the crowns on my shoulders. It does seem rather odd, though, that they should promote me within a matter of months of my demob. I can only think that it's the usual case of the right and left hands operating in mutual ignorance.

How is the house sale proceeding? Where will you live? Those and other questions spring to mind when I think of you. I'm looking forward to Christmas all the time. Frankly, I'm sick of what I'm doing, and I'd just as soon be demobbed.

What are you going to do now that you've left Rimmington's and you're free to roam? I can't picture you as a carefree socialite, or as a lady of leisure, who champions the local orphanage and browbeats disrespectful tradesmen and left-wing politicians. Do tell me about your plans.

I'll let you into a secret, shall I? When I'm demobbed, I intend to speak nicely to the hierarchy at my old college at Cambridge – I imagine there'll be government funding of some kind available – and return to the hallowed cloisters to study archaeology. Even allowing for all the mud, clay, peat and honest soil to be excavated, it has to be a cleaner existence than the one I'm leading now. So, there – you're the only person I've told, including my family.

Take care.
Love,
Alan.

16

December

Wind, Rain And Rabbit Pie

The sale of the house was confirmed, contracts were exchanged, and the handover date was set for early January. More than anything, Dot longed to be free of the spectre of death duty. She simply wanted to discharge it so that she could address the rest of her life. She still had no idea where she wanted to live; for the time being, she would put her furniture into store and live in a hotel until she felt inspired.

Christmas was a nonsense, at least, socially. Kate, Jack and Baby Maurice had moved to Bridlington, and Connie's extended family would keep her busy throughout the brief holiday. Alan was due home on the 23ʳᵈ, but he would naturally spend most of the time with his parents. For that, he deserved her sympathy rather than her resentment. She was therefore surprised to receive a phone call from him on his arrival home.

'Dot, it's Alan.'

'Lovely to hear from you, Alan. Where are you?'

'At home. It's the usual thing: a note on the kitchen table saying, "Welcome home. Father is busy at the office. I'm busy with the WVS. Careful with the tea, it's all we've got. Love, Mother." Honestly, it's happened so often, I could write it for her.'

'Oh, dear. You're welcome to come here.'

'I'm tempted, but I should be here when they return. I'll be expected to be at home on Christmas Day, as well, but Christmas Eve is the time for their hectic social round, and I can't face that. May I be a nuisance then?'

'Of course.'

'I'd invite you over for lunch on Christmas Day, but—'

She laughed. 'You know how your mother feels about me. I don't think Peace and Goodwill would have a place at the table. Do you?'

'I wouldn't place a bet on it. So, Christmas Eve's all right, then?'

'And any other time. Take it as read.'

'Bless you, Dot. I haven't had time to do a lot of shopping....'

'Neither have I. Let's just give each other our time and our company.'

'The true Spirit of Christmas, eh? Let's do that, and "God bless us, everyone".'

* * *

Alan had brewed tea by the time his mother arrived home, bustling, business-like and in her grey-green tweed suit and red blouse, as a stalwart of the Women's Voluntary Service. She accepted a kiss from her son and proceeded to tell him about the various tasks the WVS were undertaking.

'Even though the war is over, there's still a lot of work to be done,' she told him.

'Yes, I've noticed.'

'I suppose you have.' As if the thought had only just occurred to her, she asked, 'Isn't it time you were demobbed? People are coming home all the time.'

'My thoughts exactly.'

'Even that Needham girl is back. I told her about Gwen, of course.'

'I know. She wrote to me, and we've been in regular communication.'

Inevitably, his mother frowned. 'Don't start entertaining ideas about her again, Alan. You know what she's like.'

'I know exactly. She's a very faithful, platonic friend. She came over to Hanover, you know.'

'Why on earth did she do that?'

'She's trying to discover the fate or whereabouts of her long-lost aunt, who's half-Jewish, apparently.'

'Oh.' The disapproving look intensified. 'Of course. I heard some time ago that the Needhams were part-Jewish.'

Alan could only laugh.

'What's so funny?'

'Just that you make them sound like grave robbers.'

'Oh, really.'

'I've spent the past two-and-a-half years interrogating prisoners who could find nothing good to say about the Jewish race, and now I've returned to my civilised home to hear the same kind of thing. You have to admit, it's ironic.'

'Don't be ridiculous, Alan. I've nothing against Jewish people. I was only saying that the Needham family just had to be… *different*.'

Still smiling, he stood up and said, 'It's hardly worth the trouble for this short leave, but I'll go up and unpack.' It would be easier than holding a conversation with his mother.

* * *

Dorothy stood at the butcher's counter, looking at her meat ration. Most people had done their shopping for Christmas, so she and Mr Rogers, the butcher, were alone. She asked, 'Have you anything off the ration?'

'Nothing Christmassy, Miss Needham, only prepared rabbits, and nobody wants to eat rabbit at Christmas.'

'I'm not so sure about that, Mr Rogers. I'd like to take a couple, please.'

She took her purchases and hurried home. Then, with everything in the refrigerator, she enquired about the number of the Shire Hall in Durham and dialled it.

'Durham Shire Hall. Good afternoon.'

'Is that Connie?'

'That's Dot, isn't it? You worked with us long enough. You should be able to recognise my voice, bonny lass.'

'Not when you sound like Peggy Ashcroft. Anyway, Connie, I wouldn't trouble you at work, but I need to know how to cook rabbit.'

'Just let us put you on "hold" while Ah take this call, an' Ah'll be with you.'

Dorothy waited for a short time, and then Connie came back on the line.

'Rabbit pie or stew?'

'I think I can push the boat out and make a pie.'

'Right, bonnie lass, if you've a pad and pencil handy, Ah'll see what Ah can do, seein' as it's nearly Christmas.'

* * *

Christmas Eve brought unsettled weather from the north, but Alan, who had resurrected his old Panther combination, arrived suitably protected in a leather coat and trousers.

'Come in, Alan.' Dorothy inclined her cheek for a kiss, and closed the door behind him. 'Take off your wet things,' she told him, taking his outer clothes as he divested himself of them.

'I've brought shoes,' he assured her, seeing her glance at his heavy boots.

'I expected nothing less.'

Eventually, he emerged in a tweed jacket, grey flannels and brown Oxford shoes.

'I last saw you in civvies before the war,' she said.

'At the Bay Horse,' he confirmed.

'Come through, and I'll put the kettle on. I'm amazed you managed to get your motorbike to start after all this time, bonny lad.'

'What did you call me?'

'I've been talking to Connie in Durham, and the language tends to rub off, at least for a while.'

'And why not? In response to your amazement, I spent the whole morning working on the Panther.' He looked at his nails and then hid them playfully behind his back.

'I'm flattered. Come into the kitchen and talk to me while I make the tea.'

'It'll be worth it to see you in a kitchen.'

'I'll have you know,' she said with mock-dignity, 'that I'm acquiring new skills all the time.' She filled the kettle and lit the gas.

'Two new skills,' he observed.

'You ain't seen nothin' yet.'

Changing the subject, he asked, 'Is there any news on the house sale?'

'Handover is on the fifteenth of next month.'

'Excellent. Where will you go?'

'I'm open to suggestions.' When his face registered surprise, she explained, 'I really don't know where I want to live. It's easier for people who have a job. They just find somewhere handy for work, but I'm blessed with too much freedom. I suppose I'll put the furniture into store and book into a hotel until I reach a decision.'

'You'll be homeless, like me in Lüneburg.'

'And you had lovely married quarters in Hanover.'

'I'm not allowed in married quarters now.'

'Well, you were being a little bit naughty.' She opened the caddy and spooned tea into the pot.

'Be thankful you didn't come to Lüneburg.'

'Is it really so awful?'

'It's not the friendliest working environment. For one thing the officer in charge of the post is a hidebound, ignorant lout, who resents having to share the place with an officer who's not even in the Royal Military Police.'

'Not your favourite people?' She took the kettle from the stove and scalded the tea.

'They acquired a reputation in the fourteen-eighteen war, tried to live up to it in the last war, and now, fearing that they've somehow fallen short of their objective, they're trying to make the worst of things in peacetime. Meanwhile, Acting-Major Cochrane is striving to put the clock back and impose the archaic rules of interrogation as laid down in the manual. We can only hope for a visit by three spirits, such as I experienced in nineteen-forty.'

'You poor man, but you've just reminded me of something.' She disappeared into the drawing room and returned with a small package wrapped in Christmas paper. 'I know we said we wouldn't do anything about presents, but I saw this and thought of you offering cigarettes out of that box of yours to undeserving prisoners. I'm sure you'll cut more of a dash with that.'

He removed the wrapping paper to find a silver cigarette case. 'This is superb, Dot. Thank you. If this doesn't help me get a string of confessions, I don't know what will. Thank you again.'

'Don't worry if you haven't got anything for me. It was just a flash of inspiration on my part.'

'I would worry if I hadn't bought you something,' he said, taking a small box from his hip pocket and handing it to her.

'You shouldn't have.' She opened the box and took out a double locket on a chain. It was exquisitely engraved in an Art Nouveau design. 'This is just lovely,' she said, opening one side and finding it empty. She opened the other and gasped when she saw the star of David. 'Thank you, Alan. It's very special indeed.'

'You can put any photo you choose in the other side,' he suggested.

'I'll find one of Aunt Sarah. Thank you, Alan.' She leaned forward and kissed his cheek.

'I thought of your Aunt Sarah, but of course, that was up to you. I bought it in Cullington when I arrived. As you can imagine, anything with a Semitic design is thin on the ground in Germany.'

'Well, you couldn't have found anything better.' She offered him the loose ends of the chain and asked, 'Will you hook me up?'

He fastened the clasp behind her neck, rearranging her hair gently and tidily, a gesture that pleased and surprised her, but she made no comment.

He sniffed the aroma from the oven and asked, 'What are we eating, Dot?'

'Rabbit pie.'

'Really?'

'Well, it is Christmas.'

'I like rabbit pie, but I can't see the connection.'

'The connection,' she explained patiently, 'is that I'm serving it on Christmas Eve.'

'Ah.' He'd heard of feminine logic, but only as an example of a contradiction in terms.

'I spent time on the phone to Connie in Durham, learning how to make rabbit pie,' she told him. 'It was like you with your motorbike. Some things require preparation.'

* * *

Dorothy was greatly relieved that the rabbit pie was a success. She'd followed Connie's recipe slavishly, but the result was still a surprise. It transpired that neither of them had eaten lunch prior to Alan's arrival, so they made it an early dinner, and it was all the more enjoyable for being different.

It also gave them an opportunity to listen to the Festival of Nine Lessons and Carols from King's College, Cambridge. With the wind and rain buffeting the windows, they found it unusually comforting.

'I'd like to go there, some time,' said Dorothy when the service ended.

'Cambridge?'

'Not the university, but Cambridge itself. I've never been there.'

'That could be the answer to your quest for a purpose,' he said.

She gave him an odd look. 'Visiting Cambridge? I'm sure I'd enjoy it, but it would hardly be pilgrimage.'

'No, I meant the university. If I remember rightly, you got a particularly good School Certificate.'

'No,' she said, 'it doesn't appeal, whereas I could maybe see myself owning a bookshop or a teashop.'

' "My aunt owns a teashop in Horsham".'

'Does she?'

'No, it's one of those tongue twisters, like "She sells seashells on the seashore".'

She thought about it, juggling the words in her head, and said, 'I don't know of a place called Teasham.'

'You wouldn't want to know it if my aunt's shop is typical of its attractions.'

'That's true.' She crossed her legs and smoothed her skirt.

'You've just reminded me of something,' he said, getting up.

'Have I? I wasn't aware of it.'

He went out to the hall, where he'd left his wet clothes and the box that carried his shoes, and returned with two cellophane packets, which he handed to her.

'Nylon stockings,' she gasped. 'Wherever did you find these?'

'In the PX, the Post Exchange, when I visited the American base at Dülmen. I thought you'd find them useful as there's a shortage of them in Blighty.'

'Your thinking was spot-on. Thank you, Alan.'

'I'll think of you next time I go there.'

17

January 1946

A Quid Pro Quo

The prisoner on the other side of the desk was one of many who'd been identified by concentration camp survivors as members of the Allgemeine Schutzstaffel, the branch of the SS charged with striving for racial purity, largely by manning the death camps. It struck Alan, not for the first time, that Nazi policy was not without irony. Hitler was a homosexual, and yet he persecuted his own kind. Also, through a programme of sterilisation, he tried to rid the Third Reich of the intellectually disadvantaged, and yet he staffed his death camps with cretinous thugs such as the one who now awaited interrogation.

'Are you Mann Manfred Lehmann of the Allgemeine SS?'

Lehmann's response was sullen. 'Yes.'

'Were you directed to Sachsenhausen Concentration Camp?'

'Yes, I was forced to work there.'

'By whom?'

'I don't understand.'

'Who forced you to work there?'

'Scharführer Krüger.'

'The *Scharführer* who was arrested with you?'

The man looked vacant.

'Is he the *Scharführer* who shares your cell?'

'Yes.'

'Did he tell you to beat the prisoners?'

'Yes, he forces me.'

Here was a German, one of the Master Race, who was incapable of forming the past tense in his own language. Alan toyed with his swagger stick, causing Lehmann to flinch. Realising this, he put it down and said, 'Relax. I'm not going to beat you, much as you deserve it. Did you ever beat a prisoner to death?'

'Only Russian prisoners.'

'Why?'

'Scharführer Krüger forces me to do this thing.'

'Why only Russian prisoners?'

'I don't understand.'

'Why did you beat to death only Russian prisoners?'

'This is where I work, in the Russian place.'

'Only with Russian prisoners?'

'Yes.'

Alan persisted for a further ten minutes, but all he could extract from Lehmann was that Krüger had forced him to beat Russians to death. He decided to send Lehmann back to his cell and to send for Krüger.

When the guards brought Krüger in, he was as sullen as Lehmann had been.

'Are you Scharführer Hans Krüger of the Allgemeine SS?'

'Yes.'

'Yes, who?'

'Yes, Herr Major.' His attitude was still resentful.

'Were you directed to Sachsenhausen Concentration Camp?'

'Yes, Herr Major.'

'You were very powerful there, weren't you?'

'Yes, Herr Major. I was a *Scharführer*.' Incredibly, he sounded proud of the fact.

'Mann Lehmann used to beat prisoners to death, didn't he?'

'Only Russian prisoners, Herr Major.'

Alan was conscious that a theme was developing. 'Why did he do that?'

'I ordered him to do it.'

'Did you order him to beat Jews?'

'No, Herr Major.'

'Poles?'

125

'No, Herr Major.'

'Gypsies?'

'No, Herr Major. Only Russians.'

'What do you think of Russians?'

'They are barbarians, sir. They are *Untermenschen*.'

'Who ordered you to have them killed?'

'Obersturmführer Köhler, Herr Major.'

'We are holding an *Obersturmführer* of that name. Is he the officer who ordered you to kill those Russians?'

'Yes, Herr Major.'

'Guards, take this man back to his cell and bring me Obersturmführer Köhler.' Alan was aware that an *Obersturmführer* was the equivalent of a lieutenant in the British Army, but he'd learned that even the most junior officers of the SS wielded terrible power.

When the prisoner came in, he kicked one leg of the chair to move it from beneath the desk.

'Remain standing, Köhler. I have not given you permission to sit.'

Köhler favoured Alan with a look that seemed to question his right to speak to an SS officer in that manner, so Alan reinforced his order by saying, 'You will remain standing until I give you permission to do otherwise.' He looked unnecessarily at the document before him, a directive from Cochrane regarding the wearing of correct dress, and asked, 'Are you Obersturmführer Ludwig Köhler of the Allgemeine SS?'

'Yes.'

'Yes, *who*?'

'*Jawohl*, Herr Major.'

'Very well.' The German form of receipt was acceptable. 'You were posted to Sachsenhausen Concentration Camp. Is that correct?'

Köhler nodded with something that was almost a sneer.

'Answer me, Köhler, so that the stenographer can hear you.'

'Yes, Herr Major.' His response was grudging.

'A mere *Obersturmführer*.'

'In the SS, an *Obersturmführer* has the kind of power you Engländers do not understand.'

'That's interesting, Köhler.' Alan took out his cigarette case, opened it and closed it again, as if he'd changed his mind. Meanwhile, the prisoner had been treated to a waft of Virginia tobacco. Alan saw his nose twitch. 'So, you enjoyed a great deal of power in Sachsenhausen?'

'Of course.'

' "I say to one, 'Go,' and he goeth".'

'I do not understand, Herr Major.'

'It was a quotation from the Bible, Köhler. I don't suppose you've ever read it. Take a seat, by the way.'

Surprised for the moment, Köhler sat down. 'I have read *Mein Kampf*,' he said.

'A poor substitute.' Ignoring Köhler's look of protestation, he went on to say, 'The line I quoted was spoken by a Roman centurion, an officer who commanded a hundred men.'

Köhler sneered. 'Only one hundred men?'

'Do you find that less than impressive?'

'It makes me laugh, Herr Major.'

'I'm fascinated by what you say about the power of an *Obersturmführer*.' He took out his cigarette case again and opened it. 'Would you care for a cigarette?'

'Thank you, Herr Major.' He took a cigarette with the air of a man who was about to handle a rare and valuable object.

Alan lit it for him and said, 'You were a very powerful man, Köhler. If you ordered a man to do something, he would have no choice but to carry out your order.'

'That is so.'

'Scharführer Krüger tells me you ordered him to have prisoners beaten to death. Is that also a fact?'

'Only Russian prisoners, Herr Major, savages and barbarians.'

'Nevertheless, you ordered Krüger to have them beaten to death.'

In a condescending manner that Alan found sickening, Köhler said, 'Herr Major, are you really interested in the fate of those Russians? I did not order anyone to beat Jews, Poles, French or Engländers, only Russians.'

'How many Russians?'

Köhler gave a careless shrug. 'Who knows? A hundred, maybe.'

'Thank you, Köhler. Guards, will you take this prisoner back to his cell?'

Alan left the interview room and climbed the stairs to Cochrane's office. It went against the grain to seek his approval, but he was, after all, Officer in Charge. He knocked on the door.

'Yes?'

Alan pushed the door open and walked in.

'What do you want, Lofthouse?'

'I've just been interrogating the SS prisoners who came from Sachsenhausen, Cochrane: a private, a sergeant and a lieutenant, who have all denied ever having killed British, Jewish, Polish or French prisoners, but who have all confessed to the large-scale murder of Russian prisoners. Frankly, I don't believe their denial. It seems to me that they've jumped to the conclusion that we regard the Russians pretty much as they do, as savages unworthy of decent treatment. Certainly, they expect us to overlook that aspect of their unholy practice, or they wouldn't have confessed to it so readily.'

Cochrane stirred impatiently. 'Who gives a shit about the Russians, Lofthouse?'

'Keep listening, Cochrane. I don't consider it worthwhile to persist with their interrogation, when it could go on for a long time and result in their being sentenced each to a lenient term of imprisonment.'

'What do you propose, Lofthouse?' Cochrane's patience was ever limited.

'That we turn them over to the Russians.'

'Why, for the love of Mike?'

'Goodwill, and if we're lucky, a *quid pro quo*.'

'A what?'

'A favour in return.'

'How do you propose to organise that?'

'If I'm given the go-ahead, I'll write to the Russians and make the offer. The handover can be made at the frontier, and they'll have nothing to complain about. On the contrary, they should be pleased.'

For the first time, Cochrane saw an advantage. 'And we'll have two empty cells.' Everyone had a priority.

* * *

Dear Dot,
Don't bank on anything, but I may have found a way forward. I'm

about to strike a bargain with our allies, and I should shortly be in possession of the list of survivors from Sachsenhausen. I'll examine it carefully and let you know what, if anything, I find.
Love,
Alan.

* * *

He wasn't surprised when he received a prompt reply.

Dear Alan,
Well done! As soon as I've handed over the house, I'll join you in Lüneburg.
Love,
Dot.

* * *

Dear Dot,
If you really insist, I can't stop you, but the same old warning applies, and the outcome could still be disappointing. Remember that.
I'll arrange a hotel room for you. Things are far less cosy than they were last time you were here.
Love,
Alan.

* * *

Official approval came surprisingly quickly, the scheme having a certain appeal. With that settled, the cloak-and-dagger routine could be set in motion.

The exchange had to take place at night, because neither side wanted everyone to know they were doing business with the enemy. One senior British officer referred to it as 'supping with the devil', so the cover of darkness served in his case, presumably, as his 'spoon with a long handle'.

The two vehicles stopped, each on its own side of the border, and the officers of the opposing powers met. The whole operation amused Alan tremendously, but his opposite number seemed predictably solemn, as did his subordinates, and the proceedings were carried out with almost-theatrical gravity.

'Good evening,' said Alan. 'I have here the German prisoners. Have you the information I requested?'

The Russian officer said nothing, but simply held up a file.

It occurred to Alan that the Russians were more than likely under strict orders not to communicate verbally with the Western Powers. It seemed both churlish and childish, but they no doubt had their reason. 'Very good. Sergeant, unload the van.'

The sergeant opened the rear doors of the van, and the guards bundled the German prisoners on to the road.

When Köhler saw the Russians, he shouted in alarm. 'You did not tell us you were going to surrender us to the Russians! You cannot do this!'

'It's perfectly within the laws of the Geneva Convention, Köhler.'

'This is an outrage!'

'No more outrageous than what you did to their countrymen.'

'Why are you doing this to us? Why are you betraying us to the Russians?'

'Because the prisoners you murdered were Russian, and these people are feeling upset about it. It's only natural, when all's said and done.'

The guards pushed the prisoners forward, to be grasped by the Russian soldiers. When he was satisfied that the British had kept their part of the bargain, the officer handed the file to Alan, who acknowledged the gesture with the phrase he'd learned specially for the occasion. '*Bolshoi spasyba, tovariyshch.* Many thanks, comrade.'

The Russian officer remained silent and made no move to shake hands, but Alan was happy. He had the document he wanted. He just hoped it would yield the information Dot wanted.

18

Recognition And Relaxation

Dot waited for Alan to get into the car, and said, 'I am now officially homeless.'

'A homeless orphan,' he mused, 'like a great many of the people around us.'

Dorothy viewed the devastated landscape through the passenger window and said, 'This is my first visit to Lüneburg. They say it was a beautiful town before the war.'

'Let's hope it will be again. I should be horrified if I thought the politicians were going to make the same mistakes as they did last time, planting the seeds of another war.'

'You'll have to explain it to me some time, Alan. Meanwhile, where are you taking me?'

'To the Kieler Hof Hotel. It's next door to the RMP Post.'

'RMP?'

'The Royal Military Police.'

'Of course.'

Alan turned into a busy, main street and said, 'I have news.'

'Good news?'

'No, but it's not necessarily bad news.'

'Please put me out of my misery.'

He slowed down behind an army lorry and said, 'Your aunt was a prisoner at Sachsenhausen, but she was transferred shortly before the end of the war to Bergen-Belsen. The Nazis were trying to destroy the evidence before the Allies, and particularly the Russians, arrived. There were mass killings as they tried to eliminate evidence of their misdeeds, but a prisoner answering to the name Sarah Elizabeth Moore arrived, mercifully in one piece, at Bergen-Belsen on the twenty-fifth of March last year.'

'Oh, my goodness.' Dorothy closed her eyes and tried to digest the information. 'Aunt Alice said she would always land on her feet.'

'I hope so. The greatest threat between arrival and liberation came not so much from the Nazis, but from illness. With so many prisoners herded together, typhus abounded.' He glanced at her and said, 'I'm only acquainting you with the facts as they're known. I don't want you to get your hopes up, only to be devastated.'

'I've got Aunt Sarah in this locket, Alan, so that she'll always be with me, but I must find out what happened to her. It's something I just have to do. It's almost as if... don't laugh.'

'I wouldn't dream of it. Go on.'

'I was going to say that, with no one else to care about her fate, it's almost like guarding her last wicket.'

'You're a constant source of surprises, Dot. I never associated you with cricket, of all things, but if it helps at all, you're not alone.' He pulled into the forecourt of what seemed to be one of the few hotels remaining, and parked the car. 'This is the best I can do, Dot.'

'Thank you for arranging it. I'll be fine. I can manage by myself now, if you need to be away.'

'No, it's essential that I go everywhere with you.'

'In that case, it's just as well we don't squabble anymore.'

She booked into the hotel, and Alan carried her cases upstairs to her first-floor room. 'I have other news,' he said. 'It's taken a while to arrive, but the post isn't exactly dependable.'

'Good news, I hope.'

'For me, it is. His Majesty has decided to acknowledge my humble efforts, and I'm to receive the MBE.' He indicated the ribbon newly sewn on to his tunic.

'Congratulations! Alan, that's wonderful. Tell me, though – although I did know at one time – what does it stand for?'

' "Member of the Order of the British Empire", but usually taken to mean in service parlance, "My Bloody Efforts", unlike the OBE, which stands for "Other Buggers' Efforts".' He placed her suitcases on the double bed so that she could unpack.

'As I recall,' she said, reverting to the subject of Aunt Sarah, 'the list of survivors from Bergen-Belsen wasn't encouraging.'

'The last thing I want to do is raise false hopes, Dot, but a surprising number of prisoners who were able to walk, vanished as soon as the British soldiers arrived.'

She nodded. 'They were living in hell, and then someone opened a door. I can't imagine how that must have felt.'

'It made our task all the more difficult, but who was going to stand around, offering to give evidence against the SS, when freedom presented itself for the first time in what must have seemed an age?' He looked at his watch and said, 'I must go, You have my phone number, haven't you?'

'Yes, and you mustn't get into trouble on my account.'

'Get into trouble?' He laughed. 'I outrank the Officer-in-Charge. He'd better not try to make trouble.'

The thought made her smile. 'Alan, I'm so grateful for your help, it's difficult for me to express my gratitude.'

'In that case, don't. I'll take it as read.' He kissed her cheek. 'Stay out of trouble, and I'll be in touch when I know anything at all.'

'How far away will you be?'

'We're in the next building. I told you the hotel was next door. Look,' he said, pointing through the window, 'you can see the Union Flag from here.'

'You think of everything, Alan. If you're free this evening, come and have dinner with me.'

'Thanks, I will.'

* * *

'It's not wildly exciting,' said Dorothy, lowering the menu, 'but I never expected that. It's actually very similar to what's available at home.'

'That's because the British taxpayer is feeding the Germans in this sector, and that's in addition to feeding ourselves and repaying a fortune to the Americans.'

'So soon after the war,' said Dorothy. 'I suppose we have to blame President Truman for that.'

133

'Or whoever's working him from behind. The word is that the White House is home to an elaborate puppet show.' He put his menu down and said, 'I think I'll have the Thuringian sausage.'

'I'll join you with that.'

'One of the problems is that the Germans have their main meal at lunchtime, and what we think of as a lunch-type meal, *Abendbrot*, at the end of the working day, the purpose being to fuel the day-workers and allow them to relax at night.'

She smiled good-naturedly. 'Just imagine, Alan,' she said, 'there'll come a day, hopefully before long, when you'll go home to Blighty for good, and you'll probably never have to speak German again.'

'That day can't come soon enough.'

The elderly waiter came to their table to take their order.

'I'll leave the wine to you, Alan,' said Dorothy. 'You know German wines better than I do.'

Alan ordered for them both, and when the waiter was gone, Dorothy said, 'This is still my treat.'

'If you insist.'

'I once had an argument about paying. It was with a Polish airman I knew. At first, he couldn't accept the idea of an independent woman, even when I confirmed that I was, in fact, "Needham's Ketchup", as poured daily in the Sergeants' Mess by him and his fellow aircrew. In the end, I paid the hotel bill, and he paid for the meal.'

He asked casually, 'Was that a significant relationship?'

'No, it was very brief. He made his feelings known about Jews, and I bade him an angry farewell. Shortly after that, we were all posted to various places to make way for the American Air Force.'

'You once told me you were posted in disgrace to the officer-training facility – I forget its name – but you never gave a reason for it.'

She laughed lightly. 'You people are very dismissive of the junior service. Jack's just the same.'

'I honestly can't remember its name. I know the Army Staff College is Sandhurst, and the Navy place is Dartmouth, but I've had other things on my mind these past few years.'

'RAF Cranwell,' she prompted him. The story is that a particularly dismissive section officer – that's like a junior lieutenant – said something particularly cruel about Connie, who was my corporal, and then made another unkind remark about a newly-trained girl who froze with nerves on an RT circuit. I explained to her that Connie was more than capable of discharging her duties despite the accent the officer despised so much, and that it was quite common for a newly-trained girl to be affected by nerves. I told her that, prior to joining the WAAF, the girl might not even have used a telephone, never mind a transmitter and receiver. Needless to say, it didn't go down too well, and I was called in by the squadron officer, I thought, for a reprimand, but she decided to have Connie and me posted to Cranwell to instruct the new WAAF officers. She said that if I showed the same consideration for them that I'd reserved for the other ranks, I might do them and myself some good.'

Alan let the waiter bring their order, and tasted the wine, before asking, 'If you were the culprit, why did she have poor Connie drafted as well?'

'The section officer wasn't without influence. Daddikins was an air vice-marshall, and she was a spoilt brat. She got rid of Connie because she found her uncouth, whereas she's pure gold and one of my dearest friends.' She stopped to ask, 'What's so funny?'

Alan stopped laughing and told her, 'You were an NCO through and through, Dot. You protected the other ranks like a mother hen, and regarded officers as strutting amateurs.'

'That's basically what Jack said.' More seriously, she said, 'Some of the officers were all right.'

'This sausage is pretty good, too.'

'Good. Dorothy's mind was elsewhere. 'Were you serious about studying archaeology?'

'Very serious indeed. I spent three years gathering intelligence by devious methods, and the next few months using trickery and low cunning to extract confessions from dull-witted thugs. In addition to that, although I know it was a damned sight worse for the victims, I'm beginning to find the shadow of the concentration camps oppressive.'

'Very different from archaeology,' she agreed.

'I want to do something clean and honest.'

'You'll get dirty, digging up Roman remains,' she reminded him. 'You'll certainly need a good nail brush.'

'But it'll be honest dirt, the kind that can be washed away at the end of the working day.'

She nodded, now convinced by his argument. 'And you're partway there with your first degree,' she said.

'That's what made me think of it.'

'I'm a little disturbed by what you said about the shadow of Nazi atrocities.'

'In what way?'

'You're doing all you can to help me, at a time when you'd prefer not to hear the words "concentration camp" again.'

'I can grit my teeth, Dot.' He lifted the wine bottle and asked, 'More wine?'

'Please, but I don't want you to grit your teeth. I'd rather not put you through a process that you find oppressive.'

'It's different from the daily round,' he said, placing his hand on hers. 'Honestly, compared with what I hear in the course of my work, it's nothing at all.' Realising that his hand was on hers, he removed it. 'I'm sorry, Dot. I was carried away by what we were saying.'

'That's one I've not heard before, but I'm not offended.'

'I'm happy to give you what help I can. I'm very conscious that, with Jack and Kate in Bridlington, you and I are all that's left of the five who gathered at the Bay Horse that evening, when I made a clown of myself.'

She gave him the look of a disapproving parent. 'You just can't stop kicking yourself for that, can you?'

'The embarrassment has never faded,' he agreed.

'Look,' she said, 'it's a well-known fact that boys take longer than girls to mature. You were an immature boy in those days, and now you've had time to grow up, you've become realistic, sensible, kind and considerate. More than that, you're someone I like and respect.'

He held eye contact with her for a few seconds longer and said, 'As they say where I'm going tomorrow, shucks, ma'am.'

* * *

Left with her own company the next day, Dorothy spent the morning going over the progress she'd made so far and recording it in the form of a chart.

She was interrupted at about ten-thirty, when the chambermaid arrived to attend to her room. She addressed Dorothy confidently in English.

'I can return later, if you wish, Miss Needham.'

'No, that's all right. I'll go down to the lounge.'

'If you're sure.'

'Yes, it's no trouble.' Dorothy had to ask, 'Where did you learn to speak English? It's very good.'

'Thank you. I worked as a housemaid in London before the war.'

'I see. What's your name?'

'Helga.' She smiled as something occurred to her. 'You will find Germany much colder than England, I believe, and a great deal of snow has been forecast in northern Germany.'

'But I'm from the north of England, Helga. We're used to cold weather and snow there.' Dorothy picked up her work and went to the door. '*Auf Wiedersehen*, Helga.' She had to practise.

Helga smiled. '*Auf Wiedersehen*, Fräulein Needham.'

Dorothy went down to the lounge, where she ordered coffee and settled in an armchair.

Mapping her quest all the way from Orléans was probably pointless as a planning strategy, but she found that looking at it as a whole was somehow encouraging. After a while, however, she put her chart aside and spent some more time with her old German text book from schooldays. Cases and sentence construction still constituted a minefield, and there was a mountain of vocabulary to be learned.

* * *

Alan arrived sooner than she expected, bearing gifts.

'They keep trying to sell me chewing gum,' he said, and the only people I know who find the damned stuff appealing are the other ranks at the post. As far as I'm concerned, they can buy their own.' He handed her what looked like a brown-paper carrier bag without handles. 'This is called a grocery sack,' he told her. 'Americans have to work hard when they go shopping.'

'Alan, you lovely man,' she said, looking at the contents of the grocery sack. 'More stockings, cold cream and lipstick. Thank you a thousand times.'

'You're welcome. I wasn't sure about the lipstick, I mean the colours.'

'You got two of them just right, and I know of a home for the other.'

'Oh?'

She looked at it again. 'Yes, it's just right for Connie. I'll post it tomorrow.'

'I'll post it for you. Remember my warning?'

'Oh, heck, yes. I'm confined to quarters, "withering in my bloom, lost in solitary gloom".'

'Actually,' he said, looking more serious, 'that lipstick may take a while to reach... where is it?'

'County Durham. Why will it travel slowly?'

'Heavy snow in northern Germany.'

'Oh, I heard all about that this morning,' she said dismissively.

'Oh, yes? How did you get that information?'

She adopted an expression of mock outrage. 'Are you interrogating me?'

'No, I'm just asking you a question.'

'That's all right, then. Helga, my chambermaid told me. She worked as a housemaid in London before the war, which is why her English is so good.'

'Be careful, Dot. Don't tell her why you're here or who you're associating with.' He was quite serious.

'Why not? She's a friendly soul.'

'Have you forgotten your wartime security training?'

'Not all of it, but we're not at war any longer.'

'I'm serious, Dot. The diehard Nazis I told you about have spies, just like everyone else. They have sympathisers who pass information to them about possible targets.'

'I never thought of that,' she said, genuinely chastened.

'Well, now you know, so not a word. Remember that "walls have ears".'

' "Be like Dad and keep Mum",' she agreed, 'and I thought the bloody war was over.'

'They'll get the message eventually, but until then, we have to be extremely careful. Of course, it doesn't help that, now the war has been won, Acting-Major Cochrane seems hell-bent on losing us the peace.'

'What a horrible thought. What can I do to take your mind off it?'

'Have dinner with me tonight. My treat.'

'I'd love to.'

He smiled again. 'It worked, Dot. I've forgotten Acting-Major Cochrane already.'

19

Winning The Peace

Happily, Dorothy was in communication with Mr Paynter, her solicitor, who was happy for her to phone him from Berlin as it was at her own expense. She had no doubt that, had he felt the need to phone her, the charge would have gone down against the estate, anyway.

'I can now inform you that I have remitted your Estate Duty, Miss Needham.'

'Traitor.'

'I can appreciate how you must feel, but we are at the mercy of a government whose mission is to tax us mercilessly and with unrelenting vigour.'

'Actually, Mr Paynter, I'm not so upset. I mean to say, I'm not convinced about the nationalisation of industries, but the government has promised us a free health service, of which I'm heartily in favour, and as that is going to require funding, I like to think that my Estate Duty will pay for a chunk of it.'

'We're all entitled to an opinion, Miss Needham. Now, with your approval, I am in a position to pay the balance held by us into your bank account, minus my firm's charges, of course.'

'What are your firm's charges, Mr Paynter?'

'I shall naturally send you an itemised schedule of our services in this matter, but the total amounts to two hundred and twenty-two pounds, three shillings and sixpence.'

'Mr Paynter, you're worse than Clement Attlee.'

'I assure you, Miss Needham, that—'

'I was only joking, Mr Paynter. I'm sure your charges are perfectly reasonable.'

'That is our intention.'

'Thank you for handling everything. I'm most grateful.'

'Not at all, Miss Needham. I am happy to be of assistance.'

'What's the weather doing at the moment?'

'There is about six inches of snow and more is falling, Miss Needham,' he announced in the same grave manner. 'The forecast is far from promising.'

'In that case, it's possible I'll be here for some time. I'll notify the bank to that effect.'

She considered phoning the bank immediately, but changed her mind when she heard the vacuum cleaner in the next room. She picked up her German textbook and pad, and went downstairs, leaving Helga free to service her room.

She was thinking about the next stage of her search for information, when she heard a squad of soldiers being marched in the direction of the makeshift barracks. People were watching them in their various ways, despite the snow that had begun to fall. According to Alan, most Germans had adopted a kind of passive acceptance of the occupation, but it wasn't difficult to spot those who were observing the squad with resentment, if not hatred, if the terrorists had substance, and she had no reason to doubt Alan's word about that.

She smiled when she saw a child, a boy of maybe six or seven with his mother. He was watching the soldiers closely. Now, he attempted to perform a salute. It wasn't a bad try, either. Dorothy remembered WAAF recruits who'd struggled with the simple manoeuvre. She smiled at that memory, too, but her smile faded when a group of young men confronted the boy and his mother. They were clearly angry, and Dorothy was unable to see the mother's reaction, but she saw that the boy was crying, no doubt with fear. One of the group was shouting at the child while the others berated his mother, pushing her against the railings. It was the worst kind of threatening behaviour, and Dorothy dashed outside, giving no thought to the rapidly-falling snow or to Alan's oft-repeated warning. She simply wanted to rescue the poor child and his mother from their tormentors.

As she approached them, the young men's anger showed no sign of abating; the boy was almost hysterical, as was his wretched mother. Dorothy had no time to frame what she had to say in German, but she was determined to be understood.

'Leave these people alone! Can't you see what you're doing to them?'

The man stopped ranting at the little boy to ask with undiminished hatred, *'Was hast du gesagt, Engländerin?'* His fair hair was matted and dirty, and his blue eyes were filled with hatred.

'I'm telling you to leave this lady and her little boy alone!'

Speaking a torrent of German that meant nothing to her, the man seized her arms and pushed her hard against a parked car.

'Let me go!'

The man's companions now joined him, one saying with open disgust, *'Halt deinen Mund, Engländerin!'*

For good measure, another said, *'Englische Sau.'*

'I'm not a sow, and I won't be quiet.

'Englische Hure!'

'I'm not a whore, either. Take your hands off me!'

A large crowd had gathered, and fresh insults were being shouted.

The man who held her arms said something to his friends that caused them to laugh. He was making a suggestion to them, but she was incapable of making any sense of it.

'Kom, Engländerin.' He pulled her roughly towards him.

'No, let me go!' His thumbs were boring into her arms. He reeked of stale perspiration, and his breath was vile.

'Kom!'

Horrified, she struggled to resist him.

* * *

Alan and Cochrane had finally reached the end of the list of prisoners to be interrogated. It was an unrewarding process, as Cochrane took every opportunity to create difficulties. Alan's promotion had been contentious enough, but his MBE had quashed any remaining suggestion of a positive working relationship.

'Going somewhere, Lofthouse?' Cochrane had been aware that Alan was wearing his greatcoat when he first came to the office, and he'd made no comment then, but it seemed that he was looking for an excuse for further disagreement. 'You wouldn't be off to see your fancy-woman, would you?'

'I'll warn you once, Cochrane. If you ever make that kind of remark again, I shan't be so—'

There was a hasty knock on the office door, and the orderly sergeant burst in without waiting to be invited.

'What the hell do you think you're doing, Sergeant?'

'Sorry, sir. There's a riot in the street!'

'Turn out the guard.' Cochrane got up, checking his revolver for ammunition. 'Let's go and see what your precious German civilians are up to now, Lofthouse.'

Alan was already at the outside door. He could hear the excitement from where he stood. It was happening outside the hotel, but he'd no idea what it was about. With Cochrane and four redcaps at his heels, he ran towards the disturbance, and when he was a matter of yards away from the gathering, he saw Dorothy. Someone was manhandling her, and she was shouting and struggling. He elbowed his way with uncharacteristic roughness through the crowd to reach her.

'Alan!' She seemed unable to say more, but her terror was unmistakable.

'You,' said Alan in German, 'let her go! Stand with your back to that car!' He took a semi-automatic pistol from his coat pocket and pointed it at the miscreant. 'Back to the car! Move!'

Fearfully, the German did as he was told.

'Who else is involved?'

'Him and him.' Dorothy recovered the power of speech to indicate the two accomplices.

'Both of you, back against the car, now! Let me see your papers.' He took their identity papers and checked the photographs against them. Then, turning to the nearest redcap, he said, 'check their arms for tattoos.' The louts could easily be ex-SS personnel, in which case, they would have to be taken into custody.

As the MPs carried out his order, Cochrane addressed the crowd, which was now a great deal quieter. 'Ah'm orderin' you all to disperse. Go on, on your way, the whole bloody lot of you! Back to your *sauerkraut* and sausages!'

At first, no one moved; there was an uneasy stillness that was suddenly shattered by a single gunshot. Cochrane stiffened, standing as straight as a statue before crumpling and falling to the ground. Alan scanned the crowd, unsure who'd fired the pistol, and then he saw the weapon and the smoke still issuing from its muzzle. He was aware of it as he saw those closest to the gunman shrink quickly away from him, not wishing to be associated with him, or simply afraid of being caught in an exchange of gunfire. Now with a clearer field of vision, the gunman raised his pistol again, and Alan fired two shots, both of which found their mark. The onlookers moved even further aside, leaving the body a stretch of road to itself. 'Corporal,' said Alan, 'get an ambulance for Major Cochrane and take that man's body inside. The police can deal with it later.'

Captain Hall, who'd most likely arrived in response to the gunshots, was crouched over Cochrane's inert body. 'It's no use, sir,' he said. Major Cochrane's dead.'

'Take him inside.' To the others, he said, 'Have you inspected those three?'

'Not a tattoo in sight, sir,' said one of them.

'You can check the gunman when you get him inside the post.' He was suddenly conscious of two things: that the man who'd attacked Dorothy was still standing with his associates in front of the car, no doubt chastened by the gunfire, but still openly resentful, and that Dorothy was clinging to his free arm, no less distraught and desperate not to be parted from him. 'It's all right,' he told her. 'You're safe now. I want you to go into the hotel and stay there. I'll come to you when I've dispersed this crowd.' In truth, the crowd was looking far less ugly than at first; many had already moved off, such was the sobering effect gunfire had on bystanders. 'Go on, Dot, I shan't be long.' He felt her release his arm, and he turned to see her make for the hotel entrance.

The corporal asked, 'Shall we fire a burst over their heads, sir?'

'Of course not, Corporal.' Automatic gunfire was the last thing the civilians needed to hear. 'Leave it to me.' Raising his voice to address the remainder, he said, 'Listen to me, all of you. You've seen three young men terrorise a helpless woman. You've also seen a British officer shot dead, and you saw what happened to the assassin. If you want any further entertainment, I suggest you return to your homes and create your own.' He watched them walk away, leaving footprints in the fresh snow that lay on the frozen ground. 'As for you three, just what do you expect me to do to you now?'

They made no reply, but it was clear that fear was now their sole, remaining preoccupation.

Seizing the man who'd manhandled Dorothy, he drew him closer and then slammed him against the side of the car, causing his head to come into violent contact with the roof. In doing so, he came to his senses and released him. 'I should like to take you into the post,' he said, 'and beat you senseless for what you did, but I shan't, because it would do no good at all. You people have to realise that the war is over, and it's now time to start rebuilding Germany as well as London, Hull, Newcastle, Liverpool, and all the other places the Luftwaffe bombed.' Their looks of surprise prompted him to say, 'They didn't tell you that, did they? Just remember that the British Army is here simply to keep order, not to bully you or taunt you with your misfortune. You will meet soldiers whose behaviour is not so noble, and that's when you'll have to remind yourselves that maybe not every German soldier was a saint.' If that didn't qualify as the understatement of the century, he was mistaken. 'Now, go away and be thankful that I have a sense of proportion.' He watched them go, and breathed a sigh of disgust.

A civilian police van had parked outside the RMP Post, but Captain Hall seemed to have everything organised. Alan walked into the hotel, where the receptionist stiffened when she saw him.

'Everything's fine,' he told her. 'There's nothing to worry about.'

'Fräulein Needham has gone to her room, Herr Major.'

'Thank you. I'm not exactly surprised.' He took the stairs to the first floor and knocked on Dorothy's door. 'Dorothy,' he said, 'it's Alan.'

There was the sound of the key turning in the lock, and then the door opened. Dorothy stood, red-eyed and still visibly disturbed. Alan stepped inside, closed the door behind him and held out his arms to her.

When she spoke, it was in a tiny voice that sounded unlike her own. 'Thank goodness you came when you did,' she said. 'I don't know what those men would have done.'

'It's all over.' He wrapped his arms round her and held her tightly.

'I wouldn't have gone… out there if it hadn't… been for the little boy and his mother.' So long after the event, her voice still shook.

'I'm sure you had a good reason.' He could feel her whole body shaking. 'Come and sit down,' he suggested, guiding her towards the bed.

'The little boy was... terrified. His... mother, as well.'

'What happened?'

She made a visible effort to gather herself together. 'The little... boy was watching... some soldiers,' she said. 'They were marching, I think, to... the barracks. He tried... to salute them. He was... only maybe six or... seven years old, just playing at soldiers.'

'And the louts objected to that, presumably?'

'They were horrible to him.'

'So you went out to protect the little boy and his mother?'

'Yes.' Still shaking, she buried her face in the folds of his greatcoat. 'I know you told me never to go out alone, but I couldn't ignore what was happening.'

'You know, Dot, I admire you for doing that.'

'Do you?' She looked surprised.

'It was a brave thing to do.'

'It didn't feel like that at the time. I hadn't realised what horrible people they were.'

'It's not surprising. You'd never known that kind of ugly behaviour, had you?' He drew her closer. 'But it's all over.'

'I never expected anyone to start shooting.'

'That wasn't your fault, Dot.'

'Will there be trouble because you shot that man?'

'No, he'd murdered a British officer, so I shot him before he could repeat the offence.' Responding to a sniff, he reached for a handkerchief and offered it to her.

'Who was the officer who was shot?'

'That was Cochrane, the one I told you about. He was a fool, and he probably brought about his own end, but he didn't deserve that.'

She seemed naively baffled. 'Do you really mean he was responsible for his own death?'

'Yes, didn't you hear the way he spoke to the crowd?'

'Not really. I was distracted.'

'So you were. I'm sorry.'

'What did he say?' Now that she'd recovered from the immediate

146

upset, she seemed unaccountably curious about the incident, at least from Alan's point of view.

'It wasn't what he said that angered the crowd, as much as the way he said it. He only ever spoke to German civilians as if he despised them, and that's no way to win the respect of a defeated nation.'

She blew her nose hard, producing a trumpeting note.

'That was good, Dot. Now that you've mastered "The Last Post", do you think you could manage "Reveille" as well?'

'I don't usually make that noise when I blow my nose.'

'I shan't tell a soul,' he promised.

'You know, Alan,' she said, smoothing down the creases she'd made on his greatcoat, 'you're ever so good to me.'

'I know, and we both know you don't deserve it.'

'Please be serious. I'm trying to tell you how much I appreciate everything you've done for me.'

'Well, I could hardly leave you at the mercy of those louts.'

'I mean *everything* you've done.'

'You're welcome to all those things as well.' He stood up and asked, 'Will you be all right, now, if I leave you?'

'I imagine so. I certainly shan't leave the hotel, whatever happens outside.'

'Good.'

'Will you join me for dinner tonight, Alan?'

'I'll be happy to.'

'My treat?'

'If you insist.'

20

Times Remembered

Alan waited until Dot was seated and then took his place opposite her.

'I did wonder,' she said, 'if the menu might be more appealing elsewhere, but I've been very good and stayed indoors.'

'You'd only have been disappointed. The food's the same wherever you go in the British Zone.' After brief consideration, he said, 'With Cochrane gone, I could invite you into the Officers' Mess, but I don't think you'd find the company as agreeable as you did in Hanover.'

'It's no matter.' Dorothy had the air of someone about to make a disclosure. 'This morning, I told my solicitor and my bank manager I'd most likely be abroad for some time,' she said, 'and now, I find myself planning a return home.' She paused, expecting a response. When none came, she went on. 'I realise now that I've been incredibly naïve about this business of Aunt Sarah.'

'Why do you call yourself naïve?'

'Oh, good. I'm glad you're listening. I mean that, with so many people emerging from the concentration camps, I've rather assumed that information would be forthcoming, and now I realise I'm at another *impasse.*'

'Another of those things, eh?'

'I'm told it's what the French say instead of *"cul-de-sac"*.'

'English is full of French phrases that the French completely disown. Apparently, they never say, *"double entendre"*, but they do occasionally recognise *"un double sens"*.' Having made that point, he asked, 'Why were you surprised that I was listening?'

'I'm sorry. I've always worked on the supposition that if a man says nothing, he's not listening. Of course, it's silly of me to generalise; in fact, it's a deplorable habit, but I'm as guilty as anyone.'

'I was waiting for you to say more. In any case, I find that women usually respond too readily. Someone has to take a more leisurely approach to listening, or there'd be bedlam around each corner.'

The waitress arrived, and Dot gave her order.

'The Thuringian sausage, please,' said Alan.

'You really care for Thuringian sausage,' remarked Dorothy when the waitress was gone.

'It performed wonders for J S Bach.'

'Wasn't he the composer who had two dozen children?'

'Twenty, actually.'

'Well, something seemed to agree with him.' Without warning, she asked, 'What makes you say that women respond too readily?'

He gave the shrug of a man whose argument is already won. 'The evidence is there to be seen.' Adopting an effeminate delivery, he began. 'Woman A says to Woman B, "Just guess who I saw the other day." Woman B asks, "Who?" Woman A says, "Gladys Thompson, and you'll never guess what she was wearing." Woman B says, "The last time I saw her, she was wearing a bright orange cardigan that just drained her complexion." Woman A says, "She should never wear orange." Woman B says, "Orange and green. They're both completely wrong for her." Woman A says, "Disastrous colours for her complexion, and that's not all." "No," says Woman B, "Everybody knows what she and that so-called friend of hers get up to." "Really?" By this time,' said Alan, 'Woman A has completely forgotten what she was going to say about Gladys Thompson, which is doubtless good news for Gladys Thompson, but it's no way to tell a story.' He tasted the wine and pronounced himself satisfied.

'I disagree.'

'That's your prerogative, Dot.'

'On a purely common-sense level, I disagree. Women respond to help each other tell a story.'

'It didn't help with the Gladys Thompson story.'

'Only because it was your story and your agenda.'

Without changing his expression, he asked, 'Did your decision to go home have anything to do with that commotion this morning?'

She hesitated, clearly considering her reply. 'It probably helped me arrive at a decision,' she said.

He nodded, again without commenting, and then said, 'Home is obviously England, but where, exactly, is your home?'

'It's wherever I make it.' Possibly accepting that some amplification might be in order, she said, 'I'll take a room in an hotel to plan the rest of my life. I need to buy a house, obviously, but before that, I have to decide on where I want to live, given that my friends from before the war are somewhat scattered.' Then, maybe conscious that the spotlight was on her, she asked, 'How far have you got with your plan to return to Cambridge?'

'I shan't be returning to Cambridge, after all,' he told her.

'Oh? Was it something they said?'

'Yes, it was. Apparently, both Cambridge and Oxford are "doing their bit" for returning servicemen and women, to the extent that there's no room left for me.'

'Oh, what rotten luck.' Reaching across the table, she took his hands in hers, probably without thinking. 'Here you are, still serving in the Army, and Cambridge is full of demobbed service personnel. It's hardly fair.'

'Because of that, I've spread my net a little wider,' he said, conscious of her hands on his.

'Not *red brick*, surely?' It was the gentlest tease.

'Why not, if Cambridge won't have me?'

The waitress brought their order, interrupting the conversation for a short time, and then Dorothy asked, 'Where else have you tried?'

'Several universities, actually, and the one that looks the most promising is Leeds.'

'That's handy. You could live with your parents.' She made the suggestion only partly in jest.

'I could, but I don't intend to.'

'Go on, Alan,' she urged him playfully. 'I could come and visit you, and really set the cat among the pigeons.'

'Wouldn't you just? Seriously, though, we should keep in touch, and I can let you know about anything that might crop up.'

'I'd appreciate that, but would that be your only reason for keeping in touch?'

'You're teasing, Dot.'

'Not in the grown-up sense, I assure you. I don't go in for that kind of thing.' She regarded him seriously for a moment and said, 'When I saw your mother recently, and she told me about Gwen, she was as distant as ever. I'm sure she was feeling the loss on your behalf, quite understandably, but it was still as if I were the *femme fatale* who has to be hissed every time she comes on stage, and I couldn't help wondering after all that time just what crime I'd actually committed.'

'Oh, Dot,' he said wearily, 'it's always the same with mothers and their sons. She knew I was keen on you – I think everyone knew that – and she formed the belief that you'd been somehow less than ingenuous in your treatment of me. I had nothing to do with that, believe me. She arrived at that conclusion with absolutely no prompting.'

'So I stand wrongly accused, although It's not the first time, I can assure you.'

Alan picked up the bottle and topped up her glass. 'Your only offence where mothers are concerned was to be born with the ability to attract and charm their unsuspecting sons. That's all it was as far as I was concerned.'

'Just physical attraction?'

'That's all. I didn't know you then. You were simply the girl who was pretty enough to have me jumping through hoops, except that I don't imagine you've ever behaved like that.'

'Believe it or not, it hasn't been easy.'

'Being irresistible?'

'Yes, seriously. Aunt Sarah told me something very important a long time ago. It was that a pretty girl has a huge responsibility. She meant it as a caution, and I tried to heed it, but sometimes the damage was unavoidable.'

'Have you a photo of her in your locket?'

'Yes, just a minute.' She opened the flap with her thumbnail and held the locket so that he could see the photograph.

'It's uncanny,' he said, looking from Dorothy to the photograph and back again. 'You might almost be sisters.'

'Except that she's now in her forties. This was taken before the war, obviously.'

Looking at the photograph again, he said, 'She's stunning all right, and it was very wise of her to give you that advice.' Handing the locket back to her, he said, 'I imagine there have been quite a few cases of unavoidable damage. They're a fact of life, after all.'

'That doesn't make them less regrettable.' She drank the last of her wine and stared at her glass thoughtfully. Alan signalled the waitress to bring another bottle.

'I shouldn't talk about a man in his absence,' she said, 'but I feel guiltiest of all about Jack.'

'Jack? I didn't know you and he had....'

'It was short-lived, and it was over before he was ready, which is why I feel so guilty about it. Jack was an old friend who deserved better than that.'

The waitress arrived with the wine, which Alan tasted briefly before registering his approval.

'When did this happen?'

'It must have been early 'forty-four, shortly after I was posted to Cranwell, but long before he and Kate got together.'

Alan was aware that something was missing. 'But I had the impression that Jack and Kate were as happy as....' He struggled to find a suitable and decent simile.

'They are. As far as Jack is concerned, our little fling is a dim memory. That's if he thinks of it at all, which I doubt.'

'In that case,' he said, filling her glass, 'why do you still feel guilty about it?'

'I think it's for the same reason you feel guilty about Maurice.'

Her reply was unexpected, and he had to think about it. 'You told me Maurice had probably forgiven me for everything.'

'That's what Kate told me. She was very emotional about it at the time.'

'Kate, emotional. There's a thought.' She would be emotional about the big things, obviously, such as losing Maurice, but it wasn't a state he associated with her.

'You can't imagine that, can you? Dry-eyed fortitude is a

characteristic she and I have in common, although you've seen another side of me since this Aunt Sarah thing came up.'

'You've had much to be emotional about,' he said, patting her hand. 'The thing is, though, however forgiving Maurice was, I still regret my behaviour towards him.'

'And I regret hurting Jack, even though he's obviously forgiven me for it.'

'It seems to me,' he said, 'it's the way we remember it that creates the problem.'

She let him top up her glass and said, 'If the bearing of guilt ever became an Olympic event, you and I would leave the competition way behind.'

He nodded. 'We have to stop doing it, because I'm sure it's not healthy.'

'Neither is getting through two bottles of Sylvaner, but we're well on the way to doing that without giving it a moment's thought.'

'I'll pay the bill,' he offered.

'I thought it was my treat.' She seemed unsure.

'It may have been, but it's mine, now.' He held up his hand to summon the waitress.

'I'll have my turn later.'

As the waitress approached their table, Alan said, '*Die Rechnung, bitte, Fräulein.*'

She returned quickly with the bill. Word had gone around that the English *Herr Major* was not only courteous towards the staff, but generous as well. Alan opened his wallet and counted out notes to cover the bill. Adding another, he said, '*Ihre Trinkgeld, Fräulein. Vielen Dank.*'

'*Danke schön*, Herr Major.'

'*Bitte schön, Fräulein.*'

'You're very popular here,' said Dorothy when the waitress was gone, 'and it's hardly surprising.'

'It's all to do with what I said about winning the peace, rather than losing it, which was what the late Major Cochrane seemed determined to do.' Seeing Dorothy shudder involuntarily, he said, 'I'm sorry, I shouldn't have mentioned him.'

'It's all right. Did you have lots to do at the post?'

'Quite a lot. We got the Polizei to take away the German's body, we dealt with Cochrane as decently as we could, and I wrote a report about the whole thing. Needless to say, Major Cochrane will be remembered as an exemplary and upstanding officer. There's no reason why his family should have to bear his shame. In any case, the Military Police would never allow criticism from an outsider to see the light of day.' As he spoke, he saw that her eyelids were beginning to droop. 'I'll see you to your room,' he said, 'and I'll come round in the morning to take you to the airport.'

'Thank you. I'm all right, really.' She took his arm and allowed him to take her to the stairs. Partway up the stairs, she asked, 'What's the German for "lift"?'

'As in "elevator"?'

'Mm.'

'*Der Aufzug.*'

'I wish someone would persuade them to install one.'

'We're nearly there.'

'Goody. You know,' she said in increasingly slurred speech, 'I do believe I've had just a little too much to drink.'

'That's my fault,' he said, steadying her in front of her bedroom door. 'Have you got your key handy?'

'Mm.' She opened her evening bag and began searching.

'Can I help?'

'Very likely. You strike me as a resourceful kind of chap.' She watched helplessly while he retrieved her key and opened the door. 'Are you going to stay?'

'No, I must leave you, flattered though I am by your invitation.'

'Must you?' There was genuine disappointment in her tone.

'Yes, you're tired and obviously affected by this morning's episode, and as if that weren't enough, you're three-parts tight as well.'

'Is that all?'

'It's enough.'

'Will you do one more thing for me? Will you unhook my dress?'

'Okay, turn round.' Sensing helplessness, he rotated her through a half-turn and carried out the desired operation.

'Can you find the zip fastener?' She articulated the words carefully and with some difficulty.

'Yes,' he said, running it down to her waist.

'Thank you. I didn't want to sleep in my frock.'

'Quite understandable.' He slipped the straps over her shoulders and let the garment fall to her feet.

'This is where it gets difficult,' she warned.

'Nothing I can't handle.' He slipped one arm beneath her shoulders and the other behind her knees to lift her and deposit her on to the bed. 'Finally, your shoes,' he reminded her, removing them, 'and that's as much help as I can decently offer you.' He drew half the counterpane across the bed and covered her with it, realising that she was as undressed as she was going to be.

'You really are a gentleman.' The words came as if from far away, and it seemed that the events of the day and the excess of wine had finally overtaken her.

'Good night, Dot,' he said, kissing her forehead. 'I'll be over at ten in the morning.' He just hoped she would be fit for the journey.

21

February

The Customer is Always Right

With the whole country to consider, Dorothy nevertheless booked a room at the Bay Horse in Cullington, where the familiarity of her surroundings gave her a temporary sense of security in her new status.

The flight from Lüneburg had been far from pleasant, but she was aware that no journey could ever be seen as enjoyable through the cloud of a hangover.

It was her first for a long time, although they hadn't had all that much wine. Alan was typically apologetic, having ordered the second bottle, but Dorothy wondered if her lingering reaction to the incident might have intensified its effects. One thing still puzzled her, however, and that was her surprise discovery of her frock from the previous evening, hanging neatly in her wardrobe. She could only vaguely remember arriving at her room, and Alan, courteous as ever, had told her nothing about it that was even remotely embarrassing.

Now, however, she had to take charge of her new life, and excitement beckoned in two forms. Her car, a nine-year-old MGVA sports saloon that had been carefully laid up for the duration of the war, now stood in the hotel's coach house that served as a carpark, tantalisingly ready to go wherever the sparse petrol ration might take it. Before that, though, she must take the train to Addlesden-in-Wharfedale to meet the estate agent whose name Mr Paynter, her solicitor, had given her. It was only a name he'd extracted from the *Yorkshire Post*, but the unknown quantity seemed to add an extra sparkle to the lure of new surroundings.

* * *

February was hardly the best time to view a landscape, and the weather was of no help at all, but Dorothy found the terrain familiar and unspoilt, a welcome change after the medieval ruins of Lüneburg and her confined existence in a German hotel.

As the train approached Addlesden itself, the countryside appealed to her more and more, so it was with something akin to childish delight that she climbed down on to the platform with its exquisitely-tended floral decorations.

Having had her ticket punched, she walked through the exit and found the taxi rank empty. In the light of fuel rationing, it was never a surprise. Catching the eye of a porter, she asked, 'Do taxis call here often?'

'Where do you want to be, love?'

'Cooper's Estate Agents. Do you know them?'

'I do, love, but you won't need a taxi to get there. Do you see where I'm pointing?'

Dorothy followed his finger and picked out the estate agent's sign. 'Thank you.'

'You're welcome, love. Are you looking for somewhere to live?'

'Yes.'

'You'll happen need more 'n one estate agent, then. There's George Brewer's just across t' road from Cooper's.'

'Thank you again. You've been very helpful.' She dug into her purse and gave him a half-crown piece.

'Much obliged, love. I hope you get on all right.'

Dorothy took the short walk to Cooper's and walked in. A woman and a young man were each seated behind a desk. The young man saw her and greeted her.

'Good afternoon, madam. Can I be of assistance?'

'I'm sure you can. I'm looking for a house in or around Addlesden. I'm thinking in terms of probably four bedrooms and a garage, or at least garage space.' At this point, the woman looked up, possibly realising that this could be a lucrative sale.

'We have several properties on our books that might appeal to you, madam,' said the young man. 'Would you like to take a seat while I show you some?' He took a large file from a shelf above his head and laid it down in front of her.

'Thank you.' Dorothy opened the file and was about to read the details of a very attractive property, when the woman approached the table and clicked her fingers at the young man.

'You're showing this lady the wrong binder,' she told him curtly.

'These are the houses with four bedrooms, Mrs Cooper.'

'I can see that. Start with the next one, four and five bedrooms.'

'Just a minute,' said Dorothy. 'I asked about houses with four bedrooms, and this young man was about to show me some when you interrupted us.'

'I was simply pointing out,' said the woman with scarcely more politeness than she'd shown to the assistant, 'that he was going about it the wrong way.'

'I want to look at houses with four bedrooms,' insisted Dorothy. 'Is that so much to ask?'

'I was merely pointing out to an employee that we do this differently at Cooper's.'

'That may well be the case, but when I came in here, I wanted to look at houses with four bedrooms, not five. However, it seems that the client's wishes are of little consequence at this agency, so I'd better look elsewhere.'

As she got up to leave, an office door opened, and a young man with round spectacles and a look of concern emerged. He asked, 'What on earth is going on?'

'I was trying to find a house,' Dorothy told him, 'and this young man was being extremely helpful, but then this... person... interrupted us very rudely to criticise his methods. I have to say that it's a long time since I saw anyone gain a person's attention by snapping her fingers, and I find it as distasteful as ever.'

'This is my wife.'

'Then you have my sympathy. I, on the other hand, am a prospective buyer who has decided to look elsewhere. This young man was to have benefited from the sale – I'm assuming you pay your staff commission as well as abusing them – but now, unfortunately for him, the sale will not take place.'

'Just a minute,' said the man. 'It seems that we've got off to an unfortunate start—'

'As understatements go, that one ranks highly.' She smiled at the woman's undisguised annoyance.

'Can't we reconsider the matter and start again?'

'You can reconsider to your heart's content, Mr Cooper, but you'll find yourself doing it alone.' Dorothy closed the file in front of her and stood up to leave. At that point, Mrs Cooper recovered the power of speech and said, 'This is ridiculous, a storm in a teacup.'

'Wait a minute,' said her husband. 'I'm sure this misunderstanding can be cleared up.'

'There's no misunderstanding,' Dorothy told him, 'at least, from my point of view. Mrs Cooper appears to have lost you a sale. That's something you need to consider.'

Tight-lipped and clearly outraged, Mrs Cooper opened the door for her to leave.

As Dorothy passed through the doorway, she said to no one in particular, 'Now, which was that other agency? I remember now. It was Brewer's. Goodbye, everyone.' She crossed the road to the Brewer agency.

This time, a man of maybe forty or so with thinning, fair hair greeted her warmly. 'Good afternoon, madam. How can I help you?'

'Are you Mr Brewer?'

'Yes.'

'My name is Dorothy Needham, and I'm looking for a house with, I should think, four bedrooms and maybe three reception rooms. I think they call them that nowadays, don't they?' She removed her gloves to avoid the usual confusion.

'Yes, Miss Needham, that's what drawing and morning rooms are called nowadays.' He delivered the information with a conspiratorial smile that marked him out as friendly. 'Please take a seat and tell me more about what you're looking for.'

'Ideally, I'd like a place in or around Addlesden, a detached house, preferably, and I have no property to sell.'

'That puts you in a strong position.'

'Yes, I believe so.'

'In that case, let me find some properties for you to look at. You can do that at your leisure, and I'll organise tea or whatever you prefer.'

'Tea would be lovely, thank you.' She opened the folder he'd placed in front of her and began browsing.

It was a new experience for her, and she was a little over-faced by the details, at first, but she found three that looked promising.

'How do you like your tea, Miss Needham?' Mr Brewer set the tray down on the table beside her.

'Oh, with milk but no sugar, thank you.'

'Have you visited any other agencies yet?'

'Yes, I called in on the Cooper agency. It was a name that had been given to me, but I decided not to take matters any further.' She could see his eyes twinkling, and she felt obliged to explain. 'Mrs Cooper disagreed with me about my needs, whereas several years at Rimmington's Department Store have taught me the value of the old-fashioned adage that the customer is always right.'

'I quite agree.'

'It was a shame,' she said, 'because there's a young man there, who seemed very able and obliging. Unfortunately, his approach didn't win Mrs Cooper's approval. I think she wanted him to persuade me to consider something more expensive than I had in mind.'

'I shan't do that Miss Needham,' he assured her, placing a cup of tea beside her.

'I never imagined you would, but whilst you're here, can I show you some houses that have caught my attention?'

'By all means. I see you've found two with vacant possession.'

'What does that mean? I sold a house recently, but I'm afraid I'm very much a beginner when it comes to buying.'

'Don't worry, Miss Needham. "Vacant possession" means that there's no one living there, so you don't have to wait for anyone to move out.' No doubt sensing her continued hesitation, he said, 'I'll be happy to help you through the process, as I'm sure, your solicitor will.'

'I've been rather at the mercy of solicitors and bankers since my mother died,' she admitted.

'Did that happen recently?'

'Fairly recently.'

'I'm sorry.' It was a genuine response.

'Thank you.'

'If you like, we can have a look at two of these houses this afternoon.'

'Could we really?'

'There's no reason why not. I'll just have a word with my secretary, and then we'll go house seeking.'

* * *

Two viewings later, they drove back to the agency.

'I've decided,' said Dorothy. 'It's the house in Nursery Lane.'

'That was a quick decision.'

'I love it. It was waiting for me all along.'

'In that case,' he said, pulling up outside the agency, 'you may have some bargaining room. It's been on the market for some time.' He walked round the car and opened the door for her to get out.

'I noticed Cooper's sign next to yours.'

'Yes, it was on their books before the vendors came to us hoping for a quicker sale. Mr Cooper is a reasonable sort of man, but he married recently and took his new wife, whom you've met, into the business.'

'I imagine she won't be too pleased.' She followed him into the agency.

'It's a cut-throat business, Miss Needham,' he said with the familiar twinkle in his eye.

'Is it really?'

'No, but it would be if Mrs Cooper had her way.'

They arrived at a figure for an offer, and Mr Brewer phoned the owner of the house. After a brief chat, he came off the phone and said, 'He's happy to accept your offer.'

'Excellent. What's the next stage?'

'I'll put up a sign saying, "Sold Subject to Contract" and you should put your solicitor in touch with me. You'll need a survey, but that's straightforward enough.'

She had to ask, 'How will Cooper's find out about the house being sold?'

'The owner will tell them.'

'You know, Mr Brewer, I can only imagine that Mr Cooper's main weakness is his taste in women, although I'm sure he'll have realised that by this time. I can't take any pleasure from knowing that I deprived him of a sale, when he has enough trouble on his hands.'

'That's a very commendable attitude, Miss Needham. In any case, Mrs Cooper will be the agent of her own undoing.'

22

Lüneburg, March

A Not-so-Dead End

Given the choice, Alan would always interview suspects rather than victims. Victims preferred to forget, if such a miracle were possible, the very incidents of which suspects needed to be reminded.

As he drove to the Priory to interview Father Ignatius Schneider, he tried to rid his mind of the horrors associated with the enquiry. They would wait until he could ignore them no longer. In the meantime, he thought about his last evening with Dorothy. He'd been thoughtless in ordering more wine. Clearly, she was only just recovering from her ordeal outside the hotel; that alone probably caused her to drink more than usual, and he should have realised that. Even so, he smiled at the memory of her leaning against him as she climbed the staircase, and then asking him to unlock her door because she couldn't focus on the key. Her ultimate act of inebriation, though, was to invite him to spend the night with her. If anyone had told him, seven or eight years earlier, that he would turn down such an offer, he would have dismissed both the suggestion and the possibility as the stuff of fantasy. That was one relationship that had changed for good.

He turned into the Priory gates and switched off the Jeep's engine before lifting the heavy wire recorder off the passenger seat.

He knocked on the stout door, waiting several seconds, and was about to knock again, when the door opened to reveal a frail figure in a priest's cassock.

'Major Lofthouse,' he said in English, 'come in out of that cold night.'

'Thank you, Father.' Alan followed him into a study heated by an open fire that seemed to be fuelled by broken remains from the ubiquitous bomb damage.

'I would offer you a drink, but I have none.'

'I've brought something for you, Father. I believe you're fond of Irish whiskey.' He took a bottle from his greatcoat. He'd used all his contacts to locate and procure it, knowing that the priest's testimony was vital, and he felt, in any case, that the wretched victim of Bergen-Belsen deserved any luxury that came his way.

'How very kind of you, Major Lofthouse. Let me find two glasses.'

When he returned, Alan said, 'We can converse in English or in German, Father. I leave the choice to you.'

'I like to practise my English. Maybe, when I am tired, we can revert to German.'

'With pleasure, Father.' He accepted a glass of whiskey from the priest, and said, 'We're about to discuss matters that I'm sure you would rather forget. It's very noble of you to do this. May I put the recorder on your desk?'

'Please do.'

Alan placed the wire recorder on the leather-topped writing desk and opened it, plugging it into the nearest socket.

'I am prepared to do this in the interests of justice, Major Lofthouse, not out of revenge. That is the Lord's prerogative.'

'Exactly.' It had often occurred to Alan that very few people were aware of the difference between the two. 'Are you ready, Father?'

'Yes.'

Alan switched on the recorder and said, 'This is Major Alan Lofthouse of the Intelligence Corps interviewing Father Ignatius Schneider on the fifth of March, nineteen forty-six. Father, you were arrested in nineteen forty-three and taken to Dachau Concentration Camp. Is that correct?' He handed one of the two microphones to the priest.

'That is correct.'

'And I believe you have given your testimony to the United States authorities regarding that period of your imprisonment.'

'That is also correct.'

'In March, nineteen forty-five, were you transferred to Bergen-Belsen Concentration Camp?'

'I was.' The tiny, wizened priest answered with surprising confidence.

'Who was in charge of the Priest Block at Bergen-Belsen?'

'There was no priest block at Bergen-Belsen, as there was at Dachau. I was held in the block reserved for German dissidents.'

'I stand corrected, Father Ignatius. Who was in charge of the German Dissidents' Block?'

'Obersturmführer Heinz Baumann of the Allgemeine SS.' The priest enunciated the name confidently.

'If I were to show you a photograph of Obersturmführer Baumann would you be able to recognise him?'

'Yes, I should.'

'I realise this may be painful for you, Father, but please take as long as you need.' Alan took the photograph from his inside pocket and showed it to Father Ignatius.

The priest's voice trembled as he said, 'That is Obersturmführer Heinz Baumann of the Allgemeine SS.'

'Thank you, Father.' Speaking into his microphone, he said, 'Father Ignatius has identified photograph two-zero-one-zero-five-four-seven-one positively as that of Obersturmführer Baumann.' Returning his attention to the priest, he said, 'Would you like to tell me more about Baumann, Father?'

'Yes, Major Lofthouse.' His eyes were closed as he said, 'He was an agent of Satan.'

'Can you be more specific?' The prosecutors needed hard facts rather than spiritual condemnation. He poured another drink for the traumatised priest and listened to a catalogue of almost unbelievable barbarity and sadistic cruelty, only interrupting occasionally, when he had to clarify the evidence for official purposes.

Presently, Father Ignatius asked, 'May we proceed with the interview in German, Herr Major?'

'By all means.' Alan continued, as requested, in German. 'For how long did this regime last, Father?'

'For one month, but it felt like an age.'

'Of course, How did it end?'

'British tanks entered the camp, and the soldiers began making arrests.' He paused briefly, no doubt reliving the event. 'Baumann escaped, I believe.'

'Only temporarily, Father. We caught him on the road to Munich and arrested him. He will be tried in a British court in Lüneburg.'

'I'm pleased to hear it, Herr Major.'

'Is there anything else you'd like to tell me about Baumann, Father?'

'I don't think so. I have told you what I remember.'

'And I am extremely grateful to you.' Alan leaned over and switched off the recorder.

'Now we can converse as human beings.'

'You and I have always been that, Father.' Consorting with so many prisoners and suspects as Alan did, he found the knowledge comforting.

'I mean rather than as investigator and victim.'

'I take your point.'

'You speak German remarkably well, Herr Major.'

'It's kind of you to say so, Father. I spent quite a lot of time in Germany before the war, and I've been involved in procuring information and interrogating prisoners for most of the war.'

'Are you a professional soldier, Herr Major?'

'No, Father, I was conscripted in nineteen thirty-nine.'

'In that case, the Army must surely release you before long.'

'I hope so, although my extended service has been useful. I can't say quite how useful at this stage, but I've been able to use the time well.' For no better reason than that the priest was a confidant both by calling and by nature, he told him the story of Dorothy's quest, ending with the knowledge simply that her aunt had been transferred with thousands of others to Bergen-Belsen, but that her name was not among those of the survivors. 'That,' he said, 'is sadly where the story seems to end.'

Father Ignatius was silent for a spell, clearly turning something over in his mind. Finally, he said, 'I'm not so sure, Herr Major. I cannot be certain, but come with me to the Convent of the Sisters of Mercy tomorrow morning and we shall speak with the Mother Superior.'

'Will I be allowed in the Convent, Father?'

'Yes, if I take you there. I have to say mass for the Sisters, and we shall speak afterwards.'

* * *

Alan arrived promptly the next morning, and drove Father Ignatius to the convent.

Having ascertained that Alan spoke fluent German, the Mother Superior asked, 'Are you carrying a weapon of any kind, Herr Major?' She was elderly and wore glasses with very strong lenses. Her manner was quite unequivocal.

'Not this morning, Reverend Mother.' In anticipation of such an objection, he'd left both his revolver and pocket pistol at the Post. In those uncertain times, he felt almost naked without them, but he had to respect the order's pacifist convictions.

She nodded her appreciation and led them into a chapel, where the sisters were assembled.

'Take a seat at the back of the chapel,' Father Ignatius told him. 'Feel free to take part in the devotions, but I must tell you that, as you're a protestant, I am prevented from offering you the Holy Sacrament.'

'I understand, Father.' Alan took his place at the back and well away from the sisters, who regarded him nervously as an outsider and one of the occupying force.

His Latin, though neglected for the past several years, was sound, and he had no difficulty in following the mass and joining in the responses. Finally, however, he sat and waited until all the sisters had been served with Holy Communion and the mass was brought to its close, before responding to a beckoning signal from Father Ignatius.

'Will you join the Sisters, the Reverend Mother and me for breakfast, Herr Major?'

'Thank you. I'm grateful for your invitation.' He made a mental note to send some provisions over to the convent at a later date.

They took their places in the refectory, where they were served with bread, British margarine and marmalade.

'Major Lofthouse is trying to trace an English prisoner, who may have escaped from Bergen-Belsen when the British Army arrived, Reverend Mother.' Turning to Alan, he said, 'Perhaps you could tell us more about this person, Herr Major.'

'Certainly, Father. Her name is Sarah Elizabeth Moore, she has dark hair, brown eyes and a rather noble face. I realise, of course, that years of deprivation and ill-treatment must have marred her appearance, but I can only describe her from the photograph I was shown.' As an afterthought, he said, 'Not that it makes much difference, but I omitted to say that she is also half-Jewish, which was the reason for her imprisonment.'

'You are correct, Herr Major,' said the Mother Superior. 'It makes no difference. She is still entitled to God's mercy.' She turned and said something to one of the sisters, who took her leave of the gathering and left the refectory.

'The sisters cared for a great many survivors of Bergen-Belsen,' said Father Ignatius.

'Then they have my utmost respect and admiration.'

The Mother Superior acknowledged his remark with a grateful smile.

After a short time, the sister returned with something that resembled a large account book, which she placed in front of the Mother Superior.

'These were the prisoners who passed through our hands, Herr Major. Regrettably, not all of them survived. Most were suffering from typhus when they were liberated, and they lacked the strength to resist it.' She leafed through the book, reading the entries carefully until she came to one that seized her attention. 'Sister Theresa,' she said, 'your handwriting is illegible. Perhaps you would enlighten me.'

The offending sister left her place to do as she was asked.

'This entry,' prompted the Mother Superior.

'I am sorry, Reverend Mother. The entry reads, "Sarah Elizabeth Moore, English".'

Alan could scarcely breathe. He asked, 'Does it say what happened to her?'

'She recovered from the typhus,' said the Mother Superior, 'and she left our convent on the twenty-seventh of April, nineteen forty-five, just twelve days after she came to us.'

It seemed a lot to ask, but Alan had to find out what he could. 'Is there any way of discovering her destination after she left the convent?'

One of the sisters lifted her hand and said, I may be able to help you.'

'Go on, Sister Katherine,' prompted the Reverend Mother.

'She was taken by a Jewish organisation to the Belgian border, Reverend Mother.'

Alan asked, 'Do you know the name of the organisation, Sister?'

'I'm afraid not.'

'There's no record of it here,' said the Reverend Mother, 'but we were concerned with nursing our patients back to health. We gave no thought to where they went after their recovery.'

It was quite understandable, even if it left Alan with another dead-end. He had something, however, to tell Dorothy. Most importantly, he could tell her that Sarah had survived Bergen-Belsen, and that was worthy of celebration.

23

April

Fortunes Come and Go

Amid all the unexpected turmoil involved in buying the house in Addlesden, Dorothy was ever thankful for the services of Mr Paynter, her solicitor, and the estate agent, Mr Brewer. There was quite enough to organise, and when a business letter arrived, postmarked Thornton, Bradford, she put it on one side, knowing it was from the company. It was most likely to be a notice of a meeting of shareholders, although she would be surprised for one to be called so soon after the end of the financial year.

In fact, it wasn't until that evening that she opened the envelope, guiltily aware that, for some considerable time, she'd given even less thought than usual to the family firm.

Dear Dorothy,

Her name was in Uncle Thomas's handwriting, a nice touch.

An extraordinary meeting of shareholders is called for Friday, 26ᵗʰ April, 1946, at 10:30 a.m. here, in the Board Room. It is essential that all shareholders are either present or represented by proxy, although, in view of the serious nature of the matter to be discussed, the former is preferred. Please confirm your intentions as soon as possible.
    Yours,

Thomas Edward Needham, Chairman.

Thoughtfully, Dorothy returned the letter to its envelope. She knew that profits had been hit during the war, when the contract to supply the Air Ministry had reached its end, the new contract going to one of the company's competitors, but things couldn't be so bad, surely. People had to eat, whatever happened. At all events, she would have to wait until the meeting to find out what was happening. In the meantime, she took out her pen to confirm that she would be present at the EGM.

Having signed and sealed the letter, she put it into her bag for posting. As she did so, she saw Alan's letter and took it out to read again.

Dear Dot,

I hope you're well and that the move is going according to plan.

I have news. I've learned that your aunt survived Bergen-Belsen! Do you remember my telling you that a number of prisoners fled the camp when the British Army arrived? I've since learned that your aunt was among them. She was taken into the Convent of the Sisters of Mercy, who told me that, whilst in their care, she recovered from typhus, which was rife in the camp, and she left the convent bound for the Belgian border with an organisation committed to helping Jewish ex-prisoners return to their homes. I made enquiries and wasn't at all surprised to learn that the organisation is called Exodus. I am trying to make contact with them, but it's a slow job. I'll let you know if and when I learn anything new.

Take care, and good luck with the move.

Love, Alan X

It was too wonderful for words to hear that Aunt Sarah had survived, and there was every chance she was still alive somewhere in Belgium, which was more wonderful still. It just had to happen when Dorothy was moving house and up to her ears in contracts and deeds. She'd naturally written to Alan, telling him how grateful she was for his efforts. If only she didn't feel so helpless.

* * *

The next day, she received another letter from Alan.

Dear Dot,

I'm coming home briefly on Friday, 26th. Leeds University have invited me to call on them, so keep your fingers crossed for me.

Unfortunately, at this stage, I've no further news about Aunt Sarah. I'll explain more fully when I see you. I know you're busy, but do you think we might meet?

Love,

Alan X

Finally, the move was settled, and Dorothy was able to call the removal firm holding her household effects in store, and ask them to carry out the removal. Her next job was to write to Alan.

Dear Alan,

I will certainly keep my fingers crossed for you, although I can't imagine you'll need it. On that day, I have to attend a extraordinary meeting of shareholders, but I'm sure you'll want to spend that evening at home with your parents, anyway.

If you can, come over for dinner on Saturday, 27th, and I'll try not to get blotto again! Bring your overnight things. The neighbours don't know me yet, so there'll be no scandal! The address is "Lark House", Nursery Lane, Addlesden-in-Wharfedale, and my new phone number is Addlesden 168.

I look forward to seeing you again.

Love,

Dot X

* * *

The move went more smoothly than she'd dared hope. Instead of being fazed by everything, she found herself standing outside the front door, casually directing the removers to the appropriate rooms and watching her new home take shape.

During the operation, she was occasionally conscious that the youngest member of the removal team kept looking in her direction, and the mystery was solved when one of the older men said to her, 'Young Brian's wondering if he's seen you in the pictures.'

'I doubt it. I haven't been to a cinema since the war.'

'No, he thinks he's seen you in a picture.' He called out, 'Brian, come here.'

'I hope you're not going to embarrass the poor boy.'

'It's all part of growin' up, miss, He'll take it in his stride. Here, Brian, now you can ask the lady who she is.'

The boy blushed painfully, looking as if he'd rather be anywhere than outside 'Lark House', explaining himself to the lady of the house.

'I didn't want them to embarrass you, Brian,' she said, looking at the team now assembled for the entertainment. 'Just tell me who you think I am.'

Eventually, the tongue-tied youth managed to speak. He asked, 'Were you in *The Wicked Lady*, miss?'

'No, I wasn't, but I'm very flattered that you thought I was.' Inclining her head towards the rest, she said, 'Don't let these men tease you.'

After a while, she made tea for them all, carrying the mugs out on a tray. 'Just a minute,' she said, disappearing into the kitchen again and emerging with a cake tin. 'I saved up my coupons for these,' she said, removing the lid. 'Brian, you can have first choice.'

One of the men asked, 'Why him?'

'Because he was the only one among you to pay me a compliment, and it was a sincere compliment, too.'

'We'll tell you owt you like, miss. We're not shy.'

There was naturally a chorus of agreement, which Dorothy dismissed. 'That doesn't count,' she said. 'Enjoy that cake, Brian. You've earned it.'

When the removal was complete, she tipped the men, including Brian, who was no longer embarrassed. 'Now, see that you treat him properly,' she told them, 'or he might embarrass you, one day.'

It had been a day of fun, and that was a bonus. Friday still beckoned, however, and the signs were less inviting.

* * *

Dorothy parked her car at the factory and called at reception.

'The directors are all in the Board Room,' the receptionist told her bleakly. It was unlikely that the staff had been told anything, but they could pick up the signs as well as anyone, and now Dorothy was feeling pessimistic, too.

She made her way to the Board Room and found the door ajar, so she pushed it open.

'Dorothy, come in and have some coffee.'

'Thank you, Uncle Thomas.' She accepted a kiss from him and greeted the others present, all of whom were family members on her late father's side. They chatted easily, bringing one another up to date with their personal lives, until the clock showed that it was time for the meeting to begin.

'Take your seats, please,' said Uncle Thomas. 'Looking around, I see that almost everyone's here, which is just as it should be.'

Dorothy had already noticed the absence of Aunt Alice, who had presumably asked the board to vote on her behalf.

Uncle Thomas took a long breath and asked, 'George, would you like to acquaint the shareholders with the situation?'

As Company Secretary, Uncle George took centre stage and referred unnecessarily to his notes. 'As you know,' he said, 'The Air Ministry contract ended in February nineteen forty-four and was not renewed. We also lost out to the competition with regard to the Admiralty and War Office contracts. Since then we have been assailed by rationing and shortages to the extent that last year we recorded a significant net loss. The situation has not improved. In fact, it is fair to say that Needham's Pickles Limited is in a far worse state than at any time in its history.'

The silence with which his report was received was a measure of the mood of the gathering.

'Thank you, George,' said Uncle Thomas, once more rising to his feet. 'Our situation has not gone unnoticed by the competition, and we have received two offers, summaries of which I'm about to circulate.' He fanned out the copies and passed them to each shareholder, rather like a croupier dealing cards. Dorothy took hers, but waited for her uncle to speak again.

'As things stand,' said Uncle Thomas, 'the company cannot go on trading, and we have a straight choice, which is either to become insolvent or to accept one of the offers before you.'

A member of the family Dorothy knew only slightly said, 'This offer from Barker's is derisory.'

'I agree,' said Uncle Thomas. 'I only put it before you because I wanted you to see the range of options, such as it is.'

'So we go under or allow ourselves to be taken over.'

'That's the choice, I'm afraid.'

A distant cousin asked pettishly, 'Who's responsible for this downturn?'

'It's not a "who", but a "what",' Uncle Thomas told him. 'The war and the fact that the competition have greater buying power.'

'What's the war got to do with it?'

'Seven years of food rationing, for one thing.'

Dorothy remained silent. Everyone knew that women didn't understand business, although she knew rather more than the cousin who'd just revealed his ignorance. Also, on reading the summary of the offer from Maynard's Foods, she'd noticed that they were prepared to guarantee all but management jobs. As she saw it, the management would doubtless come out of the takeover quite well. The workforce needed safeguarding, and if that was what Maynard's were offering, she was in favour of that option. It was a sad fact that no one else had remarked on it.

Uncle Thomas asked, 'Are we agreed that Maynard's offer is preferable to insolvency?' He had to ask. 'Have we a motion, then, that we accept Maynard's offer?'

A motion was put forward and seconded. 'Right,' said Uncle Thomas, 'all those in favour please raise your hands.'

The motion was carried unanimously, and the meeting ended.

'A sad business, Dorothy,' said Uncle Thomas.

'And I've just bought a house.'

He looked at her in surprise. 'Not a large one, I hope?'

'Not at all, but I did need somewhere to live. I'll send everybody my new address and phone number.'

'Where is it?'

'Addlesden.'

'Very nice indeed.' Returning to the subject of the takeover, he said, 'I really don't know what to do about Sarah's holding in the company.'

'I didn't know she had a holding, Uncle Thomas.'

'Yes, it was purchased for her as a gift several years before the war, and now, the likelihood is that she died in captivity—'

'No, she didn't. She survived that, and she's still alive, possibly in Belgium. I found that out recently.'

'Good grief. I suppose I'd better exercise my duty as trustee and sell her shares on her behalf. That's unless she's likely to return soon. What do you think?'

'I don't know. It's anybody's guess, but the shares are her property.'

'Quite so.' Recovering from his surprise, he addressed Dorothy's situation. 'After Maynard's have paid out, you should still be comfortably off, Dorothy.'

He was probably right, but she wasn't impressed. 'You know, Uncle Thomas, I gave up my job to someone who had more need of it, and I don't regret it. All the same, though, I think I'll go back to earning an honest living if I can.' She had it in mind to speak to Rimmington's.

* * *

When the phone rang, she knew it would be Alan, because no one else knew her number.

'Hello.'

'Dot, it's Alan. Guess what? I've been offered a place on the MA course in Archaeology.'

'Congratulations. We'll celebrate it, naturally, but haven't you already got an MA?'

'Yes, but that's a first degree. It's the way they work at Cambridge.'

'That's as clear as mud. You'll have to explain it to me properly when you come over.'

'What time shall I come?'

'Any time. I'll be here all afternoon.'

'I'm looking forward to it. What's your news?'

'You might well ask. When I got up this morning, I thought I was a wealthy woman. Needham's is going to be taken over. I should be all right, but I want to go back to some kind of work again.'

24

Rabbit Pie – And A Surprise

Dorothy called the Shire Hall in Durham City and checked that she was speaking to Connie.

'You never recognise me voice when Ah put it on, do you?'

'No, you fool me every time.'

'What are you stuck with now?'

'I haven't got quite enough fats and flour to make a pastry crust.'

'What are you makin', bonny lass?'

'Believe it or not, rabbit pie.'

'Again?'

'It worked well last time, but now, I'm struggling to make a crust.'

'Just hang on while Ah take this call.'

Dorothy heard her say, 'Shire Hall. How can I help you?' It was almost like being back at one of the RAF stations where they'd served together.

After a moment, she said, 'Right, Ah'm back. Are you all right for potatoes?'

'Yes, there's no problem there.'

'Okay, what you need to do is forget about pastry, and put thin slices of potato on top instead. Have you got any cheese?'

'Yes.'

'Okay, when you take the pie out of the oven, grate some cheese over the potatoes.'

'What a good idea.'

'Ah'm full of 'em, bonny lass. Are you making this pie for the same fella?'

'As it happens, yes.'

'Oh, yes?'

'No, it's not like that.'

'We'll see. Anyway, I have to go. Best of luck. 'Bye.'

''Bye, Connie, and thanks again.'

She would write to her with the news that she was no longer one of the idle rich. She had that to look forward to.

* * *

She'd just finished making the pie when Alan arrived.

'I almost didn't recognise you in civvies,' she said, accepting a kiss on her cheek and welcoming him into the house. She remembered his tweed jacket from his last leave, at Christmas.

'I almost didn't recognise myself.' He looked around him, but the hall gave little away.

'Let's get rid of your bag and then I'll give you a tour. Follow me.' She led the way upstairs to the second double room. 'Put it in there for now,' she told him. 'There's the main bathroom and there's a cloakroom downstairs. Come down, and I'll show you the rest.' She showed him the kitchen, dining, breakfast and drawing rooms. 'We have to call them "reception rooms" now,' she said.

'Is that because we have a Labour government?'

'No, I think it's just progress.'

'I got the impression you were turning hard left, Dot.'

She gave the matter brief consideration and said, 'I do lean to the left, but I'm in favour of gradual change.'

'You're an old-fashioned Liberal,' he told her.

'But I'm in favour of the free health service they've promised us.'

'It sounds like a good idea, and long overdue,' he agreed.

Remembering her duty as a hostess, she asked, 'What can I offer you?'

'It's a bit early for anything grown-up, isn't it? Could you manage a cup of tea?'

'I think so. Come and tell me about your interview while I make it.'

He followed her into the kitchen. 'You know, Dot,' he said, 'despite clothes rationing and shortages, you still manage to look elegant.'

'Flatterer.'

'I must have told you before now, if you wore a sack tied with string, you'd still have "style" written all over you.'

'Thank you.' She filled the kettle and set it on the gas. 'A youngster who came with the removal men thought I was Margaret Lockwood. He was really sweet.'

Alan narrowed his eyes and viewed her from various angles. 'In a certain light, perhaps,' he said.

'Nonsense. Anyway, tell me about your interview.'

'It was little more than a cosy chat. I'll have to do some work in the field as well as the academic stuff, but that's no hardship. In any case, it's what archaeology's about.'

'Doesn't the hardship depend on the weather?'

'No, everyone crowds into a tent when it rains. It's all very civilised. I must say I'm looking forward to it.' He added hurriedly, 'The course, that is, not crowding into a tent.'

'I'll believe you.' She reached for the tea caddy and counted two, and then one for the pot.

'You're surprisingly domestic, nowadays, Dot.'

'Don't you believe it. I was on the phone to Connie before you arrived, picking her brain again.'

'What are we going to eat this evening?'

With an air of mystery, she said, 'I thought I'd keep it as much like last Christmas as I could.'

'Rabbit pie?'

'Sort of.'

'Good, but why "sort of"?'

'I hadn't the ingredients to make pastry, so Connie suggested I topped the pie with slices of potato instead.'

'My mouth's watering already.'

'It should go well with champagne,' she said, pouring boiling water into the teapot.

'Are you serious?'

'Perfectly. I said we'd celebrate your success, didn't I?'

'You're the limit, Dot.' Suddenly, he remembered something. 'I brought you an offering,' he said. 'It's in the pocket of my mackintosh.' He went into the hall and returned with the priceless merchandise.

'Stockings,' she said, as a weary traveller might view an oasis. 'Bless you, Alan.'

'I had to call at the PX to get some Irish whiskey for a man I was interviewing.'

'Is that a new tactic, to get them drunk so that they spill the beans?'

'No, I said "interviewing", not "interrogating". He was a pitiful scrap of a Catholic priest who'd been a prisoner at Dachau as well as Bergen-Belsen. It was through him that I found out about Aunt Sarah surviving the war.' He went on to tell her about going to mass in the convent, and how the nuns had been able to establish that Aunt Sarah had survived.

'I'm so grateful to you for that, Alan,' she said, pouring tea into two cups. 'I couldn't believe it at first. The trouble is, now that I know she's alive, I really want to find her.'

'We're at the mercy of this Exodus set-up, unless....'

'Unless what?'

'One thing I haven't tried is the Belgian immigration service. I'll get on to them when I get back to Lüneburg.'

Dorothy shook her head in dazed disbelief. 'Where would I be without you?'

'You didn't say that eight years ago.'

'A great deal's happened since then.' She loaded a tray with tea things and said, 'Let's take our tea to the draw... sitting room.' She carried the tray through and set it down on an occasional table. 'Is there any suggestion yet that demob might be on the horizon?'

'Not so much as an idle rumour. They dealt with the big names from Bergen-Belsen last year at the Lüneburg Trials, but we're still finding the lesser horrors that escaped the net. We caught one on the road to Munich. He was trying to escape via one of the rat lines, but he'll stand trial next month. He was the one the Catholic priest told me about.'

It all sounded very mysterious. 'What are these rat lines?'

'Escape routes for war criminals. They're called "rat lines" because rats desert a sinking ship, or so I'm told.'

'But where do they go to avoid capture?'

'Anywhere where they're still welcome and where there's no extradition treaty with Britain. Most of them head for South America.'

Dorothy knew very little about South America, but she felt strongly that any place was too good for Nazi war criminals.

* * *

Again, to Dorothy's surprise and relief, the rabbit pie was a success.

'You know,' said Alan, 'I'm not sure that I don't prefer potato to pastry. Please pass on my appreciation to your friend.'

'It'll be a pleasure.' She lifted the bottle from its ice bucket, a relic of the former family home, and asked, 'More champagne?'

'Why not? This is a better celebration than I came home to last evening.'

'I'd offer to make coffee, but that was one thing I wasn't able to find.'

'One day, Dot, everything will be back to normal. There'll be no more rationing, and Major Lofthouse will be consigned to history.'

'Shall we finish the champagne in the dr... sitting room?'

'You really are confused, aren't you?'

'Yes, let's take it to the drawing room, the way we used to.'

'Let me carry it.' He picked up the ice bucket with its stand. 'You bring the glasses.'

Dorothy took one end of the sofa, inviting him on to the other. 'Now,' she said, as he sat down. 'tell me about last evening.'

'Oh, there's so little to tell. I arrived home and told my mother I'd been offered a place, and she said, "That's nice, dear. I believe you'll be able to claim some kind of allowance from this wretched government. You may as well get something out of them. They take enough in taxes." Thereafter, she told me all the latest news from the WVS. At least, I think that was what she was doing. I wasn't really listening.' He helped the memory on its way with a sip of champagne. 'Then my father came home, and I told him. He said, "Well done, Alan. You haven't lost your touch, then?" I assured him I hadn't, and he asked, "What's for dinner, Clara?" She told him, "The usual." If my mother can get the sausages and the flour and eggs, they have toad-in-the-hole on Fridays.' He laughed at the memory. 'So much for a celebration.'

Amused, Dorothy said, 'Toad-in-the-hole's not bad.'

'Except that it was "the usual".' On brief reflection, he said, 'My mother's never had much to say to me about my... achievements, but she boasts about me to anyone who'll listen.'

Dorothy laughed. 'I know.'

'Of course, you and she go back a long way. That was another thing,' he said, suddenly remembering. 'She asked me where I was going today, so I told her and I got the usual response. "Be careful, Alan. That young woman's not good for you." Well, I was so unimpressed by the reception I'd almost received, that I told her just how I felt.'

'What did you feel, Alan?' It was important for Dorothy to know.

'That you were very good for me, that I'd enjoyed the time we spent together last Christmas, that your visits to Hanover and Lüneburg had kept me sane, and that I was looking forward to this evening because it would be a time of real enjoyment and true friendship before I returned to the squalor of bombed-out Germany.'

Reaching for his hands, she asked, 'Did you really say all that?'

'Almost *verbatim*,' he confirmed, 'and I meant every word.'

'And is that how you see me, as a true friend?'

He hesitated. 'Yes. No, more than that, really.' With a wistful expression, he said, 'Life can be a bugger, you know.'

'It can,' she agreed, 'but in what particular way is it a bugger for you?'

'Oh, you know. Just generally.'

He made to remove his hands, but she held them firmly. 'Alan,' she said, 'we both know you're more articulate than that.' She moved closer, looking straight into his eyes. 'Why is life a bugger because I'm more to you than just a friend?'

Almost squirming, he said, 'You should be doing my job, Dot. You'd wring a confession out of a Nazi the minute the guards marched him into the room.'

'So, start talking, buster.'

He laughed in spite of his discomfiture. 'Who was that supposed to be?'

'One of those gangster people. I don't know, but tell me before the suspense gets too much for me.'

'I need lubrication.' He removed one hand from her grasp to pick up his glass and take a hefty draught. As soon as he put his glass down, she reclaimed his hand. In his embarrassment, he closed his eyes and said, 'You're determined, aren't you?'

Her uncompromising half-nod confirmed that she was.

'I was afraid you might be.'

'This,' she said, 'is the man who confronted an angry mob in Lüneburg, rescued a damsel in distress, and dispersed the mob single-handed.'

'I wasn't exactly alone.'

'Let me remember it my way. Now spill the beans, and I promise I'll treat you gently.'

He hesitated, and then, seeing no alternative, gave way. 'I really don't want another one-sided embarrassment.' Now that he'd said it, he looked strangely relieved, his awkwardness stemming possibly from having taken so long before making his confession. Her response was clearly a complete surprise.

'Who says it's one-sided?'

'I just thought….' It was just possible that he no longer knew what he thought.

'You do too much thinking.' It was kindly advice, and she was still holding his hands.

'Probably.'

'Are you going to kiss me?' Her voice, her eyes, her perfume and her proximity conspired, and he was unable to resist them.

'It wasn't my intention when I stepped off the train, but it does seem rather a good idea.' He touched her lips tentatively with his, still somewhat bewildered by the course events were taking, and became aware of an enthusiastic response that seemed to draw him on with little conscious effort on his part. He teased each lip in turn before engaging fully with her so that they were in complete unity.

After a while, she asked, 'Alan?'

'Yes?'

'That last night in Lüneburg, did you hang up my frock?'

'Yes,' he said, kissing her again, scarcely able to believe it was happening. 'Military training, you know. The only creases allowed are the ones you put in with an iron.'

'Did you take off my shoes and leave them tidily beside my bed?'

'Very likely. I hate to see untidy shoes.' He wondered why she wanted to talk at such a time.

More diffidently, she asked, 'Did I offer myself to you?'

Without hesitation, he said, 'Not as I recall.'

'You're a liar and a gentleman. I distinctly remember asking you to stay the night. You were very chivalrous, I remember.'

'You were very… relaxed after quite a lot of wine. It was my fault.'

'In that case, you'll have to do a penance.'

It seemed a funny sort of game, but he went along with it. 'What do I have to do?'

'Take me to bed. Is it a lot to ask?'

'No,' he said, almost croaking in his sudden good fortune. 'I daresay I'll manage it.' He rose to his feet and offered her a hand up.

'You are the embodiment of courtesy.' She kissed him and led the way upstairs. 'I'll leave the washing-up for morning,' she said, 'or afternoon, or whenever we get up.' Passing the second bedroom, she asked, 'Do you need your bag?'

'Only for my sleeping draught.'

'What?'

'Joking. One thing occurs to me, though….'

'It's all taken care of. At least, it will be, shortly.' She pointed him to her room and said, 'Excuse me for a minute.' She disappeared into the bathroom, leaving Alan to close the curtains and undress.

She returned, carrying her stockings, which she draped over the back of a chair. 'Will you unhook me again?'

'Of course.' He parted the hook and eye, and ran the zip fastener down for her.

'Are those your uniform pants?'

'Drawers, cellular, officers',' he confirmed, 'the only kind I possess. Please don't mock.'

'You're quite right. I mustn't.' She lowered her dress and stepped out of it, reaching into the wardrobe for a hanger.

'Allow me.' He arranged the dress on the hanger, checking that it was perfectly centred and that the hook and eye were fastened. Meeting her questioning look, he said, 'It's to make sure it hangs straight and doesn't sag.'

'You never fail to surprise me,' she said, lowering her underskirt so that she could step out of it and drape it over the chair with her stockings. 'It'll be all right,' she assured him, letting him take her in his arms. They kissed while he unfastened her brassiere and suspender belt. 'That was sneaky,' she said, hooking her fingers round the waistband of his drawers, 'but so is this.'

'And this,' he said, wresting his attention away from her breasts and performing the final unveiling.

'Come and join me.' She pulled the bedclothes back in invitation.

He took her in his arms, revelling in the feel of her naked body against his, and they kissed unhurriedly, content for the moment to enjoy the new intimacy.

'I'm glad you're not impatient,' she said.

'Anticipation is a delight in itself.' He kissed her chin, then her throat, and finally her exquisite breasts, where he carried out a leisurely exploration, occasionally teasing her nipples so that her breath came and went in involuntary shudders.

Reaching downward, he ran his hand slowly back and forth over her thigh, tracing the crease where it joined her lower abdomen, and sensing the arousal it was causing.

He kissed her lips again while she made her own exploration, and it became a game of equals, each intent on giving and experiencing the ultimate sensation.

* * *

They lay together in the darkness, spent and unexpectedly happy.

'I knew there was something missing from my life,' she said. 'We shouldn't have waited so long.'

'Ah, but the wait was worthwhile.'

'So it was, and now you're going to buzz off back to Lüneburg and leave me like the maiden in the rhyme.'

He raised himself on one elbow, trying to make out her features in the dark. 'No,' he admitted, 'you've got me there.'

'The maiden all forlorn,' she reminded him, 'the one who milked the cow with the crumpled horn.'

'Poor cow. Milking by hand would have been kinder.' Addressing the immediate problem, he said, 'It won't be for much longer, I hope. In any case, you're a lady of leisure, so you could come back with me.'

'If you remember, my circumstances are somewhat changed from those you remember.'

'Are they drastically changed?'

She hesitated, thinking about her reply. 'I suppose I'm cushioned against hardship,' she said, 'which is more than a great many people can say, but I'm still determined to do something useful.'

'Have you had any ideas yet?'

'One idea, which should hopefully be enough. After the board meeting, I spoke to Rimmington's, and they suggested I apply for the Assistant Buyer's job in Footwear. It hasn't been advertised yet, but it will be very soon.'

'Wonderful. May I kiss the Assistant Buyer in Footwear?'

'No, she hasn't left yet. Kiss me instead.'

He did, with much feeling. Then, more practically, he said, 'I'd better see what I can find out about Aunt Sarah while you still have some free time.' He added, 'In case you need to come over.'

25

A Kinder Name

It was as well that the British Army could find little for Alan to do, because he spent much of his first morning back in Lüneburg on the telephone to the Bureau d' Immigration in Brussels. An officer told him that, having assumed their peacetime role once more after six years of occupation, he and his colleagues had found their records in disarray, and that individual cases were difficult and sometimes impossible to trace. Alan was unimpressed, knowing that, as well as displaying less admirable characteristics, the Nazis had been a model of bureaucratic efficiency.

'I'm not asking about something that happened during the war,' he insisted, 'but about some refugees from Bergen-Belsen, who entered Belgium during the month following liberation on the fifteenth of April.'

'I tell you,' said the officer, 'the Boche left things in a kind of unholy mess you simply can't imagine.'

'After the Germans left,' said Alan patiently, 'Bergen-Belsen was liberated. Nothing the Germans did to your system can have any bearing on this group of refugees. They would be received by Belgian officers, not by the Germans. It happened eleven or perhaps twelve months ago, when Belgian records were back in Belgian hands.'

'I do not understand, Major Lofthouse.'

'Neither do I, monsieur.'

'What I fail to understand, Major Lofthouse, is why you wish to trace these people, who would not, in any case, be allowed to remain in Belgium unless they were Belgian citizens.'

Alan breathed the sigh of one whose patience is completely expended. 'I wish you'd told me that in the first place,' he said.

'But that was not the question you asked me, Major. You asked if we had a record of their arrival, and that is, unfortunately—'

'Impossible to retrieve because of the chaos created by the Nazis, I know. Tell me one thing, though. If they weren't allowed to remain in Belgium, where would they go next?'

For once, the immigration officer was able to answer Alan's question confidently, even if his answer was less than helpful. 'They would either return to Germany, or they would be required to continue through Belgium, reporting at certain police stations until they reached France or the Netherlands.'

Not surprisingly, Alan's request for a list of likely police stations earned the same reaction as his initial enquiry. 'Thank you,' he said, adding truthfully, 'you've probably been as helpful as you could ever be.'

His quest continued with calls to a series of German border control posts, beginning with those nearest Bergen-Belsen, and by mid-day, his efforts were rewarded.

'Sarah Elizabeth Moore arrived here after attempting to enter Belgium,' his informant told him, 'and she was taken with other survivors to the displaced persons' camp at Adendorf.'

'I'm most grateful to you.' He imagined Dorothy might easily share his gratitude, but his next line of enquiry had to be to the DP camp itself, where, once again he became entangled in bureaucracy.

'Look,' he told the junior officer in the records office, 'all I want to know is if you have a displaced person in the camp, called Sarah Elizabeth Moore.'

'I have to ask you, sir, what your relationship is to the person in question.'

'I'm not related to her. I'm enquiring on behalf of a friend, a niece of Miss Moore.'

'Then because of regulations, I'm afraid I can't help you, sir. If your friend were to contact us, it would be a different matter.'

Alan swallowed his impatience. The subaltern he was speaking to wasn't responsible for Army regulations any more than the officer in charge of the place was. 'All right. The lady's niece is currently in England. I'll speak to her shortly. Thank you, Lieutenant.'

'I'm sorry I couldn't help, sir.'

'Don't give it a second thought.'

He'd never get away with making an international call without what the Army might regard as a good reason, but Aunt Sarah had waited five years. A few more days would make little difference, although the system seemed unnecessarily cruel, or so it seemed to him as he took out his writing paper.

Dear Dot,

Progress at last! I'm told Aunt Sarah is in a DP camp in Adendorf, *a short distance from this post, and if that isn't the supreme irony, tell me what is.*

I've spoken to someone at the camp, but, because I'm not related to her, they won't even confirm that she's there. I suggest that, when you come, you bring evidence of your relationship to her, such is the level of bureaucracy in this matter. Even so, hopefully we'll get a result after all this time

I keep thinking about the time you and I spent together on my last leave. It was the most wonderful thing for me. I hope it was for you, too.

Let me know when you're due to arrive, and I'll meet you at the airport.

Lots of love,

Alan XX

* * *

Dorothy read the letter twice, and then her eyes filled with tears. Alan had actually found Aunt Sarah. It was unbelievable, yet it was true. She would dig up all the evidence she could find of their relationship. First, however, she had to find out about a flight so that she could let Alan know.

She spent some time on the phone to Farrar's Tours and resolved to buy her ticket that afternoon. Meanwhile, she had to reply to Alan's letter.

Dear Alan,

You are amazing! Thank you, thank you, thank you for everything! I'll be on Flight 784, arriving at 1020 on the 2nd of May.

Last Wicket Pair

As you're wondering, yes, it was the most wonderful thing for me, too. Some things are meant to happen at an appointed time, and I'm glad we waited.
   Lots and lots of love,
   Dot XXX

* * *

She hurried into town and, through Farrar's, secured her seat with the airline. The industry was awaiting the formation of British European Airways, so not everything in post-war Britain was bleak and dreary. With a new development, a new airline and a new relationship, she couldn't help feeling optimistic.

Returning home, she hunted out every piece of documentation she could find, every letter and photograph, especially those of them together. Also, she put some clothes together. She and Aunt Sarah had been about the same size before the war. She would be emaciated after her imprisonment, but she would still need clothes.

Finally, Dorothy spoke on the phone to Uncle Thomas, who would provide the final piece of evidence.

Having made all arrangements, she took a little time to review the events of the past few days, and in particular the evening and night she'd spent with Alan. The whole thing had been quite magical. She'd meant every word she'd written to him. It really was as if it had been preordained to happen at the right time, and she was overjoyed that it had.

* * *

Another new development was the rebirth of Yeadon Airport as a passenger facility. Throughout the war, it had been used by the nearby Avro aircraft factory to send its Lancaster bombers to their operational destinations, but now that the airport was once more in civilian hands, Dorothy could drive less than ten miles from her home to catch a domestic flight to Croydon.

With the onward flight, her spirits rose even higher, and the thought that she could be making the return journey with Aunt Sarah beside her was so exciting, she hardly dared hope.

* * *

Eventually, the aircraft made its descent through patchy clouds and into bright sunshine. Dorothy felt the wheels make contact with the tarmac, and the aircraft reduced speed and taxied to the terminal. It was a little after ten-twenty, so she expected Alan to be waiting for her.

When she'd cleared customs and security, she looked around for him, but there was no sign. All she could do was wait.

After some time, a corporal in the Royal Military Police came into the terminal and, seeing her alone, approached her. He saluted and asked, 'Miss Needham?' His immaculately-set red cap seemed to draw attention to a pair of large and protuberant ears.

'Yes, I was expecting Major Lofthouse.'

'Major Lofthouse has been unavoidably detained, Miss. He sent me to meet you.' He delivered the message like a child on an errand.

'I see. Will you take my case, please? It's rather heavy.'

'Very good, Miss.' He lifted her suitcase and said, 'Follow me, please, Miss.'

'Where are you taking me, Corporal?'

'To the Kieler Hof Hotel, Miss. Those are my orders.' He pitched the suitcase unceremoniously into the back of a Jeep and took the driving seat. In the absence of an invitation, Dorothy climbed into the passenger seat just as the corporal started the engine and selected first gear.

'It was good of you to wait for me, Corporal,' she said.

Seemingly a stranger to irony, he said, 'I couldn't wait long, Miss. There's too many troublemakers around.'

'I know. I was there when Major Cochrane was killed.'

'Were you, Miss? How did you come to be there?'

'It's a long story, Corporal. Suffice it to say, my life was also in danger until Major Lofthouse arrived.' In the absence of an adequate explanation, she had to ask, 'Will Major Lofthouse be unavailable for long?'

'I think he's out all day, Miss. He'll be collecting some suspect they've caught, you can bet.'

They passed the familiar bombed ruins on the road into Lüneburg, and Dorothy asked, 'Does it happen often?'

'Not so often nowadays, Miss. Most of 'em have either been caught or they've escaped down the rat runs. That's what we call their escape routes.'

'I know.'

He passed dangerously close to a civilian on a bicycle, causing her to swerve and treat him to a well-deserved torrent of German abuse.

'I don't understand a word these Jerries say,' said the corporal.

'I do, and she described you very accurately.'

'Oh.' Her observation appeared to have passed him by, because he made no real response, but swung carelessly into the gateway of the Kieler Hof Hotel. 'Here you are, Miss.' He let the engine run and made no attempt to leave his seat.

'Will you give me a hand with my case, please. As I said earlier, it's rather heavy.'

'Right, Miss.' Switching off the engine, he picked up her case and asked, 'Do you want me to carry it into the hotel, Miss?'

'That's the way it's usually done.'

He went ahead of her, leaving her to catch the door before it swung back against her, and placed the case in front of the reception desk. 'Will it be all right there, Miss?'

'I'm sure one of the porters will be along soon.'

'Right, Miss.'

'Thank you for coming to meet me, Corporal.'

'That's all right, Miss. Goodbye.' He saluted and turned to leave.

'Goodbye, Corporal.'

She found that, in his usual courteous way, Alan had made the reservation for her, and she was grateful for that. Otherwise, it was only right that duty should take priority, but she hoped she would see him before long.

* * *

Shortly after five-thirty, there was a knock on the door. She opened it and welcomed Alan into her room, where they stood and kissed enthusiastically.

'I'm sorry I couldn't meet you,' he said eventually. I was supposed to go to the French Zone tomorrow, but I surprised them by turning up today. I hope Corporal Turner was a satisfactory substitute.'

'No one could be an adequate substitute for you, but he did the necessary, even if he set off almost before I was in my seat, and I had to remind him about carrying my case.'

Alan nodded sadly. 'And he was the pick of the unit. If it's any consolation, I drove to the French Zone with two of Turner's less-civilised comrades for company.'

'Poor you, but you still haven't explained why you went today instead of tomorrow.'

'It was to get it out of the way. I'll let the prisoner languish in his cell until Saturday, and then I'll interrogate him, and that leaves tomorrow and some of Saturday free.'

'Free for what?'

'For us to visit the DP camp, of course.'

'Alan, you're so good.' She kissed him again.

'I try to be.'

'One thing puzzles me.'

'You're lucky it's only one thing.'

'No, seriously, why do they call them DP camps?'

'Semantics, basically. A DP is a Displaced Person. It's a kinder and more respectful name than "Refugee", and it's probably good that they've changed the name, because there's been little kindness or respect in their lives these past few years.'

'I don't know what to expect when I see her.'

'The best thing you can do is not expect too much.'

'I'll try not to, but it's difficult. I'm just thankful I have you to lean on.'

26

Another Adjustment

Dorothy had learned recently about the proliferation of DP camps in various parts of Europe, and she knew that many of them had been set up in schools, old military establishments, and sometimes in bombed buildings. The camp she was now visiting, however, was purpose built. Her first impression was that it differed in appearance from a PoW camp only by the absence of watchtowers, searchlights and barbed wire. The accommodation consisted of identical wooden huts, whilst armed guards patrolled the entrance, albeit for the protection, rather than the containment, of the residents.

Alan returned the sentry's salute and showed his identity card. 'We're here at the invitation of Captain Collier,' he explained.

'I see, sir.' The sentry spoke to his supervisor, a corporal, who pointed to the orderly office and sent him on his way. The corporal saluted Alan and said, 'The sentry's gone to alert Captain Collier of your arrival, sir. He should be here very soon.'

'Thank you, Corporal.'

They waited for only a few minutes, before a harassed-looking captain in the Pay Corps left the orderly office and approached them. Saluting Alan, he said, 'Good morning, sir. Good morning, miss. I'm Captain Collier, the Adjutant. Please come this way.'

The corporal opened the gate, and they followed the adjutant to a building that was much larger than the orderly office. When they drew nearer, they saw the sign that identified it as the Medical Centre. Collier let them in and took them to a small office, where he invited them to take a seat.

'Before we can proceed, Miss Needham, I have to satisfy myself of your relationship to the person in question. Major Lofthouse tells me that Sarah Moore is your aunt. Is that correct?'

'That's right.'

'Have you brought some evidence of your relationship?'

Dorothy opened the foolscap envelope she'd brought, and emptied its contents on to Captain Collier's desk. 'I don't suppose the letters tell you very much at all, Captain, but here are some photographs of us together.' She took out the photos, and Collier referred to what could only be an official photograph of Aunt Sarah. He also looked carefully at Dorothy before nodding cautiously.

'I imagine the Nazis took her passport and any other papers in her possession, so you must know very little about her.' Sifting through the documents, she found the one she wanted. 'This is a copy of a share certificate in my aunt's name, and a letter from the Chairman of the family firm stating that Sarah Elizabeth Moore is my aunt.' She handed the documents to Collier and waited.

'Needham's Pickles,' he remarked, 'a household name.'

'Make the most of it,' advised Dorothy. 'The firm is being taken over, possibly as we speak.'

'What a shame, Miss Needham.'

'I quite agree, but have I convinced you of my *bona fides*?'

'Oh, yes. There is one more stage in the process that we must address, however, and that is the medical briefing.'

'What?'

'You need to be acquainted with your aunt's state of health, both physical and mental, and I'm about to arrange that for you.'

Dorothy found his reference to mental health disturbing, but all she could do was wait while he made a call on his internal phone. Eventually, he was connected with the person he was trying to contact, and she heard him say that he had the niece of Sarah Elizabeth Moore with him, and that she would appreciate a meeting. Coming off the phone, he said, 'I shall now ask you to wait outside until Major Wilmot, one of the medical officers, joins you.' Turning to Alan, he said apologetically, 'When that happens, sir, for reasons of medical confidentiality, you will be required to remain outside the room.'

'That's understood, Collier. It makes perfect sense.'

'If you don't mind my asking, sir, what has been your role in this enquiry?'

'Help, support, and I suppose I've opened a few doors.'

'He's too modest, Captain.'

'I'm sure. Miss Needham, I hope everything goes according to plan.' He shook hands with Alan and opened the office door. 'Please take a seat out here.'

They accepted his invitation and waited for the medical officer.

What they'd seen of the block was extremely clean and tidy, as a military establishment should be, and Dorothy could only hope that the DP quarters were kept as scrupulously clean. Decency as well as hygiene demanded it, and respect was long overdue for the residents. It had already occurred to Dorothy that, whilst 'displaced person' was an improvement on 'refugee', it still sounded distant and impersonal. She continued to ponder that thought whilst Alan, as sensitive as ever, sat with her, silent but supportive.

After ten minutes or so, a medical orderly came to them to ask, 'Miss Needham?'

'Yes.' Dorothy rose to her feet.

'Major Wilmot will see you now, Miss, but alone, I'm afraid.'

'That's fine,' said Alan. 'I understand.'

'Thank you, sir. Please come this way, Miss.'

Dorothy followed the orderly into another office, where a serious-looking man in a white coat and with greying hair rose to greet her.

'Miss Needham, I'm Major Wilmot. I'm delighted to meet you.'

'How d' you do, Major Wilmot.'

'Please take a seat. You've convinced Captain Collier of your relationship to Sarah Moore, but I'd like to hear a little more about that relationship. How would you describe it Miss Needham?'

Dorothy had told so many people about her friendship with her younger aunt that she had no difficulty in obliging. 'She's the youngest daughter of three,' she told him, 'only about fifteen or sixteen years older than me, and our relationship has always been one of close friendship. For various reasons, she was less than popular with her sisters, my mother included, but I've always loved her. It's fair to say that, during my childhood, she provided a significant part of the affection in my life. Now, I only heard of her disappearance when I was discharged from the WAAF last year, and that was when I set about finding her.' She blinked as she felt tears forming. 'Apart from a surviving sister, who cares nothing for her, I'm the only family she has left, and I'm determined to care for her.' She felt in her bag for a handkerchief, but before she could find one, Major Wilmot produced one of the large, white, man-size variety.

'Thank you, Major Wilmot. I'm not usually so emotional, but it's been a long search, and it means a great deal to me.'

'Don't give it a moment's thought, Miss Needham. I quite understand.' He sat back in his chair, clearly thinking about what he was going to say. Eventually, he said, 'Your aunt has been starved and ill-treated for four years. She's naturally weakened by illness and malnutrition.'

'I believe she had typhus at the time of her liberation.'

'Yes, I believe so. It was rife in Bergen-Belsen.' He thought briefly and said, 'It may be difficult for you to recognise her at first. Equally, she may not recognise you. The horrors she's experienced in Nazi hands have affected her mentally. It was only to be expected.'

'What kind of damage are you talking about, Major Wilmot?'

'Before I can answer that question, just tell me one thing. Do you intend to take her into your home?'

'Of course. She has nowhere else to go. In any case, I wouldn't want her to go anywhere else.'

He nodded, reassured. 'You see,' he said, 'She's become institutionalised. Every decision has been made for her, to the extent that she's become extremely passive.' Recalling one event, he said, 'We had to find her needles and thread, because fine needlework had become so much a part of her life. It's quite possible it was her embroidery and *petit-point* work that enabled her survival, using her skill to supply the guards with gifts for their wives and mistresses.' Returning to the unpleasant legacy of camp life, he said, 'Also, she reacts to given stimuli, not as a healthy person might, but as a frightened victim. Her whole purpose is survival, so every action on her part is towards that end. She will be difficult to live with for quite some time, and you'll have to keep reminding yourself that her state of mind has been created by her tormentors. She's not to be held to account for any irrational response she might make.'

'Of course not.'

'I'm glad you understand that.' Looking at his notes, he said, 'Another thing is malnutrition. She must be allowed to return gradually to her normal weight. Now, I appreciate that over-eating isn't the easiest thing to achieve in time of rationing, but it's still possible, and an extremely unhealthy thing to do. Her stomach has shrunk through starvation, so it must develop gradually. You'll be given guidance on that, but how you cope with regard to rationing will be up to you and your personal ingenuity.'

'I see.'

'Can you remember what she was like before the war? I mean in terms of weight?'

'About size ten, I'd say.' Then, realising that a man might not find that at all meaningful, she said, 'Much as I am now. She and I were physically very much alike.'

He smiled. 'I'm beginning to see the likeness, Miss Needham.' As something else occurred to him, he asked, 'Have you brought her any clothes?'

'Yes, but with no idea of her measurements, I've simply brought some things of mine. They can be altered after we arrive home.'

'Good, although I should advise you against taking your aunt home immediately. She'll need time to adjust to another big change. You'll have to trust me on that. Also, we have to provide certain documents, including a temporary passport.'

'I can see that.'

'Good. Now, unfortunately, I have to ask you about your circumstances. I imagine you have a job?'

'No, I've been living as an independent person since I was discharged from the WAAF, having resigned from my pre-war job. I was considering returning to work, but that can wait. I have a private income, now somewhat reduced, as is my aunt's, but keeping her in reasonable comfort won't be a problem.'

'That is good. If you're ready, Miss Needham, 'we'll go and have a chat with Sarah.' He led the way out of his office, briefly acknowledging Alan with a handshake before leaving the block and passing between several huts until they reached their destination. They picked their way between people walking, talking and wandering aimlessly, and Major

Wilmot explained that it was quite common for ex-detainees to shun enclosure. He opened the hut door and went in, motioning Dorothy to wait behind for the time being. Her pulse quickened when she heard him say, 'Hello, Sarah. How are you today?'

There was no audible response, but then Dorothy heard Major Wilmot say, 'I've brought someone to see you. There's nothing to worry about, she's a friend.' He beckoned to Dorothy, who entered the hut warily, and then in sudden disbelief, because the woman almost cowering behind her bed in what was presumably temporary clothing looked nothing like the Aunt Sarah she remembered. She had grey hair that might once have been dark, but that was the only feature Dorothy recognised. Otherwise, her shrunken features and wasted body belonged to a complete stranger. As she stared, however, her eyes fell on a long scar on her left forearm. It was the same burn scar she'd carried from childhood, and that acted as a prompt, because the longer Dorothy looked, the more familiar her aunt's features became, pinched though they were. She'd expected her to look starved, but the initial impression had been horrifying.

'Aunt Sarah,' she said, 'it's Dorothy.'

'Dorothy?' There was no hint of recognition in her tone.

'Florence's daughter. Don't you remember?'

Sarah repeated, 'Florence's daughter,' and her voice, as much as anything, convinced Dorothy of her aunt's identity.

'Do you remember your sisters? Alice and Florence? I'm Florence's daughter Dorothy. I've been looking for you for a long time.'

'Dorothy?' It was as if she were searching her memory.

'Don't worry, Sarah,' said Major Wilmot. 'We'll come back later. Perhaps Dorothy would like to leave some photos for you to look at.'

'Of course.' Dorothy took out the documents she'd brought to prove her relationship to Aunt Sarah, and selected photographs of the happiest times they'd spent together. 'Here you are,' she said, laying them on the bed. 'Photos from the old days in Cullington. Have a look through them, and we'll see you later.'

'Cullington.' There was only the merest suggestion that the name meant something to her.

Outside the hut, Wilmot said, 'Leave her to think about it. She has to adjust in her own time.'

'I take it psychiatry is your specialism, Major Wilmot.'

He laughed. 'Is it so obvious?'

'It's a great comfort to me that you're around. When should I see her again?'

'Leave it until tomorrow. Perhaps the idea will have taken root, and you'll see progress.'

* * *

'It was more disturbing than I can describe.' Just the telling of it was making her tearful again.

'Take your time.' Alan helped her into the passenger seat of the Jeep. 'Tell me when you're ready.'

Dorothy took a long breath and began. 'I didn't recognise her at first. They're having to feed her up gradually, so she's still stick-thin. It wasn't until I saw the scar on her arm, an awful Guy Fawkes Night injury when she was a child, that I knew it was her.'

'Did she say anything?'

'She just repeated after me, "Dorothy", and "Florence's daughter". Oh, and when I mentioned Cullington, she repeated that as well, but not in a way that really meant anything. Major Wilmot says there's a chance she might make sense of those names if she's left alone.'

'I can see something in that.' He started the Jeep and drove towards Lüneburg. 'Mind you, he's the headshrinker, so he should know.'

'Please don't talk about shrinking.'

'No, that was insensitive of me.'

She placed her hand on his knee and said, 'It was a slip of the tongue. You're not remotely insensitive.' After a spell, she asked, 'Shall I see you tonight?'

'Certainly. I'll come over and stand you dinner, and then I may enjoy a well-earned absence from the Post. You've had an emotionally taxing day, so whatever happens after that, or whatever doesn't happen, is entirely up to you.'

* * *

After dinner, they went up to Dorothy's room, where she said apologetically, 'I don't know how sociable I can be tonight.'

'I don't expect you to be sociable, Dot. You've had a gruelling day, so it's just as I said earlier. I leave you to call the shots. If you want me to stay, I'll stay, but if you'd rather I left you, I'll see you again in the morning.'

'I feel so selfish,' she said, resting her head on his shoulder.

'Do you want me to stay, but just for company? I don't mind.'

She clung to him until she was able to speak. 'I don't deserve you,' she said.

'I used to think you did, but I was a different person in those days, and what I thought didn't always make sense.'

'Will you unhook me?'

'Of course I will. Turn round.'

He unfastened the hook and eye and ran the zip fastener down, celebrating the event by kissing the triangle he'd uncovered.

Turning to face him again, she asked, 'Whatever happened to the unfazed, dry-eyed, tough old Dot we used to know?'

'I think she and I learned our lesson at about the same time.' He considered that and said, 'Maybe you got there first, but who cares? It's not a competition.'

He watched her remove her dress and unfasten her stockings. With everything else he'd learnt about her in the past year, he found her no less desirable, but he subdued those feelings for the time being. It wasn't difficult in the circumstances. To be helpful, he took her dress and hung it for her in the wardrobe.

'Thank you, Alan, you're indescribable as well as being a hard act to follow.'

'Who do you have in mind?'

'Only me. I'm never as particular as you are when I hang up my clothes.'

'It's the Army,' he told her, unbuttoning his battledress blouse. 'As soon as I'm demobbed, I intend to relax disgracefully and become an untidy layabout. It'll be expected of me when I'm a student.'

'I bet you won't.' She took off the rest of her underclothes and slipped beneath the bedclothes. 'I bet you won't wear cellular drawers, either.'

'You said you wouldn't make fun of me in them,' he complained.

'All right, I shan't.' By association, she remembered her first day in the WAAF. 'When I joined up,' she said, 'we had to have a Free From Infection inspection.'

'So did we,' he said, folding his shirt.

'But I was wearing expensive silk-and-merino mixture French knickers, and the doctor told me to lower my "drawers". It was the first intimation that the life I'd chosen was less privileged than the one I was used to.'

'And it did you no harm,' he said, joining her beneath the sheets. 'In fact, I bet you were terrifying as a sergeant.'

'An ogress in uniform,' she confirmed.

'Tomorrow, you'll be a loving, caring niece with all the patience of a saint, and I admire you for it already.'

She raised herself so that he could wrap his arms around her. 'I'm feeling much more positive about it, now,' she said, kissing him.

'Good. Keep those positive thoughts coming.'

She kissed him again and asked, 'Do you remember what I said about not feeling sociable?'

'Oh, good grief. Do you want me to get back into my drawers, cellular, officers' and leave you in seclusion?'

'Of course not. I was just going to say that I've changed my mind.'

'A woman's prerogative,' he conceded.

'I think that what would make the day complete would be....'

'A game of draughts, I know, and I left them at the Post.'

'No, silly. I'll give you a clue.' She joined him in a lingering, sensuous kiss.

'I think I'm getting the idea,' he said.

'That's right. It's time to get ideas.'

27

Where Is Home?

Once again, Captain Collier met them at the gate and welcomed them into the camp.

'There's been a development,' he told them, 'a welcome development. I believe Sarah's been looking at the photographs you left with her, and she's been talking about you. Major Wilmot's very pleased with her progress, but unfortunately, he's been called away to another patient with problems. You can see the scale of it from here.'

They could, and the numbers being cared for made them appreciate Captain Collier's and Major Wilmot's efforts all the more.

'When will I be allowed to take her home, Captain?'

'There are certain procedures to be followed, but it should be possible by the end of next week, Miss Needham.'

They reached the office, and Collier reminded Alan that he should remain behind while Dorothy visited her aunt. Then, attracting the attention of a female medical orderly, he said, 'Will you take Miss Needham to Unit Twenty-Nine and stay with her until you're sure all is well?'

'Very good, sir. Would you like to come this way, Miss Needham?'

They followed a similar route to that which Dorothy and Major Wilmot had taken the previous day, and arrived at Unit 29. Yet again, it seemed a colourless name for someone's home, however temporary.

'I'll go in ahead of you,' said the orderly, opening the door to the hut, 'just to prepare her.'

Dorothy heard her say, 'Hello, Sarah. Where's everybody gone? Are they all enjoying the sunshine? I've brought a visitor for you, a friend, so don't worry.' She beckoned Dorothy inside, and Sarah's features registered cautious pleasure.

'Aunt Sarah, it's me again. Dorothy.'

Everything seemed to happen slowly. First of all, Sarah's eyes opened wider, and her mouth attempted what was possibly its first smile for a very long time. Next, tears started, eventually streaming as if from an endless source, and then she began to sob in a way that shook her whole wasted body.

'It's all right,' said Dorothy also blinking away tears. 'Everything's going to be all right.'

Sarah emerged from behind her bed and allowed Dorothy to take her in her arms. Locked together, they sobbed on each other's shoulder, while the orderly said happily, 'I'll leave you now.'

Dorothy offered her tearful thanks, still holding the emaciated body of her aunt, overjoyed but anxious not to hurt her in her delicate state.

After some considerable time, she said, 'I'd no idea you were missing until I came home from the war.'

'Where had you been?'

'I was serving in the WAAF until September of last year.'

'What's that?'

'The WAAF?' Dorothy was sharply reminded that a great deal had happened during her aunt's absence. 'It was the Women's Auxiliary Air Force.'

'Oh.' As if she needed to consider that information in greater comfort, she lowered herself on to the bed.

'I've been looking for you ever since I arrived home,' Dorothy told her. 'Aunt Alice told me where you'd gone, so I started in Orléans and went on from there.' Now sobbing helplessly, she said, 'Everything's going... to be all right... now.' She joined her aunt on the bed.

'What will happen... now?'

Giving her the news felt like sheer self-indulgence. 'By the end of next week, they're going... to let me take you home. I'll bring you some clothes, and we'll... go from here to the airport.'

Sarah greeted the news with bewilderment. 'Where is home? My home was in Orléans.' Tears started again, and she said, 'Jeanne... died in Sachsenhausen.'

'I'm sorry, Aunt Sarah. I really am.'

'Dorothy… darling….' She seemed about to say something of great importance.

'Yes, Aunt Sarah?'

'Don't call me that. You're a big girl now.'

'What do you want me to call you?'

'Just "Sarah". You're the only friend I've got, and much more than a niece.' Then, remembering her original question, she asked again, 'Where is home?'

'It's at my house in Yorkshire, and you're welcome to live with me there for as long as you like.'

It was as if Sarah were wrestling with some problem beyond her understanding. Eventually, she asked, 'Don't you live with your mother?'

'No, she died last year. I sold the house and moved to Addlesden.'

For some reason, the news of her estranged sister's death provoked further tears. 'Your mother wasn't… very… old, was she?'

'No, but she had a history of strokes, and it was a stroke that killed her.'

'What about… Alice?'

'She's still at her house in Beckworth.'

Sarah shook her head slowly. 'So much has happened.' She looked at Dorothy with a kind of wonder and said, 'But you found out where I'd gone. That was clever of you.'

'I didn't do it all by myself. I traced you as far as the train from Paris to Sachsenhausen. After that, I needed a lot of help, and it all came from Alan. You'll meet him soon. He's serving here with the Army, and he's a very close friend.' Newly conscious of the time, she said, 'He's waiting for me at the Orderly Office.'

'Is he your special friend?'

'Yes, very special.'

'Will you marry him?'

'I don't know. He hasn't asked me.'

Looking at Dorothy as if with new eyes, she said, 'You were always a beautiful girl, Dorothy.'

'Thank you, Sarah. People used to say you and I looked so much alike, we might have been sisters.'

Sarah said wistfully, 'Not now, I'm afraid.'

'You'll soon be back to your old self, Sarah. They're going to tell me how to build you up again safely, and that's what I'm going to do.' Looking at the atrocious condition of Sarah's hair, she said, 'You'll have every kind of care I can find you.'

Changing the subject again, as she so often did, Sarah said, 'This man you told me about....'

'Alan?'

'You said he was in the Army. Does he work in this camp?'

'No, his job is to investigate and interrogate Nazi war criminals.'

Sarah closed her eyes, possibly in mute recollection. Eventually, she asked, 'Has he found Doctor Klein yet?'

Dorothy remembered reading about Fritz Klein, the Medical Officer at Bergen-Belsen, at the time of the Lüneburg Trials. 'He was tried and... dealt with... last year, Sarah. Don't upset yourself about him.'

Sarah shook her head, possibly driving the memory of Bergen-Belsen from her mind. She said, 'I'm very tired.'

'Of course you are, and it's all my fault.'

'It's not your fault, darling. You've made me happy again.' Resting her head against her niece's shoulder, she began to sob once more. 'Oh, Dorothy....'

'Everything's all right, Sarah.'

'I know it is.' She sobbed all the more with the realisation.

* * *

'It's unbelievable, Alan. She remembered me, and now she's thrilled to bits at the idea of coming home.' She chattered excitedly to him about their conversation as he negotiated the pedestrians and cyclists who seemed to have proliferated in recent weeks. 'You'll be horrified when you see her,' she warned.

'Why will I be horrified?'

'She's little more than skin and bone.'

'I've seen the film that was shot at the liberation of Bergen-Belsen,' he said. 'It was horrifying, but I imagine they'll have had time to build Aunt Sarah up since then.'

'I suppose so, but it wasn't obvious to me.' Suddenly remembering, she said, 'By the way, she's just "Sarah", now.'

'Why is that?'

'It's because I'm a big girl now, and her only friend.'

'You're now all kinds of things that I'd never have suspected in the past,' he said, turning into the gateway of the hotel. 'I must go and do my bit for justice,' he said. 'Would you like me to come over tonight?'

'Oh, please do. Do you think you can wangle another night's absence?'

'Why not? What can they do to me? If they were to court-martial me and kick me out, I'd thank them for it.'

* * *

'What are you going to do about the job at Rimmington's?'

They were finishing the wine at the end of the meal, and the conversation had been largely about how Sarah could best be accommodated.

'I've told them I'm not going to apply for it after all. It was only an innocent enquiry, anyway.'

'Tell me to mind my own business, if you like, but will you be able to manage without the extra income?'

'I daresay. The job was more about self-respect than income, and Sarah will benefit from the sale of her shares. She also has the dividends going back to before the war. Apparently, in her bohemian way, she left her bank account in England untouched while she was in France. I think she intended moving it, but other things got in the way. I know Aunt Alice banked any cheques that came for her.' Mindful that the conversation had all been about Sarah, she said, 'I never asked you how things were going with you. I know there's not a lot you can tell me, but I've been very selfish tonight.'

'Not at all. It's quite understandable.' He reflected on the afternoon's events and said, 'What can I tell you? I managed to wring a confession out of that murdering half-wit this afternoon, and what else? I know. I learned that my demob is to take place next month, to coincide with the MBE presentation.'

'You were holding out on me.'

'Not really. I'd have told you later, anyway. I was going to mention it at a suitably dramatic time, just to heighten the excitement.'

'Beast.' It was the gentlest of accusations.

'Not really. I'd invite you to the award ceremony as well, but it's relatives only, I'm afraid.' He considered that only briefly and said, 'Bragging rights for mothers.'

'It's inevitable.' She glanced at her watch and asked, 'Are you going to take me to my room and have your way with me?'

'In my usual barbaric fashion?' He narrowed his eyes in mock-consideration and said, 'It's the best offer I've had this evening, so yes, I think I should.'

* * *

'What are we going to do when you come home, Alan? I mean when you've been demobbed.'

'What we've just been doing, I suppose, as often as we can.'

She turned over and rested on her elbow to speak to him. 'Seriously, where are you going to live? The last time we mentioned it, you were less than keen to live with your parents.'

'Even less, now.'

'I mean, we are going to continue seeing each other, aren't we?' There was a hint of anxiety about the question.

'Come what may. I'm as keen as I hope you are.'

'Be serious, Alan.'

'How much more serious can I be? I love you.'

'Seriously?'

'Earnestly, genuinely and devotedly. Don't tell me I'm making a fool of myself again. I couldn't live with that.'

'Of course you're not.' She kissed him with unmistakeable commitment. 'I love you. Haven't you noticed?'

'I'm a simple soul. I was waiting to be told, but I'm very relieved to hear it.'

'So where will you live?'

'You've got me there.' He thought quickly. 'I suppose there's accommodation for students in Leeds.'

'And there's my house,' she suggested patiently.

'A veritable mansion. Are you suggesting that I come to you as a lodger?'

'That kind of thing, except that lodgers don't share a bedroom with the landlady.'

'They do in the lurid books I've caught soldiers reading.'

'I bet you've read them, too.' Returning to the important question of somewhere to live, she said, 'You'd put something into the kitty, presumably, but you wouldn't need to beggar yourself.'

It was tempting, but there was another consideration. 'What about Sarah? The doctor said it wouldn't be easy. How will she be affected by having a man in the house?'

'I don't know. I'll be able to answer that question more easily when I've had her at home for a while, I mean before you're demobbed.'

'I suppose I could always hang on to the maternal apron strings until we're sure.'

'We all have to make sacrifices, Alan.'

'Okay, let's do that and see what happens.'

They kissed rapturously until neither could delay the moment any longer.

28

September

Where The Heart Is

Coiffured, manicured and dressed now in the best that rationing allowed, Sarah was beginning to look much more like the woman Dorothy remembered. More than three months had passed since her emotional farewell to Major Wilmot and his staff, and Dorothy's patient observance of their advice on nutrition was yielding promising results. Otherwise, Sarah continued to treat life in a normal home as the novelty it must inevitably seem.

Dorothy watched her glance nervously upward, and asked, 'Is something the matter, Sarah?'

'I was only wondering if Alan's all right.'

Dorothy smiled. 'He's only having a bath. He's more than six feet tall, so he's not going to drown in six inches of bath water.'

'He was gone a long time.'

'He needed to be. If he's going to cycle to Leeds every day, he'll need to get fit beforehand.' He would also need to toughen himself underneath, and that was very much his current preoccupation.

With her mind now at rest, Sarah said, 'He's such a lovely young man. You're very lucky.'

Dorothy nodded. She was convinced of it.

'I was lucky to have you two come looking for me.'

'Try not to dwell on it, Sarah.' Only two nights earlier, Dorothy had been obliged to go to her room to help her settle after one of her frequent nightmares.

Footsteps on the stairs removed any remaining fears Sarah might

210

have had for Alan's wellbeing, although he was moving a trifle awkwardly when he entered the room.

Dorothy asked, 'Do you feel better for that, darling?'

'Most of me does.' He lowered himself gingerly on to the sofa.

'I've got some ointment you can have,' she said, unable to stifle a smile at his predicament. 'It's the stuff I used.'

'Thank you.' Perhaps in an effort to be more positive, he said, 'That was a good idea of yours to use an old chamois leather for lining. I imagine my mother's still wondering what happened to it.'

'It wasn't my idea,' she confessed. 'When I realised I no longer had my shorts, Kate suggested lining a pair of old slacks with the stuff. She even stood over me, supervising me while I used the sewing machine.'

'Whereas Sarah made an excellent job of mine.'

'It was the least I could do,' protested Sarah, 'and I'm happy to help in any other way I can. You can't imagine how grateful I am to both of you.'

'But, without realising it, you brought Dot and me together, so I reckon we're quits. Don't you think so, Dot?'

'Absolutely, and another thing we appreciate is your cooking. It never occurred to me that you might have stolen a march on me in that respect.'

Sarah laughed, a welcome sound that was becoming increasingly familiar. 'I hadn't a clue about cooking until I went to live in France. It was Jeanne who taught me.' She closed her eyes momentarily, trying not to succumb to the wretchedness she felt at her friend's death.

'But most of all,' said Alan, sensitive to her dilemma, 'we appreciate you for the person you are, and that's just as it should be.'

'As usual,' said Dorothy, 'Alan's beaten me to the line, but you know how we both feel.'

Out of genuine curiosity as well as to head off an emotional scene, Alan asked, 'Did anything exciting happen while I was working up a sore posterior?'

'Kate phoned,' Dorothy told him. 'They've just returned from North Wales. They were visiting Jack's old skipper, who's a schoolmaster, believe it or not, but they'll be here tomorrow.'

'It'll be good to see Baby Maurice as well,' said Alan, 'if only for the sake of continuity.'

With theatrical disappointment, Dorothy asked, 'Don't you want to see the result of my handiwork, as well?'

'Of course. I thought that was understood.'

Sarah was looking bemused, so Dorothy explained, 'Our old friend Kate was heavily pregnant, and her husband had to be away from home, so he asked me to stay with Kate. Well, the short version is that she went into labour, so I phoned for an ambulance. Unfortunately, there was a traffic incident in Cullington that blocked off the town centre to all traffic, including ambulances. Not only that, but the baby was in quite a hurry, and the upshot was that I had to deliver him on the kitchen floor.'

'Amazing. How clever of you, Dot.'

'Not really. Kate's a midwife, so she knew what to do. In between pushing, shouting and swearing, she gave me explicit instructions, and by the time the ambulance arrived, it was all over.'

'Well, I still think it was clever of you.'

'All right, Sarah, you're allowed that.' She thought momentarily and said, 'I wonder what my mother might have said about it.'

'As a rule, you couldn't get anything right for her,' said Sarah, 'although I speak as shouldn't, as she's no longer with us.'

'You're right, though, Sarah.'

'If it comes to that, neither could I. It was just as well we had each other.'

'Alan's lucky,' said Dorothy, 'he never had that kind of problem.'

'Not that kind,' agreed Alan, 'but I'm taking quite a hammering now.'

Dorothy smiled. 'About living in sin?'

'And living the life of an irresponsible student, although what kind of activity my mother thinks I get up to is anybody's guess.'

'If only families realised,' said Sarah, looking wistful.

Dorothy asked, 'If only they realised what?'

'I knew a girl in Sachsenhausen, who'd travelled there with her younger brother. He was very forgetful, and she had to keep nagging him because he was in her care. On the journey, she noticed that he was wearing his old boots, and she asked him where his new ones were. He told her he'd left them at home, as they needed wearing-in, and she was very cross with him. She told him exactly what she thought of him. It was just as the train stopped outside the camp, and he was taken away with the other children. She learned later that he'd been beaten to death. She never forgot that she'd spoken her last words to him in anger.'

'Try not to dwell on it,' said Dorothy, taking her hand.

Alan knelt beside her chair and stroked her shoulder. 'Try to look forward,' he advised.

'Oh, but I do. I only told you that story as a warning never to put yourselves in that girl's position.'

* * *

At the noise of a car engine and the crunch of gravel in the drive, Sarah looked immediately fearful.

'It's all right,' Alan told her, slipping his arm round her slender shoulders. 'They're our friends.'

Dorothy had already gone to the door and was greeting the visitors. Alan continued to reassure Sarah.

'I know,' she said. 'It makes no sense at all, but I just react when I hear someone come.'

'It makes perfect sense. Come and meet Jack and Kate.'

She had no need, because Dorothy brought them into the room. Kate was carrying Maurice in her arms, and he was fast asleep.

They both greeted Alan, and Dorothy introduced them to Sarah.

'We're absolutely delighted to meet you,' said Jack. 'We've been following Dot's progress ever since she told us about you.'

'Let's not forget Alan,' said Dorothy. 'I couldn't have done it without him.' Mindful of her duty as hostess, she asked, 'Tea, everyone?'

'Let me do it,' said Sarah.

'Thank you, Sarah.' Dorothy held out her arms to receive Maurice, who remained firmly asleep during the handover. 'Isn't he lovely?' She proceeded to serenade him with *sotto voce* nonsense until she realised that everyone was watching her. She asked, 'What's the matter?'

'You're a convert,' said Jack. 'All it took was an emergency delivery, and you were hooked. Are you feeling broody?'

'Give me time, Jack. This is all very new for me.'

'You wouldn't have believed it, Alan,' said Kate. 'No messing about. She was there, beside me on the kitchen floor, doing everything that needed to be done.'

'I can believe it, Kate. Dot's developed skills we'd never have imagined.'

'I keep thinking of that night at your house, Jack, when I came to change your dressing, and Dot came later.'

Jack made a play of plumbing his memory for the event. 'I'll never forget it,' he said, earning a playful punch from his wife.

'You'd just become an uncle, and both you and Dot were being sniffy about babies.'

'I just needed time,' said Dorothy.

'And now, the time has come,' said Kate, 'for us to ask you and Alan to be godparents to Maurice.'

'Both of us?' Alan's surprise was spontaneous.

'Of course,' said Jack, moving his feet out of the way so that Sarah could bring in the tray of tea things. 'You were both members of the original five.'

Alan winced. 'Don't remind me.'

'A happy memory, Alan,' said Kate.

'Well, it's quite an honour, so thank you. We'll be very happy to do that.'

'And,' said Dorothy with a flourish, 'As one good turn deserves another, not immediately, but in a year or so, when Alan's finished his studies….'

'This stage of my studies,' he corrected her.

'Well, go on, Alan, you can spill the beans.'

'Jack, I'd like you to be my Best Man, if you will.'

'And, Kate,' said Dorothy, 'I'd like you to be my chief bridesmaid.'

The twin requests were received with predictable enthusiasm. 'Of course we will.'

Kate asked, 'Who else is going to be a bridesmaid?'

'Connie.'

'I thought so. An excellent choice.'

Now happily tearful, Sarah said, 'This is truly wonderful.'

'Wait a minute, Sarah,' said Dorothy. 'We haven't finished yet. There's a job for you as well.'

'For me?'

'As my father hasn't been around these… many… years, and

because you've always meant so much to me, I'm asking you to give me away. Will you do that?'

'As part of the marriage service,' she sniffed, 'of course I will. Otherwise, I'll never let you out of my sight.'

'After recent events, Sarah, I'm not likely to let you stray very far, either.'

The End